Avelina da Silveira is a Portuguese Canadian retired teacher, a published poet and a mixed media and portrait artist. She is also a political leader of her left-wing political party, a feminist activist and a member of the municipal city council. In her retirement, she volunteers in helping children with their homework and literacy.

Avelina has two adult children and two grandchildren, lives alone and has a wonderful group of friends. She has no wanderlust and prefers to stay in her hometown of Ponta Delgada in the Azores and spends her free time reading and writing both in English and in Portuguese.

To my children, Miguel Pacheco and Vida Corvus, who are the most wonderful people in my life, and to my grandchildren to whom I offer dreams of a better world.

Avelina da Silveira

MOTHER OF STONES

AUSTIN MACAULEY PUBLISHERS™

LONDON * CAMBRIDGE * NEW YORK * SHARJAH

A CIP catalogue record for this title is available from the British Library.

ISBN 9781035856886 (Paperback)
ISBN 9781035856893 (ePub e-book)

www.austinmacauley.com

First Published 2024
Austin Macauley Publishers Ltd®
1 Canada Square
Canary Wharf
London
E14 5AA

I want to acknowledge and express my gratitude to my first readers who gave me valuable critique and suggestions. They are Carole Delaey, Leonor Sampaio da Silva and Esmeralda Cabral, all three are magnificent women and respected writers in their fields. Also, a big hug of gratitude to Susan Burkat Trubey who diligently worked on proofreading the text and gave me valuable editing suggestions. In addition, I want to thank the team at Austin Macauley Publishers for their excellent work in making this book possible. Finally, I want to thank you, the reader, for choosing to spend time dreaming with me about a world in which every person can live freely, with respect and inclusion. Until then, we fight on!

Part One

In the beginning the stones were considered magic. The First Mater was known by many names, and she walked the earth in a time called The Mesolithic. That was a time of slow technological revolution, when people started to learn how to chip stones in smaller and more sophisticated ways; when they first experimented with agriculture and domestication of animals, when pottery was first invented. This was a time of social change as well when people started to build permanent shelters. Because they did not leave written records, it is impossible to know details about their families and relationships. They did not live long lives; however, we know that they loved and honoured each other because they left us burial grounds with decorations and personal effects. This must seem strange to you with our bio implants and all the many ways that our technology makes our lives easier, but they were people just like you and me.

—Excerpt from a teaching module in the year 2387 CE

Chapter One

Spring of 11352 BCE

As far as N'kura could see from her perch above the shore, the ocean dominated the landscape. She huddled in wool fur and a straw hat, feeling as if her leg were about to burst open like a ripe melon. The ocean winds eased her fever, but the pain in her leg was a pulsating misery.

The ocean was all-encompassing, the Great Mother of All. That is what her people called the often-ferocious greatness that provided food when She was calm and soothing, She was the One of the seas and of the land. Thousands of years later, that area would be called Praia das Galés, in Portugal, and its rock formations would retain delightful pools where N'kura used to bathe and fish with a wooden spear. The long stretch of sand on calm days yielded enough bivalve molluscs to feed her small tribe and, in the low tide, there were limpets in the rocks.

Their diet consisted of seafood supplemented by berries found up the coast, seeds, roots, and the occasional rodent caught in traps. The camp was far enough from the dunes that the sand did not bother them, with two substantial streams which ran to the ocean. These streams were the only source of freshwater available and were therefore precious.

The stories told of a time when big game roamed that area, but now all they had were smaller animals. Sometimes, a traveller would come from far inland, exchange furs for polished shells and tell stories of goats and ibexes that made such good eating. By the coast, they rarely ate meat, relying on the All Mother to provide. The people of N'kura often went hungry in the winter.

Life was hard for her small tribe composed of as many people as the fingers in her hands. The last child had been born six summers ago from her body. A boy who was her people's pride. He was smart, quick and a good gatherer of food.

However, following the example of the four males in her group, he was quick to anger, and sometimes, he exploded like the waves upon a rock.

The other males were old and could not move as swiftly, but their tempers remained volatile, especially when directed at N'kura. Her other child was female, a little thing, eight summers old. Her delight. Both mother and daughter were of small stature, dark-skinned with long black hair. However, while N'kura had sparkling blue eyes, her daughter, Biba, had dark eyes like the people of her tribe.

N'kura had been a child when these people had kidnapped her. At the time, the men were young and strong, and they were able to run far. Girls were considered valuable because they would mature and breed more children to enlarge the tribe. So often there were raids between tribes for either women or resources. N'kura was a disappointment to her people because she had only bred twice. For many days, the small, hurting woman had not been in their company, ever since her accident.

N'kura had been taking garbage to the mound of shells when she slipped and fell. The sharp edges had cut shallow slices all over her body. However, one shell had dug so deeply into her leg that it took strength to pull it out. With her bleeding body, she staggered to the ocean to wash away the blood.

The women did not help her because they loathed N'kura. The three females were older, and none had a child among them. Silver Hair once had bred three babies, but they had never grown to adulthood. The other two women continued to bleed every month and sometimes twice a month with great pain. Thus, they were often cruel to the younger woman who had not been born of their tribe.

Between the men's fists and the women's verbal assaults, N'kura lived a lonely and painful life alleviated only by her daughter, Biba. However, one day soon the girl's life would change to drudgery because the males' gaze had changed when they looked at her. Biba was ripening and soon her monthly blood would flow. N'kura feared for her daughter at the mercy of four old men, with no young one to claim her.

After N'kura had been injured, her leg started to swell and become hot to the touch as it got worse. She developed a fever, feeling alternately hot and then cold. She shivered all the time. Then a great gush of pus erupted from her wound and red angry streaks spread up to her thigh. That's when the people demanded that she leave the camp, lest she bring demons to them all.

Biba was the only one who helped her build a makeshift shelter with canes and woven grass, far enough away from the camp that she could not see or hear the people. And it was her daughter who brought her a meagre meal once a day.

So now, all by herself, she wondered how long she would live because the pain and the stench from her wound were getting worse. She could not put weight on her leg, and between the fever and the pain, she was too weak to walk far.

From her promontory and between the tears that fell from her eyes, N'kura could see the stretch of white sand, rocks, the ocean in front of her, as well as the savanna behind. Only with difficulty and the help of her spear, could she start her return. The sun was descending, so it was time for her to go back to her hut.

As it was her habit, N'kura used the butt of her spear to stir the ground, looking for edible roots. On the way to her shelter, she crouched with pain to grab a thick and juicy root. Attached to it was the most marvellous thing she had ever seen. Lying on the ground in front of her was a palm-sized grey flat stone that sparkled with cold light.

She hid the stone in a fold of her grass skirt and, as swiftly as her painful leg allowed, she made her way back to the seclusion of her hut. She was exhausted from pain and fever and lay down on her furs. Placing the stone between her sagging breasts N'kura fell asleep content with her find.

The next day, it dawned clear and soft. The Great Mother of All expressed her smile with low waves and a blue sky. N'kura woke without fever, but the pain continued with each measure of her heartbeat. Finding water in a baked mud vessel, she drank deeply as she contemplated how to make a necklace with the stone. She had a thin-tipped burin and placed the shining stone on a large shell.

Sitting cross-legged, N'kura held the stone on the shell with her left hand, and with the stone bore on her right hand, she twisted it until she made a hole in the centre of the shining stone. It was easier than she thought because this stone was much softer than the stones from the ocean. As the burin drilled into the flat stone, it flaked and dusted out into the shell.

When Father Sky was at his peak, Biba came with a handful of seeds and some limpets and asked her mother what she was doing, but her only reply was that she was making a secret necklace and not to tell anyone.

Bibi busied herself by going to get water from the stream but soon got bored watching her mother work and returned to camp.

It took the woman an entire day to drill the hole. Her hands hurt from holding and drilling. Her leg was hurting and leaking pus. She wiped the mess with some grass and continued drilling until she could see through the hole in the stone. By the time Father Sun had gone to sleep, Biba sneaked out of the camp and brought her a strong string of woven grass. She hugged her mother and left in the twilight.

Alone in her lonely shelter, N'kura threaded the string through the stone and secured it around her neck. It was not heavy like other stones and rested comfortably between her breasts. She, then, had an unreasonable urge to consume the pile of dust and flakes that had accumulated on the shell. She took a pinch between her fingers and tried it. It was not bitter, but it was dry like sand.

So she poured the dust and flakes into the remaining water, stirred the mixture with her finger and half drank and half chewed the mixture. N'kura slid under her mound of furs and became oblivious to everything, except the visions she saw and felt. An exceedingly long journey through darkness and so very cold. Aeons of travel through more darkness and loneliness, searching beyond exhaustion. Eagerness to commune and become whole. Until now.

N'kura was unconscious for three days, convulsing and stinking. She sweated, vomited, shat and pissed whatever she held in her system. On the last day, she shed her skin.

N'kura woke up to her filth. She was alone; it was dark; and she was thirsty. The woman crawled out of the dank hut, rolled on the dirt and realised that she had no pain. She staggered towards the stream, entered it and drank as much as she could. She vomited.

So she walked upstream until she was sure the water was unpolluted, and she drank slowly this time. Then N'kura grabbed sand from the stream bed and scrubbed herself softly because her new skin was very tender. She again walked upstream, threw her straw skirt far into the bank and continued to scrub. That is when she realised that she had no body hair and that her leg had healed. There was no puncture damage. Exhausted, the now clean woman left the stream, found a dry and flat space to lie down and slept.

When N'kura again regained consciousness, the sun was barely above the horizon on the horizon. She felt dazed with thirst, hunger and echoes of her visions. She drank her fill of the crystalline water and walked towards the tribe naked and bald, except for the stone hanging from her neck.

The small woman expected to be welcomed by the people. After all, she was whole and clean. However, when Silver Hair saw her approach, she started to wail and scream, and the people scrambled out of their huts. They too screamed and threw stones to make her depart. N'kura did not understand until her daughter ran to her and urged her to leave.

"Mother, they think that you are a ghost or a demon. You must go! They will kill you."

"Please, Biba, come with me. Help me."

"I will meet you by the pools when Father Sun goes down. Be ready to leave and to go far away," said the daughter in earnest.

N'kura ran towards her own filthy hut to get the things that she would need to take with her. She wrapped her few belongings in the dirty skins: a pouch with polished shells that shone like mother of pearl; a stone knife; the stone burin, her largest shell and her small container of baked mud. After that, she walked to the furthest stretch of the beach, grabbed some seaweed and chewed it. She collected trumpet and whelk shells, scooped the morsels inside using a stick and ate them.

The shells she would keep because they were good for trade. With her hunger somewhat satisfied, N'kura used her stone knife to carefully force limpets from the rocks. She ate these too and threw away the shells. Finding a secluded spot with a level surface, she lay down to sleep with her necklace between her breasts.

Before nightfall, N'kura was already sitting up and waiting. She heard her daughter long before she saw her. She stood up and noticed that Biba had her own roll of furs.

"Daughter, we must hurry. Let me carry your burden."

N'kura placed both rolls on her back, made sure the weight was evenly distributed and both mother and child walked away swiftly, keeping the seashore on their right. It was already dark, but they knew the terrain well. N'kura led the way while Biba walked quickly behind. They were both saying goodbye to the only life they knew, miserable as it was. The woman only hoped they could survive.

Chapter Two

As the stream became only a small trickle of water, they followed the course of the stream until it was only a trickle. They both drank deeply before leaving this path behind. They walked towards the rising sun, away from where they had been until they were too tired to keep going. They rested for the night huddled together.

As they continued walking the next day, N'kura and Biba looked for more vegetation. They sampled the grasses and fruits along the way as they walked to see what would be edible, and they found the sweetest fruit, packing as much as they could carry. They walked for days. Their feet hurt, N'kura's back hurt from carrying the weight, and they crossed an arid land in which the trees only offered hard nuts. The woman cracked their shells with a rock, retrieved the meat and beat it to a pulp. She tried it, and it was good.

They gathered as many nuts as they could carry and continued their journey. On the way, they occasionally found streams. Each time, they washed their bodies and drank as much as they could. If the streams had fish, they would spear them or make a net out of woven grass and catch minnows. On their escape, they found no humans, only small animals scurrying around. They sometimes built traps but rarely caught anything.

After five days of walking, they decided to rest under a grove of trees. It was shady, and the fallen leaves made good bedding. There they could stay until they ran out of food. The ocean was only half a day's walk, and they could reach it easily.

Through rationing their food, the woman and the child were able to stay for three days. They slept most of the time. N'kura because she was still recovering from her ordeal and Biba because she was still a child and the long days of walking had tested the limits of her endurance. They needed the rest. When their food ran out, they walked to the shore and had their fill of molluscs and seaweed.

N'kura kept the trumpet shells because they could be used for trade, should they encounter other humans. Then, they resumed their march towards the rising sun. Later that day, they saw that trees and green vegetation spread throughout the landscape and mother and daughter smelled water. The enticing scent propelled them to walk faster until they came to a true river, a wide expanse of water.

N'kura and Biba dropped their burdens and rushed to the river. They drank carefully so as not to vomit and submerged themselves in the cool bliss of the water. They washed their bodies using green leaves as scrubbers. They stayed in the water until their fingers pruned, after that they let the air dry their bodies as they lay in mounds of green grass. When they were dry and rested, Biba collected long grass and N'kura taught her how to make grass skirts.

They left the garments to dry and proceeded to clean their bundles. The skins needed scrubbing and airing. They found scented grass and used it to scrub the furs on both sides. Next, they washed each of their stone and wooden tools. Finally, they looked for food along the water bank where they had stopped.

N'kura found a long and sturdy branch and prepared a rudimentary spear for her daughter. They gathered fallen branches and using the flint that Biba had remembered to bring, they started a fire using dry grass. They had their first cooked meal in many days of walking by filling N'kura's baked bowl with water and dropping a hot stone into it, plus the roots they gathered. When the embers were down, the woman burnt the tip of the spear, just enough to harden it.

"Yours!" declared the mother handing the spear to Biba. "Tomorrow, I will teach you how to use it to catch fish."

Biba was pleased. She was assuming adult responsibilities, and it was time for her to learn more.

The night was chilly, so mother and daughter slept close together for comfort, wrapped in the now fresh-smelling furs and close to the revived fire.

The next day, Biba practised spearing river fish, and she was successful some of the time. They ate roasted fish wrapped in leaves. N'kura then explored the new flora, so different from the one of the seashores. Leaves, thick grass, bushes and trees all thrived in the abundance of freshwater. She tasted minute amounts to find out if they were edible.

She particularly liked some stalks she found growing in abundance in the mud. There were red berries that were sweet and a bit acidic. There were also bitter berries that N'kura spat out and washed her mouth to prevent poison. She should pay attention to what the insects and rodents had already eaten. Those were safe foods.

Then, the Great Mother of All decided that the earth deserved her attention. The Sun Father hid behind dark clouds and soon rained copiously. Both mother and daughter worked swiftly to build a shelter of branches and furs on top. They kept one fur to lie down inside the hut where they huddled to conserve heat. Outside they could hear the wind and wood noises. They felt safe enough in their shelter among trees.

It rained all the rest of the day and through the night. During this time, N'kura told stories that she had heard before and others that she created. She especially told the story of her shining stone and of the visions she had experienced. Biba would remember and pass the stories to her daughters. They slept, they ate what remained of the food, and neither wanted to venture out during the storm.

When the rain stopped falling from the sky, both mother and daughter left the shelter to see if there was any damage. The river ran quicker than before, the mud was more slippery, but all their belongings were undamaged. N'kura and Biba drank the rainwater in the container and decided that it was time to move and find people. They stayed long enough to dry their furs, wrapped their belongings and set on their way.

The river ran from between the rising and the falling sun, so they followed the course, always close to the source of food and freshwater.

On the third day of following the river, mother and daughter finally found people. They were a large group of males and females. As N'kura and Biba approached carefully, they tried to look non-threatening. A man and a woman detached themselves from the group with smiles. They spoke a few words in a soothing tone, but their language was different, and mother and daughter didn't understand.

So, with gestures, words and various sounds, they tried to communicate. They seemed to be a hunting and gathering group, since on their backs the men carried several goats and an ibex, and the women had straw baskets filled with various foodstuff.

The leading man pointed to himself; said, "Molo"; and pointed to the woman and said, "Avoa." With gestures, they indicated that mother and daughter should follow them. Soon, N'kura and Biba were surrounded by smiling people who offered them water from skin bags and gave them each a ball of nuts and seeds lightly sweetened with honey. Some women touched N'kura's bald head and asked questions that she couldn't answer.

Molo and Avoa seemed to be the leaders of this band. The man was still strong and tall but showed some signs of ageing. Avoa had pendulous breasts and some white hair, however, like Molo, she looked strong and agile. Everyone in the band wore skirts made of straw or of skins, had various markings on their bodies and had decorative necklaces about their necks. They all looked well-fed, unlike the gaunt features of N'kura and of Biba.

After some fussing over the newcomers, they decided to start walking. Mother and daughter assumed that they were returning to their home, so they followed. After walking for one day and another morning, still following the river, they reached a settlement where children ran to them in glee and where small groups of adults interrupted their tasks to relieve the hunters and gatherers of their burdens.

There will be a feast tonight for sure, thought N'kura.

Biba seemed happy to meet other children, but she stayed close to her mother. As they looked around, they saw shelters made of stone with thatched roofs. Quite different from the huts that N'kura and Biba were used to. The small houses were built in a circle around a large fire pit, and it seemed that like in her own tribe, people only used the shelters to sleep or during storms.

Everyday activities and chores were done outdoors. While some adults were tasked with dressing the game and preparing the food collected during their foray, Molo and Avoa guided them towards a small group of elders sitting on large tree branches.

With gestures and a few words, N'kura introduced herself and her daughter and tried to explain that they had been walking for many days. A conversation ensued amongst the elders and between Molo and Avoa and them. After a while, everyone seemed to reach a decision to welcome them into their tribe with smiles. And why not? Both mother and daughter were potential breeders, and they looked strong and healthy, even if they were currently malnourished. They were assigned to an empty stone hut, where N'kura and Biba dropped their belongings. After that, Avoa showed them the settlement.

Neither mother nor daughter had ever seen so many people. Their number was many times the number of fingers in both hands. They were of all ages, tall and well-built. N'kura was happy to see a few boys around her daughter's age, so Biba could have some mating choices when the time came. The two newcomers saw groups of women working on food preparation and weaving grass and a group of men dressing and cutting meat with their stone tools. Some children helped with chores, while others ran around playing.

Soon a bonfire was burning brightly, and people placed woven grass mats on the ground around the fire and displayed a few varieties of dishes. Boiled grains and tubers, the same nutrients balls mother and daughter had eaten before and various tender shoots and leaves. Long thin sticks of wood were skewered with small chunks of meat and placed on coals. There was enough meat for everyone to eat a few chunks.

Avoa offered N'kura and Biba large leaves with some of each food. They accepted gratefully because they were hungry. After the meal, every one helped clean up, taking reusable utensils to the river to scrub them with sand and rinse them in the flowing water. Mother and daughter used the opportunity to drink freshwater and used sticks to clean their teeth.

The full night had fallen by the time N'kura and Biba returned to their assigned shelter. They were content with their full bellies and felt safe in this community. They slept deeply and long. The next day, mother and daughter fully unwrapped their fur bundles, placed the furs outside to air and sorted through their belongings.

They chose two handfuls of polished shells and trumpet shells, made a grass pocket for them and went looking for Molo and Avoa. In the process, they stopped and introduced themselves to the people they found and asked for directions using words and gestures. They found the couple easily enough. As it happened, they lived together.

N'kura and Biba knelt on the ground, and each made their offerings of shells which were well received with big smiles. They were made to stand and were embraced. Next, they were invited to break their fast with leftover food from the previous night. Biba was growing fast, so she ate well.

Mother and daughter spent a part of the day helping with chores and spearfishing by the river shore. Some of the children were curious and joined them, amazed at their skill. When they decided that they had enough fish, they returned to the settlement all wet and happy. Biba left her mother for the children. She had made friends and that was a particularly good thing.

Chapter Three

As time passed by, N'kura shyly learned their language enough to communicate. Biba learned faster and soon was instructing other children and young adults to spearfish and becoming the darling of many. Moons passed; seasons came and went; and both mother and daughter were well integrated and felt safe. From the women of the tribe, they learned many things, some of them were mysteries. They learned how to help a mother and child during childbirth, how to distinguish edible plants from poisonous ones, how some poisons in tiny amounts helped sick people, and how infusions of fragrant leaves were tasty and good for the digestive system.

N'kura and Biba also helped the people, teaching what little they knew about grass weaving and their style of shaping stones. They were always eager to do chores and to sit with the elderly or mind small children. Although the people still looked at times uncomfortable with N'kura's ageless features and bald head, for the most part, she became a member of the tribe and was included in gathering and hunting excursions. The mother became an expert at throwing her spear down goats and ibexes, while Biba led the youngsters in finding tasty roots and berries.

Biba's first blood arrived during the night. She felt mild pain, touched her genitals and her hand came up wet and sticky. She woke her mother who gave her a bunch of moss to absorb the blood and made her a soothing hot drink. Biba's discomfort continued, but she was soothed by her mother who hugged her and kept murmuring endearments. There was nothing to explain to Biba about menses, sex and childbirth since the newly made woman had been a witness of all during her life. N'kura felt immensely proud of her daughter.

The next day, N'kura searched for Molo and Avoa, told them the good news and asked for their advice in choosing a mate for her daughter. In a few months, she would be ready to be paired with a good young man, and she valued their suggestions. Avoa listed a few eligible youths that Biba might be interested in and explained that it was customary for the young woman's family to pay a dowry which would be kept by the bride in case the pairing did not work out.

Also, the groom's family needed to be told in advance because they were responsible for providing furs and mats as gifts to the couple. N'kura was pleased because she had kept hidden a mound of shells that served as currency. She could give most of those as dowry, keeping some for her own purposes. However, she was stunned by Avoa's next words.

"You also need a mate. You have kept yourself away from the younger males, but many have an eye on you. I would like you to consider taking Molo as your mate because I can no longer have children; you like him; and I would have a sister-wife. I know that he is not young and has lost a few teeth. But he would treat you kindly and still has the strength to protect us both. What do you say?"

"I did not think of it. My body does not crave a man, but I would be glad to be your sister-wife. And, as you say, I would be happy to have another child."

As soon as news of Biba's menses spread through the tribe, various mothers came to N'kura asking for her daughter. They all had healthy and strong sons. Of them all, Biba chose Lando who had first learned how to spearfish from her. She liked him well enough, and they were friends. Also, her young body felt hot when they were together.

Sitting cross-legged on mats outside Lando's parents' hut, the two families discussed the joining of their children while drinking a hot beverage. N'kura promised that Biba would have a dowry of shells, the number of her fingers and toes, plus all her stone tools and spear, so Lando's mother was delighted. The young man's father promised four furs suitable for sleeping and six thickly woven mats of scented grass. The family would also build a new hut for the young couple.

N'kura was pleased; however, she insisted that they would still have to wait thirteen moons before they mated so that Biba's body would be more mature and ready to breed a child. For the next round of seasons, Biba and Lando were often seen together. They touched hands and lips; they talked; and they built what they needed for their new life together.

Unlike the rough-baked mud bowls of their tribe of origin, their new people were lucky that there was a clay deposit nearby, and they were skilled at making bowls, jars and drinking vessels decorated with crosshatches. So Lando taught Biba and N'kura how to make those clay containers. They had to dry thoroughly. Then, they were packed in leaves and placed in burning coals covered with more coals. Often, the vessels cracked and were useless, but enough of them turned out perfectly that both Biba and N'kura had their own.

The round stone hut for the young couple was soon ready, the cracks covered with clay and a freshly thatched roof. N'kura was simply going to stay in her own hut because Molo's and Avoa's hut was too small for three people. Her new family would visit and stay the night when they wished, or she could visit them. It was a good arrangement for all. Molo and Avoa offered to put a new roof on her hut, which N'kura was grateful for.

Chapter Four

Throughout her time with her new people, N'kura's stone pendant had grown considerably. She had never heard of a growing stone, as if it were a living thing. She never took it off her neck and always slept with the stone between her breasts. However, she needed to weave a new grass string or find an alternative. She decided to cut very thin strips of her fur to see if it was strong enough to carry her precious stone.

Therefore she scraped the fur from an edge and, using her newly sharpened stone knife, cut an appropriate length of a thin stripe. N'kura was very happy with the result. Next, she thought of breaking her stone, so she would have a smaller one but could share stones with her daughter and her future mates.

Carefully, the woman, using a stone with a good edge and another as a percussion, separated three pieces from the mother stone, one from the bottom and two from the sides. There were flakes and very small pieces that fell from the cleaving impact. N'kura ground them and drank them with a bit of water. The next step was to drill holes in the stones, which she did using her stone bore with a sharp end and twisting it until there was a hole. Each time, N'kura consumed the powder and flakes that resulted from drilling.

She started to feel dizzy, so she lay down in her furs and slept until the next day. N'kura understood that the powdered stone had a strange effect on her, but she had a need to consume it. After sleeping, she felt strong and vital. She finished her necklaces and decided to give Biba's necklace to her on the day she formalised her union. However, N'kura did not have to wait any time to mate with Molo. So she sent Biba the message that she would mate with Bolo that night.

N'kura went to the river and had a refreshing bath. She scrubbed herself well using scented herbs and the running water. Next, in her hut, she put on her newest skirt made from a hide that Avoa had given her and took two of the necklaces with her. By the time she walked solemnly to Molo's and Avoa's hut, the whole tribe knew of her decision and followed N'kura on the path to her destination. The couple was waiting for her with a wreath of flowers which Molo placed on her head.

The bride gave each of them their necklaces. Everyone wore smiles and started hooting and hollering in joyful voices. Molo reached his hand to N'kura's and guided her to the interior of the hut. Before they entered alone, Avoa hugged her sister-wife and sat on a mat outside.

Molo had bathed just like N'kura did, and he smelled fresh and manly. However, the brave hunter became shy and N'kura kindly joined her mouth with his and caressed his member. He responded with a hug and caressed her body. Their mating was tender, and both were content with their choice of each other. When they were done, N'kura and Molo cleaned themselves and left the hut to join Avoa. The women of the tribe brought food and fermented fruit juice, and they all celebrated with joy, wishing N'kura, Molo and Avoa a fertile outcome.

During the following days, Molo visited N'kura's hut every day. He even looked younger; such was his contentment that he walked with a spring on his steps. He went hunting with a group of men to bring his new wife fresh meat. In the meantime, Avoa invited N'kura daily to join her in completing common chores or to simply be together. Both women found each other's company a sweet delight.

When the next moon arrived and N'kura did not bleed, she was sure that she was with a child. A few days later, her breasts were sore, and she became very sleepy. She was happy, but she kept the news to herself until the child was safe in her womb.

However, the joy did not last long because the hunters returned with Molo's body. He had sickened and died, they said. The men thought he must have consumed something bad because he vomited in great pain and had the flux.

Avoa was distraught and wailing as the women washed the body and wrapped him in a skin and the men took Molo's body to the burial ground. With sharpened stones and wooden shovels, they dug a shallow grave where they placed Molo with his necklace, and the body was surrounded by flowers and his spear.

N'kura decided to move in with Avoa to care for the older woman who was in deep grief. She cooked, cleaned and sat, keeping Avoa's company. At night, they slept close together for mutual comfort. When three moons had passed, N'kura spoke about her pregnancy.

She told Avoa that a child of Molo was coming, that she felt it was a strong child who would bring joy to their lives. Avoa felt her grief lessen, hugged N'kura and vowed that she would live to see the child grow. With great tenderness, the two women lived together and prepared for the child's coming.

When the time came, N'kura gave birth easily to a big girl with curly hair like her father's. While Biba had been a tiny baby, born hairless, this child was robust and ruddy. Biba was delighted to have a baby sister; Avoa felt like a loving grandmother; and the whole tribe was relieved that it had been a safe delivery. N'kura felt a placid love reinforced by breastfeeding the hungry little girl. This one would not be a meek woman, but a strong warrior. She would be called Star.

***

N'kura and Avoa started to plan for Biba's mating. So they gathered nuts, prepared fermented fruit drinks and did all the things that could be done ahead of time. The one thing that N'kura wanted was to give Biba her shining stone necklace before the mating. So, one day, she walked to her old hut where Biba was living by herself and offered the necklace to her daughter. The mother reminded the young woman of the stories she had taught her about the stone. N'kura also reminded Biba that her stone would grow and that one day when she had her own children, she was supposed to divide the stone with her most worthy daughter.

"When Molo died, the stone made me understand that it was my fault because I gave him a necklace. That's what made him sick to death. Males are not supposed to wear this kind of stone. So don't share it with Lando unless you want him to die. Tell this whole story to the daughter you choose to carry on our gift. And tell her that she must continue the line and the stories to her own chosen daughter."

A few moons later, Biba was mated to Lando, and everyone rejoiced at the happy pairing. The old hut became empty, and sometimes, children played in it. The couple seemed charmed by each other. If it were not so endearing, they would seem to be fools. Their friends teased them sometimes, but they were only jealous of their happiness.

Soon, Biba became pregnant, or thought she was. However, she suffered heavy and painful bleeding. N'kura stayed with her, applied cool wet leaves to her brow, made hot soothing drinks, boiled a bit of meat with herbs until it was tender and spoon-fed her daughter. She warned Biba and Lando not to mate until a moon had passed so that Biba would be strong for her next child.

The winter that followed was hard for the people. In the years that N'kura and her daughter lived among their new tribe, winters had been mild with many sunny days. However, in this turn of the seasons, sleet and hard rain fell from the sky and some days the water in containers had a film of ice. They could not even maintain the communal fire because it had become a waterlogged mess.

Many people sickened and died from hard coughs, wispy breathing and fevers. Especially the elderly and the children. Other people survived, but they were very weak. Tempers flared in close confinement within huts that were not built for long occupation. The people were used to living mostly outside and the constant rain, grey skies and weeping walls were a source of misery. In the few sunny days, people dragged their furs outside to air, but the mud made it difficult to keep anything clean.

N'kura made sure that her family was healthy by preparing drinks steeped with herbal remedies and forcing them outside, even in the rain. Star had become thin and that worried her mother; however, she continued to suckle well and was starting to eat pre-chewed grains. She would survive the winter. Avoa, on the other hand, was as healthy as a young woman. She would go outside with N'kura, and they would spearfish in the rain.

They would carry small pieces of wood to the abandoned hut in the hope that they would dry enough for their small cooking fires. They picked winter nuts before they would rot on the ground and harvested strong herbs and roots that would endure under so much moisture. N'kura and Avoa shared what they gathered with the neediest among the tribe, and their efforts must have helped many to survive the worst.

All they needed was sunlight and dry weather. Finally, the days became noticeably longer, and spring signalled with the appearance of crocuses. There were more sunny days, and the mud dried. The people had survived although their numbers were greatly reduced. They left the confines of their huts with shallow steps, pale countenance and stooped bodies. Even the children were subdued.

The men that remained and were strong enough left for a hunting trip. The few healthy women and the older children looked nearby for spring greens, dug for roots and speared fish. The elderly and the ill were brought outside the huts, hoping that fresh air and sunlight would help them regain strength. Few survived, but N'kura rejoiced that Avoa was among those few. With sunlight and a good diet, they all would be strong again.

The long confinement brought a wave of pregnancies among the younger women and Biba was one of them. That was good news for the tribe if all women survived childbirth and the children grew to adulthood. By the time the hunting party returned to the camp a moon later, some bellies were already showing growth. The men had lingered in the forest to enjoy the good weather and each other's company. They were invigorated by their success. Most of the meat was dried in strips and aged, but it was enough for everyone.

Star started to walk by herself by the end of spring and when Biba was delivered of a healthy daughter, N'kura was pleased that her family was whole.

***

During the spring moons, a man who had lost his mate started to court N'kura by bringing her extra meat and small furs. He was tall and sturdy with an occasional smile that showed he had all his teeth. He was called Beto and was appreciated by other men as a good hunter. N'kura talked about him with Avoa.

The older woman understood the need for more children, but she remembered Beto as a bully in his youth. She advised against the match for N'kura's sake. The sister-wife heeded her counsel and stood aloof the next time Beto brought her furs.

"Thank you, but I have enough. You take them to another woman."

Beto felt rebuked and became angry. "You are nothing but dung, ghost woman." He shouted. Since other people were watching he did not hit N'kura, but she felt his rage.

A few days later, certain of privacy under the branches of the trees by the shore, he caught her by the river, subdued the small women and tried to rape her. N'kura felt not fear, but fury. She pushed him, bit him, placed her hands on his chest and wished him dead. Since he was on top of her, she did not see her hands, but she felt a surge of energy, hot and implacable, flow from her palms to his body. He simply became a dead weight against her. She couldn't even scream because his weight suffocated her.

She twisted and pushed the body away and twisted again until she was free. Then she walked calmly to the camp and said that Beto had tried to force himself upon her, but that the Great Mother of All had struck him dead. The people believed her because N'kura was so small and Beto so large it was impossible for her to kill him with her hands. However, in the passing of time, no other male tried to court her. The fact was that she not only looked strange, but the Great Mother of All had come to her rescue. N'kura was forever different in the eyes of her tribe.

Several turns of the seasons came and went until Star was old enough to bleed. The problem was that N'kura had not aged. She was exactly as she had been when she first arrived with her daughter. People whispered and that was dangerous. It was time to leave the comfort of this tribe and search for other people.

N'kura spoke with Avoa about this and asked if she wanted to leave too. However, the older woman did not want to leave Biba and her five girls who had become her family. So N'kura went to her eldest daughter's hut and explained her predicament. Biba hugged her mother weeping but said she would help. The mother also spoke with her youngest daughter, convincing her of the need to leave.

Star, in the beginning, baulked about leaving her friends, but at the prospect of an exciting adventure, she agreed to follow her mother. This time it was a planned leaving. She would take Star with her and search for new people, but they would leave well-prepared.

On the dark moon after her decision, N'kura and Biba left with their sleeping furs well wrapped around all their essentials for survival. They wore leather skirts, took with them feet wrappers in heavier skin and tied their bundles with wide bands of leather. Now that they knew of how difficult winters could be, they also carried fur coats and hats. The bundles were heavy, and they would slow their travel. However, Star was tall and strong, almost her petite mother's height. With the bundles on their backs, N'kura and Star stepped into the night and followed the river on its course to the unknown.

Chapter Five

During many, many turns of the seasons, through all kinds of weather and terrain challenges, N'kura walked with her burden on her back and her daughter beside her. Sometimes, she found other travellers whom she approached weary but curious. They exchanged goods and information. Other times the encounters were dangerous. These times, if attacked, she would kill the man with the lightning of her hands.

Any witnesses usually fled. In the rare times that others in the assaulting group tried to attack, the woman made an arch with her lightning, and they fell where they stood. She became known as the Lightning Ghost. N'kura didn't mind because she simply kept travelling.

N'kura stopped in countless camps, and each time stayed until she had another daughter or two of an age to accompany her. When her ageless features started to disturb the people around her, she planned her exit. She always left a daughter behind with a stone and her stories, urging them not to forget and to continue the heritage with their own chosen daughter.

Occasionally, she found a sister of her soul and gave her a necklace. N'kura also exhorted these soul sisters to remember her story and to share both their stones and their mysteries. Every time she made a necklace, she consumed the powder and flakes. Every time she became stronger and more emotionally detached. She was not like other people.

Sometimes, men tried to steal a stone necklace. N'kura always had more in her pouch, so she let them place the stolen necklaces around their necks. She waited until they sickened and died and then retrieved the stones. Her collection of precious shining stones was increasing.

Each time she left her latest tribe, N'kura travelled with the ocean on her right side and the rising sun in front of her. If she had to choose between the two, she followed the sun. The people she encountered had different languages, different customs, diverse ways of dressing and different foods. The more she walked, the more interesting things were.

There were tribes who did not rely exclusively on gathering and hunting but were growing especially selected grasses around their huts. These grasses grew small grains that when ground together between stones, were nutritious and fed the people regularly. Other tribes had decided that it was better to raise small goats in enclosures than to hunt for them in the wild. And everywhere there were dogs and cats. People did not eat them, but used these animals as companions, as guards and to chase away vermin. She even met a tribe that did not walk on their two feet, but rode animals called horses.

She also saw many differences in the way people made tools. N'kura observed that many were using a black stone called obsidian to chip away small slivers that cut and drew blood easily. It was excellent for cutting food and scraping skins, but it was also used to make small blades and arrowheads that were attached to wood handles or sticks. The farther she walked, the more sophisticated were the clay vessels with beautiful decorations. She saw that people baked them in ovens.

As she walked with her latest daughter, N'kura tried to avoid warfare, but sometimes, it was inevitable. Once, she hid with her daughter for days in an abandoned, roofless hut waiting for the slaughter to end. They were lucky, but many men had been gutted with the new kind of stone knives. She warned her daughter to avoid angry men and that when the time came, she should choose a kind man for a mate.

As she continued her explorations, N'kura realised that her impetus to leave established camps and small villages was only in part due to her agelessness and bald features. She had become consumed by what she could find next. It was as if the stones wanted to spread their seed, like males or the people who grew food by their huts. She also understood that she was not quite human any longer.

Although she maintained the bodily functions of a human, including reproduction, her heart was so used to losing her daughters, her kin and places that she called home, that she felt closer to the stone that she wore than to other people. N'kura felt the urge for more stones. She had a pouch filled with them, but she wanted the stones close to her body, and she felt the need to consume more stone powder.

For the moment, her latest daughter Ishtar and N'kura were living by the sea in a place that thousands of years later would be called Constantinople. It was a large village due to the trade that flowed through its wooden-decked port and the caravans that occasionally stopped to replenish their supplies. The people on dugout boats and the foot caravans made their trade and continued on their way. Sometimes, the caravans had one or two beasts of burden, but these were still rare.

N'kura and Ishtar fell into the customs of the village. Here people kept busy doing only one type of labour, instead of the habits of her original tribes in which everyone contributed in a variety of ways. Mother and daughter became known as healers and that is how they could afford to live in the village. After their travels through countless camps and villages and from learning from the wise women of those places, N'kura had become an expert at setting bones, healing wounds and preparing various tisanes for a variety of purposes.

Even the village chief and his family used her services and were content with her healing abilities. The woman had already accumulated a small number of yellow pebbles called gold. Like her shells of so long ago, these were used for trade.

One of the stones had grown so big that it could be carved onto a torque necklace. N'kura decided to speak with the jeweller in the village because she wanted a perfect job done and she did not have either the tools or the skills. The man was fascinated by the sparkling large stone and said he would do it in exchange for a piece of the stone. N'kura refused and offered a piece of gold.

He bargained for a second piece, and the woman decided that it was a deal if he also made a ring with a spider web design. He accepted and said she could come back in three days. N'kura refused to leave. She insisted that she had to stay for as long as it took him to work on the stone and that she wanted all the dust and flakes from the process. She offered a third piece of gold, and he set to work.

It took him a full day and a night to create the torque and the ring. In the end, he returned to N'kura all the smaller pieces of stone derived from the carving process and a good amount of dust, wrapped in a small skin pouch. He received her thanks and three pieces of gold.

When she got home, N'kura placed the torque on her slender neck. It would hold, and it was comfortable. Next, she threaded her left index finger into the newly carved ring, and it fit. Finally, she dropped the dust in a drinking cup, added water and swallowed the thick paste. She was in bed for three days with visions, too weak to stand.

Ishtar regularly brought her mother water and helped her to relieve herself. N'kura had never consumed such a large amount of stone dust, but her body had craved it. By the third day, she woke up refreshed and reenergised. However, she was not surprised to know that the jeweller had died of stone poisoning. Of course, no one could figure out the source of his sudden illness and death, but N'kura felt that it was time to leave the village.

Before they left, the mother gave Ishtar the necklace that she had previously prepared. As she had done countless times before, she told her daughter the story and mysteries of the stones and warned of its dangers to men and that she had lived many times the lifespan of a regular person. She exhorted Ishtar to tell the stories to her chosen daughter and to share the necklace with her, but, for every woman's sake, she insisted that she keep secret everything about the stones.

Mother and daughter continued their journey and eventually, as she had always done, N'kura left her daughter with her own child in a welcoming tribe and continued walking with another girl-child. She walked, settled, gave birth and raised her newest daughter many more times and every time that the people started whispering about her agelessness, she left in the company of another daughter. For a long time, N'kura had gotten used to wearing seven stones around her neck, plus the torque and her ring. While occasionally she heard fantasy stories about the 'Lightning Ghost', among her multitude of daughters she was secretly known as the 'Mother of Stones'.

Chapter Six

With the passing of time, N'kura lost track of her age or of how many daughters she had left behind. This time, as they walked keeping the sea on their right side, the rising sun was at their backs.

N'kura and her latest daughter arrived at a delta which was rich in food, with exuberant vegetation and much wildlife, but she felt the weight of centuries in her body. She did not walk as fast as before, and her skin looked translucent. She was incredibly old. In the distance, she saw a village built on stilts. N'kura sat in the shade of a palm tree and spoke to her daughter.

"Akira, I cannot travel any longer. My body is old; I'm not able to carry my burden; and I have seen all I care to see. You have been a woman for several summers, and I have taught you well. Remember all that I told you and what you saw.

"Behold that village! They will welcome you, and I have already taught you much. Nevertheless, you won't carry on empty-handed. You will have all my gold, shells, tools and old leather. And above all, you will receive all my stones. It is time that you receive your heritage.

"Although you are still young, you are the only daughter of my blood that I have left. So you must become the Stone Mother. I will be with you for your transformation, and then I will let my body die."

"Mother, please don't leave me! I will be all alone."

N'kura reassured her daughter that with her wealth and skills, she would be welcome in the village and find a good mate. That she would only have daughters, live a very long time and become wealthy.

"When you are ready, my daughter, leave this place behind and follow my footsteps backwards. Find your sisters and your nieces. The further you walk back the older the bloodline will be. Tell them my story and, on the way, give the stones to women you trust with the secret. You must ensure the future. When you are very, very old and you feel that you cannot continue, make another Mother of Stones of our line."

They walked closer to the water, settled in a dry and shaded spot and N'kura told her daughter to fill a drinking cup with water. The old mother sipped some water and dumped the contents of her small skin bag into the cup. She stirred the stone dust and flakes with the water until it was a fluid paste. Then, she removed all her stone jewellery and gave it to Akira who was sitting cross-legged in front of N'kura. The young woman placed the necklace of seven stones, the torque around her neck and the ring on her finger. Finally, she consumed the contents of the cup and collapsed upon a skin rug, unconscious.

For the next three days, N'kura took care of her daughter very afraid that she might die under the onslaught of so much stone. She cleaned Akira, gave her sips of water, cooled her brow and waited. On the evening of the third day, the new Mother of Stones woke up very weak. N'kura helped Akira bathe in the water and made her a hot nourishing drink, and Akira slept deeply for another day. The mother prayed to all the gods and goddesses that she wouldn't die before her daughter was ready because N'kura was feeling the last of her strength leave her. So she lay down beside her daughter, and she too fell asleep.

When Akira woke up, she felt dazed by the images of her mother's life and of the great journey in cold black that she did not understand. It must have been the voyage of the first stone. However, she felt physically strong, revitalised, thirsty and hungry. That is when she noticed N'kura's cold body beside her.

Akira lovingly wrapped her mother's body in the furs where she had died. Afterwards, she drank deeply from the river and ate one of her mother's balls of nuts and seeds. Satisfied, she dug as deep a hole as she could manage, placed N'kura's body in it and covered the burial site with stones.

The new Mother of Stones attended to her bundles, placed them on her back and, with her bald head, she walked proudly to the unknown village. Her time had come, and it was a formidable responsibility. She was ready for the future.

Part Two

The Mater that we know, our beloved and fierce Mother of Stones, was born in the middle of the twentieth century and celebrated her four hundredth birthday not so long ago. Of course, there have been Maters, or Mothers of Stones, ever since the First One, thousands of years ago. However, this is the Mater that shaped our lives. Let us learn now about her beginnings as our Mother of Stones.

—Excerpt from a teaching manual in the year 2387

Chapter Seven

Time is a companion to our life span and an interesting linear concept. When we are young and having fun, time is a whirlwind in a carousel. If a task or an experience is boring or painful, time stretches according to the intensity of discomfort or of pain. However, as we get older, time speeds and passes in the blink of experience. Nevertheless, there are lucid moments in our lives when time feels suspended, and we know that nothing will ever be the same. That was about to happen to Sofia.

On the island of Sao Miguel, Azores, it was a rainy winter day when Sofia went down the stairs of her large home to get the mail. She noticed the rain and wondered if the mail would be wet. Besides the usual bills, there was a fancy envelope, the kind that is thick with texture, with her address handwritten. "Peculiar…" she wondered. The return address was that of a law firm in Lisbon. 'Stranger and stranger'.

Sofia climbed the steps. There were seventeen, she had counted numerous times when lack of exercise reminded Sofia of her age. Today, though, there was a bounce in her step as she climbed the stairs and continued through the long corridor to sit in her favourite chair in a small sitting room and began to open the odd envelope.

Dear Senhora Dona Sofia de Lima,

Our law firm is pleased to inform you that you are the recipient of an inheritance. Due to the importance of this bequest, we have taken the liberty of sending two of our senior staff to meet with you at your earliest convenience. Please contact our office for a place and time that best suits you.

Sincerely and with best compliments,

(Scratchy signature),

Unknown female name followed by several phone numbers, fax and email.

"What the fuck!" Sofia's first emotional reaction was suspicion and anxiety. "This must be one of those catfishing frauds that the internet talks about. No way! Could it be true?"

What followed was a couple of hours of frantic internet fact-checking. She even called her best friend to help confirm that there was indeed a legitimate law firm with that name. It seemed genuine. Sofia was not by nature a mistrustful person, but this was extraordinary and out of her comfort zone. So, even though the law firm did exist, she felt she needed to be cautious. So she got a paper and pen to jot notes and called the first number on the list.

The line was answered by a professional-sounding secretary with a 'You have reached the law firm of…' followed by a list of partners. As soon as she introduced herself, the secretary immediately told Sofia that her call was expected and to please hold for a transfer. A mature-sounding female voice picked up the line and introduced herself as the managing partner. The interaction was brief, but the voice sounded very respectful and confirmed that she had sent the letter and that two of the firm's partners were already on the island ready to speak with Senhora Dona Sofia de Lima. The phone call confirmed that indeed there was an inheritance and that it was very important that Sofia met with the two lawyers. She was reassured that all her questions would soon be answered, and a meeting was arranged for the next day at mid-afternoon.

Sofia felt exhausted. She was unnerved by this unexpected turn of events, and she wondered who would leave her a legacy. Her family was not wealthy, she really did not know well her mother's side of the family in the United States, but they had their own children, nephews and nieces. Her parents had passed away years before and so had her younger sister.

Sofia lived alone in the house she had inherited. She had several good friends on the island of Sao Miguel, Azores. Her two children lived in different European countries with their own children and their busy lives. Never too busy, however, to forget to call Mom regularly. Sofia visited her children occasionally and, in their turn, they came to the island to visit and enjoy the summer beaches.

Sofia loved her retired life after teaching and researching sociology. She had worked mostly at a local university and spent a lifetime of social activism. In her youth, she had been fierce and irreverent; now, she was a respected local politician and spent some of her free time volunteering with vulnerable women. She really loved her life on the island and was fortunate to have a good enough pension to live with comfort. In a moment of lucid expectation for the following day's meeting, Sofia was certain that her life was about to change. She did not know how she felt about it.

At the appointed time, Sofia was ready. She checked the hot tea and newly purchased cookies set in the living room. It was her parents' furniture. She never bothered with decoration. Why spend money buying new things when the old ones are just fine?

Of course, the walls needed new paint, but the weekly cleaner kept everything dust-free and that was good enough. The bell rang, and she invited in two women. One was older than the other and introduced herself as Ana. She had lovely long grey hair, was very slim with stylish clothes and a tentative smile. The younger woman said her name was Leonor. She also looked very attractive but with a heavier body, very artistic glasses and a broad smile. Both women followed Sofia to the living room and were delighted at the tea and cookies.

"Thank you for taking the trouble. It's very kind of you!" said Leonor, taking the leading role.

"Please be comfortable and explain to me what this is all about." Sofia sat across from both women and waited.

"To begin with, here is our identification and credentials. Please feel free to take photos for your records." Both Ana and Leonor placed their documents on the coffee table and Sofia did just that. She carefully checked their ID and their professional credentials and took pictures with her phone. When Sofia was done, the three women sipped their tea and Leonor, once more took the lead.

"We want to tell you some background before discussing your inheritance. But, before that, we need you to sign a non-disclosure agreement because everything we are about to tell you is an absolute secret. If, after we briefly tell you the story and about your inheritance, you choose not to accept the responsibilities that come with it, we will deposit in your account a substantial sum as compensation for your trouble. We will leave, you will have a good chunk of money to do as you will, and you will be silent about this for the rest of your life."

Sofia was surprised. She took a deep breath. "Well, what can I say? This seems like a lot more than a simple inheritance, however now I am genuinely curious. If I reject what you are about to tell me, I will still receive an undisclosed amount of money. So it's a win for me, I guess. How much money do I receive if I refuse to accept the inheritance?" Sofia thought all might as well be clear.

"About the value of your house. You can always say that a rich old aunt left you the money. Do you agree?"

Sofia looked at both Ana and Leonor. They were earnest and looked truthful, and there was a lot of money involved. So she decided: "Please give me the document to sign."

Ana sat forward and started to speak in a very thoughtful manner.

"A very long time ago, a woman started a kind of sisterhood centred around stones that were not stones but a dense amalgam of nanobots. I know it sounds inconceivable, but the woman simply found the first stone, which likely came to Earth as part of an asteroid, or it was deliberately sent. We don't know.

"A nanobot is an exceedingly small (nanoscale) self-propelled machine, especially one that has some degree of autonomy and can reproduce. Scientists have guessed that there are many potential applications if one day such machines can be engineered. However, it has been among women, secretly, for millennia. Well, Leonor and I are part of this network of women spread throughout the world. Yes, we work at the law office, we are lawyers and partners in the business, but we owe allegiance above all to the network.

"We call it Telea, Latin for web because there are many tendrils throughout the world and, at its centre, there is a leader we call the Mater. She used to have other names throughout history. She has always been known as the Mother of Stones, but since Roman times we simply call her the Mater. She is not a spider in her web consuming her prey.

"On the contrary, the Mater is the source of energy that sustains and defines Telea. Her power is absolute because the Mater is able to connect the multitudes of women. She feels us, nurtures us and multiplies us by sharing new stones. Many women share their own stones by dividing them and giving them to trusted females, but none has the power of the Mater."

"I'm sorry," interrupted Sofia, "but what do these nanobots or stones do? And what about the women in this Telea? What kind of lives do they have? Can men receive stones?"

"Once a woman receives a stone, she must wear it next to her skin. Usually as a necklace. The nanobots enter the skin through absorption, spread throughout her body and keep it in optimum condition to the end of her long life. Not all women's bodies accept the nanobots. Some reject them and, unfortunately, sicken and die. There is no treatment for a nano rejection. The same happens to transwomen and men. The stones are keyed to double X chromosomes."

"May I see your stones?" asked Sofia. Both women took out equal necklaces with a very dark, semi-shining surface. They were flat ovals that looked like marcasite, broken patterns of dull and shine. "Okay. Thank you!"

Leonor added to the explanation: "Most women in Telea live normal lives. Many are married with female children. They cannot carry males beyond the first couple of weeks of gestation. Many women live in female communities, such as nunneries—that is how we survived through the ages—live alone or with female sexual partners.

"Most women in Telea live everyday lives and have jobs, hobbies and interests. We tend to live well into our eighties or nineties in good health. Once a year, women get together to reinforce their bonds of community and further charge their energies, especially if the Mother of Stones is among them."

"How do they do that? I mean, how does the Mater recharge energy?"

"Sorry, that part will only be disclosed to you if you agree to the terms of your inheritance. So, let's continue." Leonor sounded stern. "Some women work full-time for Telea or for its hundreds of social enterprises, such as schools, hospitals and women's shelters. A few women work as security.

"Some, like us, work as lawyers, accountants or financial advisers and in a variety of occupations that sustain a very large and secret organisation. I regret, but this is about the extent of what I may share with you in terms of background information."

"What can you possibly want with me? I may be insane, but I actually believe you. You have the stones; you have the financial means to come and speak with me and to offer me a whole lot of money. You could be part of an elaborate hoax, but I believe you. However, what does any of this have to do with me? What is my inheritance?"

Both women looked at Sofia, leaned forward in their seats, and Ana answered: "We, in the representation of Telea and its council of ministers, want you to be the next Mater, the next Mother of Stones."

Sofia stood up quickly and declared: "I need a cigarette and a stiff drink. Do you want to join me?"

She didn't wait for them to reply. She efficiently served scotch, got her cigarette pack and a lighter and walked back and forth in the living room, puffing vigorously. She didn't say a word. Just smoked, lit another one, poured another drink and, like the previous one, gulped it down. It was just too much information. Sofia was a planner, a thinker and generally serene about life, but she felt overwhelmed.

The afternoon was turning into the evening. Usually, she would be preparing dinner about now. However, she couldn't think about food. Sofia took deep breaths and felt herself calm down. She sat down, looked at Ana and at Leonor and asked the age-old question of all whiners: "Why me?" It sounded like whining, but it made no sense, and she needed a lot more information.

"Why would you want me to be the Mater? Don't you have one? How would I become the Mater? I'm just a 67-year-old retiree who never heard of you or of Telea until now."

"The last Mater died about two years ago," Leonor explained in a soothing voice. "We spent the time until now searching for you and for other candidates. Two of them died in the test to become the Mater, but you were always our best choice. It just took time to find you. Why would you be a potential Mother of Stones? Because you are a direct descendant of the first one and a mitochondrial heir."

Ana continued the explanation. "Through genetic testing of the available corpses of previous Mothers of Stones, we determined that they all carry the same mitochondrial DNA. That means that they were all descendants of the same mitochondrial mother. The first one to find the stone.

"Your maternal great-grandmother was one of us. Isolated on the island of Flores, without her peers for support, she nevertheless lived a full life as a farmer's wife. She had seven daughters. Each daughter had more female offspring, just like your mother had three daughters. You have a daughter and a son.

"Your daughter has a daughter, and just like that, the flow of mitochondrial DNA continues. Once we suspected that you were a potential Mother of Stones, during your last blood tests we surreptitiously gathered a sample and tested it. We were proven right.

"Since the twelfth century, we have kept meticulous records in Europe. Unfortunately, historical upheavals, such as war, famine and disease, have often eradicated whole genetic lines. Yours survived. However, there are other reasons for choosing you. Please, Leonor, since you were part of the search committee, can you continue?"

"Of course! Besides your genetic inheritance, you have a combination of traits that make you a perfect candidate. You are a strong woman whose life was difficult. You know how to deal with successes and failures. You are a natural leader as evidenced by your previous profession and your political activism.

"You are highly educated. You enjoy administrative tasks. You are very creative, and the proof is in the books you published and the art you create. Some Portuguese operatives interviewed several women as if they were just gossiping. We learned that you are well-liked and respected.

"You work as well in teams as you do by yourself. Also, you have no family responsibilities. You could dedicate your time exclusively to Telea. You would be wealthy beyond your imagination. You would have personal power and authority over all the women that comprise Telea. It would be the culmination of your life's work."

"Well, well… thank you for the praise, but, at my age, how could I take over such enormous responsibility?"

"Very simply, you will have an extended life and time enough to use your passion to change the world. However, as we told you before, not all women survive the transition to Mater. There is a danger that you could die. If that unfortunate outcome occurs, your children will receive a very large inheritance from you.

"As of this evening, you will receive the money we promised just simply because you listened to us. We will return tomorrow at the same time to hear your answer. Please keep in mind the absolute secrecy of what we have discussed."

Leonor and Ana stood up, thanked Sofia for her time and left the house. Sofia saw them walking in the night down her street towards the centre of Ponta Delgada.

***

Sofia did not call her best friend that evening. She sent a message to Carrie saying she needed to rest. The house felt confined, and her mind was in turmoil. The house was cold and damp. Dinner was forgotten.

So she decided to take a hot bubble bath. It was a long bath with flickering candles. She did not read her novel, did not watch television, did not check her social media. In fluffy pyjamas, wrapped in a blankie, Sofia sat for hours in her comfortable chair thinking and, at times, letting her mind wander. She drank and smoked the evening away until she realised she was getting drunk, and the ashtray was overflowing with ashes everywhere.

She climbed the stairs to her bedroom, took her pills and imagined that perhaps in the future there would be no more pills to worry about. Brushed her teeth and peed in the adjoining bathroom. She looked in the mirror. A grey-haired woman, slightly obese looked back.

Her wrinkles were not very pronounced; her eyes were bloodshot from the stresses of the day and too much alcohol. Her face was pleasant; unfortunately, her body had seen better days. Well, nothing hurt and that was the most important thing. Now, what would the future bring?

Under her winter comforter and the lights turned off, Sofia kept thinking. There was still so much to learn about Telea and her role in it. What if she died? She was not afraid of that but felt sorrow for the pain her children and friends would endure. If she survived, the future could hold amazing things, and Sofia could dedicate her life to any project she desired.

The possibilities were endless and appealing. She would be rich; she would live a long and healthy life. The decision coalesced in her mind. She would do it. She would become the next Mother of Stones. But what was the test they talked about? Sleep finally overtook her as thunderstorms raged outside.

Chapter Eight

As it was her routine, Sofia woke up at noon, drank two cups of coffee and a glass of orange juice and took her morning pills. After a shower, she dressed carefully and put on her make-up and jewellery. In some way, it was protection from the vulnerability she felt. What further challenges would the upcoming conversation bring? She tidied up the house, cleaned ashtrays and washed dishes.

The house was, as usual, silent. The day was bright and colder than usual. She added a cardigan to her outfit and, while waiting, Sofia checked her bank account online. Yes. There it was the money as promised. Thus, this was not an elaborate hoax. Nobody would dish out that much money if they didn't mean business. She logged out, had yoghurt and cereal and wasted time on social media while waiting.

Her brain was too restless to read. Her e-reader was fully charged. With age, her eyesight had been deteriorating for years. Sofia wore stylish eyeglasses, but still needed to increase the size of the fonts to be able to read comfortably for hours. It had been a long time since she had read a paper novel.

In her later years as a researcher and teacher, Sofia had been glad of online articles. She could download them to her tablet, increase the size of the font and take notes on a paper pad. She knew there was note-taking software, but she had never bothered to learn. Yesterday, Ana and Leonor mentioned long life and health. Perhaps her eyesight would improve. Sharply, on time, the doorbell rang. They had arrived.

Both women were dressed for the weather with scarves and coats. Once more, Sofia offered them tea and cookies, Leonor and Ana sat on the same seats as the day before, and the conversation began. Leonor took the lead.

"So, Sofia, I'm sure that you thought long and hard about our discussion yesterday and all the explanations we offered. With that limited information, we need to know what your decision is. Only if you accept the duties of being the Mater, can we move forward with further explanations. As you may have checked, the money we offered for your attention to this matter and for your lifelong silence has been deposited. From now on, you must tell us your decision, and there are two possible paths ahead.

"In the first one, you reject the offer, we drink your delicious Azorean tea, and we leave. You will never see or hear from us again. The money is yours. We suggest that you invest it for your old age. If you choose to accept our offer, then you will sign another document of acceptance and acknowledge that we have informed you of the risk of death in the test and transition to become the Mater. What do you choose?"

Sofia looked both in the eyes, took a deep breath and answered, 'I accept the offer to become the Mater, and I accept the possible risk of death. I also expect that in the eventuality of my death, my children will be financially stable for the rest of their lives. That is the price you pay for the risk."

Ana exhaled, and Leonor leaned over and took Sofia's hand. "I'm so very happy that this is your decision." She took a document from her briefcase, placed it on the table and asked for Sofia's full signature. Sofia read the text carefully, left the room to get her identification card, filled in the details of her ID and signed her full name: *Sofia Luisa Machado da Silva*. She felt a bit breathless, wary and, at the same time, eager to know what would come next.

Ana placed the signed document in her own briefcase, turned to Sofia and to Leonor and said, "Now we can answer fully any questions you might have, and we plan in detail the next few days."

Sofia just needed to know: "When you say I will have a long life, how long are we talking about?"

Leonor smiled. "The last Mother of Stones was born in the South of France in 1762, before the French Revolution. She died two years ago. However, instead of choosing her successor as her predecessors had done, she lingered fragile for over two decades. That was, in my opinion, selfish of her and caused great damage to Telea because she was not able to fulfil her duties.

"The council of ministers took over the management of Telea, but they couldn't or wouldn't maintain its vitality. We desperately need you. In your case, we expect that you will be able to live three or four centuries. We also expect that you will surrender your stones to a successor when the time comes so that Telea can go seamlessly from one Mater to the other. However, we won't be able to force you to do so because your power is absolute. We can only advise you when your time comes."

"Assuming that I will successfully become the Mater and that I live all those years, what happens to me when I surrender the stones to the one that comes next?"

"You will die quickly and painlessly," answered Leonor with a flat tone of voice. "But that is many, many years in the future. In the meantime, you must become the Mother of Stones. Ana, how long will it take for our team to arrive in São Miguel?"

"Two days. The full team has already been assembled in Arles, Provence. They will have quite a bit of technology to bring with them, and we need to find a house suitable for our needs quickly. Since it is winter, there will be quite a lot of local lodgings available for tourists. By tomorrow, I will find a large house away from neighbours."

Sofia looked alarmed. "What kind of technology? Why do we need a house? Mine is big enough. What will you do to me?" This was totally not what she was expecting, and it sounded menacing.

Leonor explained calmly: "Today is the last day that you will ever sign your full name because you will disappear. Some members of the team will fake your death. Perhaps your car flying off a ravine into the ocean or some other scenario. Don't worry about that. They are experts."

"Wait! Why do I need to pretend to die? Can't I simply become the Mater without fooling people that I'm dead? And another thing, I like my name." Sofia found herself whining again. It was embarrassing.

"What do you think would happen if suddenly a younger version of yourself were to appear in Ponta Delgada? What will happen in twenty years when you don't age? You will have to disappear many times in your lifetime because you simply cannot live in the same place for longer than a decade. The transformation into the Mater will return you to full health as you were in your prime. That will make you look younger; you will be stronger and more agile.

"You will also have other changes that no one can foresee. The last Mater became a genius in navigating turbulent times, and she could predict patterns in social and economic developments, long before they occurred. She steered us into safety and further prosperity. If you survive, as we expect, you will come through the ordeal differently. The test is the same for millennia, but the results are always surprising."

Ana added, "You will be addressed as 'the Mater' or 'Mother of Stones' for the rest of your life, just as every other woman who came before you and every woman who will come after you. The Mater also signifies stability and continuity. You will no longer be Sofia, but a different entity. You will certainly not be fully human any longer. How could you live centuries and still be the same human being? Does this upset you, Sofia?"

"I just didn't think through the implications. It's a lot to consider, and it's unsettling. I only hope you are really good at creating this fraud because the police are going to investigate, and there will be intense scrutiny. Oh, my goodness! I will never see my children or grandchildren. They will be devastated when they hear about my death."

Leonor, once more, took charge of the conversation. "You don't need to worry about your children. They will be fine, and they will be wealthy. As time passes, you can get regular reports on their lives if you wish. For the rest, the logistics are our responsibility, but you need to prepare your body.

"You will need to purge your intestines, and you can only consume clear liquids. We will bring you the medication for the purge after we leave you. You can drink your whiskey and smoke your cigarettes for now, but you will never be addicted again once you become the Mater. For the next two days, don't leave the house because you will need to use the toilet frequently.

"If you need to contact us, call any number in the letter you received from the law office. We will return your call. Please remember the absolute secrecy involved. You cannot give any hint to anyone that you are going to disappear. Do you have any questions?"

"Yes. If I die, after you have set up the fake death, what will happen to my body?"

"We will dig a really deep hole," replied Leonor with some mirth in the tone of her voice.

Chapter Nine

After they left, Sofia once more sat silently. She was hungry but knew she couldn't eat. So she drank the cold tea, returned to her usual seat and decided to call Carrie, her best friend. They chatted about the latest Netflix series, although they never liked the same things. They talked about how Sofia was not feeling well and about Carrie's latest sewing project. They said goodbye in their usual way.

Shortly after, the doorbell rang. It was Ana with the cleansing medication and two boxes of pineapple gelatine. Enough for two days. "How are you feeling?" she asked kindly.

"I don't know, but I'll be okay. Just a lot to process. See you in two days!"

"Actually, this is goodbye for now. I will leave when the team from Arles arrives because I will need to return to the office, write a fake report and pretend that nothing special happened here. I will resume my work and go back to my wife and to my life. A word of advice: after you survive the transition, it might be a good idea if you keep Leonor with you.

"She is the leader of this sequence of events, and she is also the regional director of the Portuguese Telea. Leonor is much older than I am and has invaluable experience. She received her stone when she was in her twenties, so she has aged slower than most. You will need a friendly face in the beginning."

"Thank you for the advice. I just need to survive first. I hope that I see you again. Goodbye!"

Sofia prepared the gelatine, set it in the fridge and decided to call her children. Their conversations were affectionate but brief. It was dinnertime, and their young ones were demanding their parents' attention. Sofia ended the calls, got herself a shot glass, her favourite scotch whiskey and started to cry. She mourned herself.

The old woman she would never be, the grandmother that would disappear. There was also fear of dying. What would they do to her body that required purging? She poured the drink and sipped. Then it was time to set things up in the bathroom for the expelling of the contents of her digestive tract.

Back in the kitchen, Sofia prepared the medication and hurried up to the bathroom. Shortly after it began, she resigned herself for a couple of miserable days of drinking the awful liquid and shitting. Such was the end of her known life.

Two days later, Sofia received the expected phone call. She felt a bit weak and lightheaded. Leonor told her to drive to the town of Furnas with only her purse, nothing else. They would meet by the fumaroles and hot springs. Sofia walked around her house, saying goodbye to it.

She looked at her artwork, at the memories and photographs. What would her children do with her personal possessions? What would they do with her property? Well, it wasn't her business anymore. She used the bathroom first, grabbed a bottle of water, locked the house door, walked to her car and drove. It was only a forty-minute drive.

By the time Sofia arrived in Furnas and although it was an overcast day, there were already tourists wandering around. She parked the car near the hot springs and fumaroles and walked around. Soon she found Leonor who asked for the keys and directed her toward an SUV. Sofia complied and soon they were driving again towards the lake. With the four-wheel drive engaged, they turned left and drove up a very steep dirt road until they reached a dead end with a gated entrance.

The property had very high walls around the gate and dense foliage. Leonor opened the gate and Sofia was amazed at the mansion inside. It was clearly a nineteenth-century home with a large embossed front door and beautiful curtained windows gracing two levels. Two wings extended out from the main hall, and it had a luxurious garden around the driveway where four cars were parked.

"Please let me smoke my last cigarette," begged Sofia. Leonor entered the house while Sofia smoked, and she stared at the exterior. She hid the butt under an azalea bush and went to meet her destiny.

Leonor introduced Sofia to ten women in the grand hallway. There were too many to remember their names, and she was feeling dazed. However, she found medical, security and support personnel. Sofia was guided to a large room at the back of the house, close to the kitchen. It must have been a dining room of sorts, but it was now furnished with two medical beds and various equipment.

She was asked to undress and put on a medical gown. After she was done, Sofia sat on one of the beds and Leonor gave her what looked like an ancient Celtic torque necklace. It seemed to be made of nanobot amalgam, solid all around. Leonor placed the necklace around Sofia's neck. It felt warm and surprisingly comfortable.

Then, Leonor offered a heavy ring of the same material. It appeared to be a signet ring with a web carved on the flat surface. Sofia put it on her left hand, where her wedding ring had once been. She started to feel dizzy. Leonor shook her lightly and placed a mug in Sofia's hand.

"Before you pass out, you need to drink all this thick fluid. It has a large amount of suspended nanobot dust mixed with hot chocolate. You will drink it, and then you can have some water if you are still awake. We are here for you. You are not alone. We will take care of you."

Sofia forced herself to half swallow and half chew the stuff. It wasn't bad tasting, but Sofia was starting to see things in visions that came very fast, like a movie in fast forward. The movie in her head accelerated and that's all that there was.

A maelstrom of images and foreign sounds that would make sense one day. The acceleration continued and continued. By then, Sofia was enthralled in her visions. Someone closed her eyes, but the visions continued.

Leonor stepped aside for the nurse to place a catheter and an adult diaper. After that, she found a vein in the back of her hand, placed an IV filled with a simple saline solution, covered Sofia in the soft comforter and let her be.

After three days, Leonor started to worry. Sofia had been cleaned several times, washed and changed many times. Sweat covered her body, and she trembled. A few times there had been seizures which the doctor suppressed with medication.

By the fifth day, Leonor was very worried. Sofia's skin was dry, but the EKG was irregular, and her brain activity showed constant REM sleep. Occasionally, she shivered. It was a good thing that they had brought several comforters to keep her warm.

On the sixth day, Sofia's heart resumed its regular rhythm and her brain showed activity consistent with deep sleep.

On the seventh day, early morning, Sofia opened her eyes. She said she was thirsty and received ice chips. She fell asleep again and by late afternoon she woke up lucid wanting to get out of bed. The body that came through the ordeal was not the same, though.

She had lost most of her body hair, her skin was shedding in large swaths and her voice was rough. Sofia had lost a good amount of weight; her belly was loose; her breasts were long and pendulous. She still had a long way to go.

The nurses filled the ancient bathtub with warm sulphurous and ferreous water that poured from the tap. It was typical of Furnas. The doctor knelt by the bathtub and gently removed the shedding skin. A whole basin of tissue. It was a good thing that the tub had a filter on the drain.

They refilled the tub several times and finally let her soak unmolested. Sofia was dry and warm when she consumed a light soup. Then, she returned to bed and slept until the next day.

During the following week, Leonor helped the new Mater regain strength. The doctor pronounced herself satisfied with the progress. "For the next few days, sleep as much as you need or want, walk around the house and then go outside. The weather is chilly, so make sure you bundle up. Walk around the garden for as long as possible. Your diet will become more diverse and richer in minerals. We expect to leave this place in a couple of weeks."

***

The Mater followed instructions. She didn't speak at all about her visions, which now took the form of nightly dreams. She slept with the torque and her signet ring, and she wore them constantly. She needed fourteen hours a day of sleep the first week, then less in the next days. She still shivered all the time even in her slumber, her muscles quivered all over.

The doctor guessed that it was the way the nanobots were toning the body. She wasn't cold or uncomfortable. The constant trembling progressively abated during those two weeks.

It was in the second week when she looked at herself in the mirror that she noticed a peculiar thing. Considering the state of her physiognomy after her ordeal with her bald head and pink tender skin, the Mater imagined herself as a young Sofia. It was just a reverie, but the muscles in her face shifted, and she looked like her former twenty-year-old self. That was startling! Then it shifted back to her worn face. The Mater tried it again and concentrated.

The beautiful and youthful face that looked back stayed in place. She visualised herself as a very old woman. Again, the muscles shifted, and her face acquired deep wrinkles and mottled skin. Even her back curved. She concentrated and kept the look. The Mater opened the bathroom door, wrapped in a huge fluffy bath towel and called for Leonor and for the doctor. They came in a hurry and froze when they saw her face.

"What happened? How did it go wrong?" Leonor moaned.

The doctor came over and tried to sound professional, but her voice was shaky. "How do you feel? Yes, please tell us what happened."

Instead of replying, the Mater imagined herself as a twenty-year-old, concentrated and her face transformed again. "I believe that I acquired the ability to change my look. Isn't this awesome?"

They were stunned. The doctor did a quick physical check and remained speechless. Leonor immediately saw the possibilities. "This must remain a secret from Telea at large. Only your most trusted advisors should know of this ability.

"This means that you can remain in a place far longer because you can age yourself, and it also means that you can disguise yourself better. With a change in wigs, with make-up, and your shifting ability you can become a totally different person at will. This is unprecedented! How wonderful!"

The Mater asked them to wait in the sitting room and, after dressing herself, she joined them in her natural state, pink-faced and bald but surer of herself. She sat close to Leonor and the doctor.

"To begin with, I will need a scarf for my head. Second, I'm sorry, but I never caught your name, doctor. It's terribly rude of me to not address you properly."

"I'm Justine Clairvaux. I'm French Canadian, and it has been my honour to assist you. I have been part of Telea for fifteen years as personal physician to the previous Mater. I would really like to be your personal physician if you trust my professional skills."

"Well, Justine, I don't see why not. You have cared for me in this crucial time, and you are kind. I would like you to review all the in-house research on nanobot absorption, intercellular diffusion and its effects. I want to know everything that twenty-first-century science has to offer on this matter. So, yes, as my first official decision as the Mater, I want you both, Justine and Leonor, as my advisors, and you will sit on the council. Will this inconvenience you, Leonor?"

"No, the opposite! I'm delighted. I'm single and unattached to any community. I can move to your court right now, except for a brief trip to Torres Novas to get some personal effects."

"How interesting… I will have a court? I guess it makes sense considering that each Mater lives centuries, my predecessors' worldview would be that of the time when they lived. By the way, Justine, how did the previous Mater adjust to the accelerating changes of the last centuries?"

"She had difficulties with the twentieth century. Her mindset simply could not grasp the immense changes, so she focused on giving energy and on increasing her wealth. Aeroplanes terrified her, so she travelled by train and only in Europe and the Middle East. The rest of the world was neglected. Everything and everyone that she cared for had disappeared, and she slowly became a recluse, and then, for the past twenty-six years, she had not even received visitors or interested herself in Telea matters.

"She should have released the stones a long time ago, but she was also desperately clinging to life. Didn't want to let go. So we monitored her health, let her be and the council managed Telea. That's why we are all ecstatic about your arrival. We trust that you will renew Telea, bring fresh ideas and lead us forward in the coming centuries."

The Mater looked to Leonor and asked, "How are my children? And what about my fake death, did it go smoothly?"

"Your death as Sofia went as planned. Your body was never found due to fierce waves on the day of the accident. When the sea calmed, divers found part of the wreckage and one of your car plates. That's how you were identified as the driver. The police entered your home, checked your Facebook account and spoke with your friends. Through your best friend, Carrie, they found your children's contact information.

"They were notified and both your daughter and your son are on the island dealing with their grief and with bureaucracy. I'm sure they are having a hard time, but I'm certain they are also stunned at your wealth. Our legal team will provide appropriate provenances for the money. Don't worry. You are no longer Sofia. You are the Mater. And we are very competent at what we do."

"How is Carrie? I worry that at her age, this could be too much for her. Sometimes, losing a best friend can be as bad as losing a spouse."

"Your best friend seems to be a tough cookie. She even arranged a memorial service for you, with lots of drinking, crying and laughing. It was very well attended." Leonor reassured the Mater, who still seemed preoccupied.

"In three days, we leave. Where are we going? What are the next steps?"

"Before anything else, tomorrow we will buy you very basic clothes because you have been wearing sweats for long enough. When you are ready, in France, we will call upon a dressmaker, a shoemaker and a wig maker, if you wish, to provide you with a proper wardrobe. Remember, you are the Mater. Arguably, the most important woman in the world. You must dress the part." Leonor paused to ascertain Mater's reaction.

"I understand. However, I will also need comfortable clothes to wear at home."

"First, we will go to Paris so that you can confirm that you are the Mater. You will meet with our banker and with Telea's legal team. From there, we will drive to Arles, in Provence, where our base has been established for the past century. You'll love the place! It's beautiful, full of history. Van Gogh lived there for about a year and produced some of his most exciting and luminous pieces.

"The previous Mater chose the property outside Arles because she loved flowers, and the house sits on a working flower plantation. You will see the setup when we get there. However, if you don't like the place, you are free to choose anywhere else in the world to live. Except the Azores or Portugal for the next fifty years. Even with your face-shifting ability, we can't risk anybody recognising you."

"What happens when we get to Arles?"

"That is totally up to you. I suggest you choose the first week to meet the staff, rest, visit the town and call a council meeting. At that point, you will need to decide who to trust and who to dismiss. Have private conversations. I don't know the women in the council, so I can't give my opinions. Come to think of it, even if I knew them, I would not volunteer my thoughts on the matter because you are the one who needs to trust your feelings and your observations and come to a decision about each woman."

The Mater was feeling tired, so she ended the conversation and went to bed. She needed to think and to have a long nap. Each day seemed filled with new information. She was not feeling overwhelmed; nevertheless, she needed to continue to adjust to the new person that she was. The Mater understood that she needed to become assertive as new information came pouring in, but she also needed to be kind to herself.

Sleep helped, even though she continued to process data in her sleep, as her dreams made clear that she was the repository of thousands of years of lived experiences. When she arrived in Arles, she would ask to see Telea's archive. The new person that she was felt emotionally distant. Even the news about her children did not elicit gut reactions or grief. It must be the result of her transformation. She welcomed it.

The Mater also realised, before sleep took her consciousness, that she needed to be careful because she would be navigating unknown shores, dealing with women who had kept power for too long. The council worried her, but she knew that when the time came, the Mater would make the right decisions. She would be guided by her expanding knowledge of her predecessors, her instincts and her escalating capacity to deal with information.

Chapter Ten

On the day of departure from São Miguel, the Mater was woken by Leonor quite early. It was still dark. She was dressed in black pants and a black turtleneck sweater, under a silver puffer coat. Her torque was hidden under the sweater, but the signet ring was prominent on her left hand.

"I don't think I'm going to be able to stay awake. I will catch some sleep whenever I can."

"Don't worry about that. We are taking a private jet from Ponta Delgada to Paris, and then we'll have a motorhome waiting for us at the airport to take us to Arles. You will be able to sleep as much as you like," reassured Leonor.

The Mater snoozed in the back seat next to the doctor with Leonor driving to the airport. The medical equipment had already been removed the week before, so all the other people divided themselves through the other cars with their possessions. Although there was a consistent rainy mist, the drive was uneventful. At the airport, they were ushered quickly through security and walked through one of the gates to a parked private jet.

When the Mater entered the aircraft, she was surprised by how roomy it felt. It was a twelve-seater with a bedroom in the back. A pleasant flight attendant served everybody coffee and pastries after take-off, and the Mater retired to the bedroom. How wonderful to be able to fly like this!

It seemed like she had just fallen asleep when the Mater was awakened and told to take her seat and buckle the seatbelt for landing. They landed at Le Bourget Airport and as promised there was a motorhome waiting for them. It was a long, white vehicle with enough seats for everyone and a bed at the rear. Leonor explained that the rest of the group would stay in the motorhome while she and the Mater were driven to the bank.

A black limousine was on the other side of the motorhome. They climbed in and the motorist drove to their destination, a non-descript large building close to the centre of Paris. It looked solid and respectable, but there were no signs that it was a bank. By the main door, there was a small copper plate with the name *Banque de la Toile*.

Leonor pressed the doorbell and very quickly a young man opened the door and invited them into a magnificent office. It was large, with antique furniture and a beautiful Aubusson rug. Artwork covered the walls, and there was comfortable sitting around a fragile-looking table. A small, middle-aged man with some girth approached the door, bowed briefly and welcomed them.

"I am Antoine du Pressy. I'm the banker for La Toile. Who do I have the honour of meeting?"

"I'm the Mater, and this is my advisor, Leonor. I have come for my inheritance."

"Of course, Madame. I'm not surprised because the beautiful Leonor called me yesterday to inform me of your visit. After we finish our business, the lawyers for Telea have come to meet you. Just a moment and please have a seat " The Mater gave her coat to Leonor and sat at the table while Leonor stood standing behind her.

Antoine opened a cabinet behind his desk, brought out a box and placed it on the table. From his pocket, he removed a small triangular prism clearly made of nanobot amalgam and gave it to the Mater.

"This is the key. Please open the box," asked Antoine.

The Mater couldn't see a lid in the usual place. She lifted the box to get a better look. It was a rectangular wooden prism without any seams, however there was a triangular slot on one side. She slid the key into the slot, and nothing happened. It couldn't turn or slide any further.

The Mater concentrated on the problem. Imagined the box opening. Suddenly, there was the noise of a mechanism engaging, and the box opened. Inside, there was a jewellery box that once opened revealed an amazing necklace which would sit over the breastbone. There were six flat pieces of stone, with a large one in the centre and diamonds between each one.

"Oh my!" exclaimed the Mater. She lifted the necklace, found the platinum clasp and placed it around her neck over her clothes. When she stood up, both Leonor and Antoine were bowing from the waist. It was confirmation that she had come into her inheritance and recognition of her power.

"Please stand straight. This is not Versailles and I'm not the Sun King "

"No," replied Antoine, "you are much more. You are the Mater, the Mother of Stones. Please wait." He left the room, presumably to get the lawyers, and the Mater gave Leonor a hug.

"Now it's time to embrace my heritage," said the Mater, as three women entered the room and bowed deeply to her.

"Please stand straight. I think that we need to update the etiquette for the twenty-first century. A nod is enough. Now, what papers do I need to sign?"

The women came closer to the table and introduced themselves as senior lawyers for Telea. A woman named Gisela Stein explained: "We are the legal witnesses that you are the Mater and the Mother of Stones. Nobody could have opened the box without the strongest power of nanobots. You wear the stones. You are our Mater.

"We carry documents, indeed, that attest to that fact and all witnesses must sign. We also carry a proclamation that we have a new Mater. You need to approve the text and sign it. We will keep the original in the archives and send PDFs to all corners of the world with the appropriate translations."

The Mater read the text of the proclamation printed in English on very heavy paper: *From this day forward, Telea has a new Mother of Stones. I am her. I am the Mater.*

Simple and to the point. This was the first time she was going to sign her new name. The Mater needed a moment and asked Antoine for a clean sheet of paper and a pen. She practised several forms until she felt sure that the letters flowed easily. Using the same pen, she signed her name and handed both paper and pen back to Gisela.

"We will keep both items in the archive, and I will have the pleasure of seeing you at your convenience in Arles. I am a member of the council and, if it pleases you, I would like to continue to do so. I'm an expert in all legal matters pertaining to Telea, and I can be of great help to you if you accept me."

The Mater looked at Gisela and nodded. "Thank you. I believe we are done for now. I'm eager to be on my way. Antoine, I expect to see you soon with a full report of the finances of Telea."

She gathered her coat, shook hands with Antoine, Gisela and the remaining lawyers and left the building for the waiting limousine which would take Leonor and the Mater back to the airport and her waiting personnel.

At Le Bourget Airport, in the parking lot, all the women gathered around the Mater, made brief bows and asked to hold her hands. The Mater felt a swell of affection for these women who had been so supportive and part of her transformation. As she held each woman's hand in turn, she felt energy flowing from her to the waiting women. Each reacted differently.

Some gasped, others wept; one went to her knees. The Mater embraced each of them and looked around, afraid that they might be seen by curious onlookers. They seemed safe. It wasn't a busy airport, anyway. It catered only to the super-rich with their private planes.

The Mater and Leonor had a quick meal in an elegant restaurant in the terminal. The others had already eaten and used the facilities. They looked revived after receiving a transfer of energy from the Mater, but it was already mid-afternoon, and there was the long drive to Arles ahead of them. This time Leonor didn't take the wheel as she was unfamiliar with the roads. One of the security women drove them down. Her name was Lila and her accent sounded Eastern European.

The Mater lay down on the bed at the rear of the motorhome and forced herself to relax. So that's how it felt to give energy! She had felt their awe, their expectations, their surrender to her power. This was a dangerous thing. So much power and such immense authority in one person. It could easily slide into tyranny, and it would certainly isolate her from the rest of humanity. Very dangerous.

As Mater, she must remind herself every day that she was the caretaker of every woman in Telea, she was their servant, only exalted because of the stones. She must not allow her own power and that of the council to be misused. She must be vigilant. However, she was still human enough to need friends. This would also be a minefield. Who to trust?

***

The previous Mater had apparently behaved as if she were a queen and had a court with a council of ministers and advisors, but she was an absolutist. The one, whose previous self, had been Sofia, had been a fervent socialist and feminist. While absolute power was seductive, it jarred with her core beliefs. The Mater understood that she was the nucleus and the head of a very powerful organisation that spanned the globe.

Telea was extremely wealthy, thanks to the efforts of her predecessors, but that was the extent of her knowledge. She needed details, she needed to understand the logistics, the traditions of thousands of years of existence. That was her task for the foreseeable future. She required data and information. And then she hoped to transform Telea into a participatory democracy. However, that was still years in the future.

The Mater also understood that Telea dealt in centuries and that any large organisation had layers of bureaucracy and carried the weight of inertia. If there were hundreds of thousands of members throughout the world, how would she make individual voices count? And how many precise members did Telea have? So much to learn! She hoped it wouldn't take decades for her to learn enough to make decisions that mattered. The Mater decided that now was as good a time as any to engage in conversation with her fellow travellers. So she left the bed and sat on an empty chair beside a heavy woman, and they talked.

She was Priscila, from Wales, and worked in housekeeping in Maison de la Toile and had been a member of Telea since her teenage years. Her mother had given her the necklace stone like her own mother had done before. At her mother's suggestion, Priscila contacted Telea looking for a job. She worked in several houses until she landed a job at Arles. Priscila was in her forties but looked younger, as all women of Telea. The Mater asked her about her life at Arles, did she have a companion and was she well treated at the Maison de la Toile?

Priscila volunteered that she had a good life and was very well paid, but that the previous Mater had never spoken to her except to give orders. She lived in town with her husband and had two daughters. One of them was old enough to be at the University of Aix-Marseilles. She came home most weekends and wanted to be a teacher. Priscila thought that was a good vocation.

Since her daughter already had her necklace, perhaps she could work at one of Telea's schools when she graduated. Her husband worked at the flower plantation all year round, both in the fields and at the perfume laboratory. He always came home smelling of flowers. Priscila smiled. The only thing she didn't like was wearing a stupid-looking uniform. "Sorry to be so blunt, but maybe you will consider updating our uniforms to be modern and better suited to physical labour."

"What tasks do you have to do and what sort of uniform would you like?"

"I do general cleaning in the house. It's a very large house, and we are only four cleaners. One works in the kitchen full-time helping the cook, one does the bedrooms, including your suite, and Emilie and I work in the rest of the house.

Once a year, when we do deep cleaning, we hire extra hands from Arles. As for the uniforms, I would love to wear modern comfortable pants, tunics and good running shoes. Nothing on our heads."

"I'm sure that we can accommodate your request. I too like to wear comfortable clothes to work. We will choose the design together."

The Mater stood up, walked to the middle rows and asked to have a seat. The woman on the aisle quickly gave her a seat and went to sit beside Priscila. Her companion was a stunningly beautiful woman. She had very dark skin and a shaved head. She had almond-shaped eyes with long eyelashes and wide lips. The Mater started the conversation by asking her to speak about herself.

Emani Assanti was originally from Kenya. She had grown up on a farm and was the only daughter in a Luo family of six siblings. While her mother wanted her to learn the traditional skills of a woman, her father allowed her to play with her brothers and go to a nearby school. She was quite athletic.

When she was thirteen, her family had arranged for her marriage, but Emani, with her teacher's help, ran to Nairobi and was sheltered in a Telea school compound. She continued her studies and learned martial arts. When she was eighteen, she was given the choice of joining Telea and continuing her martial training or receiving a dowry. Emani chose Telea and received her necklace.

"Telea has special military training grounds in several countries. Finally, Telea sent me to Serbia for a private military contractor course. In this case, I was one of the few women among men. It was hard. Very hard.

"Not due to the course, but because I didn't feel safe among men who were full of testosterone. I had a few dicey situations, but thankfully, I left unscathed. I kept alert and didn't drink alcohol or do drugs. Didn't really socialise.

"There was a woman who left after being raped. Everything was hushed up, so I don't know the details. I left soon after. Now, I work full-time for Telea, escorting and protecting women. There are hundreds of Telea military and security specialists throughout the world.

"I'm stationed at Maison de la Toile. There is a dozen of us on the grounds. We live in the house and rotate our shifts, disguised as groundskeepers, and all of us are highly trained and efficient. You can trust us with your life."

"Thank you! I do trust you. Did you get any education in humanities or sciences, in addition to your military and security training?"

"Well, of a sort. We need to understand the context where we operate, so, before an assignment, we receive detailed briefings on geography and terrain, cultural norms, power structures and everything else we need to do our job safely.”

“How does the military hierarchy work?”

“Well, I’m young. I have only been with Telea for two decades, so I don’t know how it should operate under an active Mater. My understanding is that the minister of interior affairs in the council also functions as a military leader. She issues orders to the regional security leaders who assign tasks and personnel. Manuela, over there, is our regional leader, and she works closely with the minister. She’s from Brazil.”

“You are an intelligent woman, experienced and thoughtful. What would you do differently?”

“I would have a designated military and security minister. The world is a dangerous place for women, so we need to have a more active role in protecting our communities worldwide. We are simply too short-staffed. We don’t have enough warriors or enough military and security training grounds. I suggest you use our martial arts schools and our athletic clubs to recruit a lot more young women.

“Also, focus on women in Southeast Asia and South America. Many teenagers have been abused and exploited. They burn with anger that needs an outlet. Rescue them. Train them. Send them on missions. That’s what I would do.”

“I think that you have just been promoted to chief recruiter if that suits you. What do you think?”

“Oh, thank you, Mater! I won’t let you down, but I will first need to select an army of recruiters from among our ranks. I will keep you posted, and you will make the final decisions.”

“Great! I will let you be.” The Mater moved up to the front and again asked to take a seat. Her next target was one of the nurses. Doctor Justine sat on the other side of the aisle. The nurse was an older-looking Asian woman.

“Hi! I’m Kyong, and I notice that you have been making the rounds, so to speak.”

“Yes, I want to get to know my fellow travellers who were so helpful during my transition. Thank you for all your help!”

“Well, that is what nurses do. What would you like to know?”

“Anything that you want to share. I’m especially interested in your career and Telea’s presence in health care throughout the world.”

"I'm Korean, and my mother died when I was a child. During the time of the Korean war, my family fled to the south. My mother was a young woman who sold her body to Americans, so we could eat. Not surprisingly, I was born in 1953. My mother didn't live long.

"When I was four, she died of a drug overdose. My grandmother and I walked to Seoul and begged on the way, and she appealed to Telea because she wore a necklace. We found ourselves in a grocery store, and I still remember how hungry I was when I was offered food. The owner sent a messenger to the clinic de la Toile, and we were given shelter and life in the compound on the outskirts of the city.

"I was a bright student and very obedient. By the time I was fourteen years old, my grandmother talked with the teachers, and it was decided that I was to be given a necklace. They explained to me the secrecy and suggested that nursing would be a good career for me. And so, it was. I graduated when I was nineteen years old.

"And I was posted in Yeosu, in the far south. Today it's a vibrant city that attracts many tourists, but at the time it was a small town, and Telea ran a health centre there. I worked there for about a decade, and then I was sent here to France to further my studies. By then, my grandmother had passed away, peacefully, in her sleep.

"I specialised in tropical diseases and worked in various Telea health centres and hospitals in the developing world. I had some affairs, but never settled with anyone. I enjoyed living with my sister nurses. I loved the sense of community.

"Finally, I returned to France and ended up working at the Jeanne d'Arc Clinic in Arles. It's a well-equipped health centre, and the work is not too taxing. I no longer do shifts, so it's a pleasure to come home at the end of the day to a residence I share with three other Telea members. I even have full weekends off."

"I'm glad that you have been living a full and interesting life. What happens to Telea members when they get old and frail?"

"If they have a family, then they make the decisions that suit them. The majority of us end our days in Telea nunneries or nursing homes. In the old days, nunneries were very popular in Catholic countries because, in a male-dominated society, they could be female oases. The ones that belong to Telea are, in general, non-denominational but with all the outward signs of devotion. We needed to be like chameleons and disguise ourselves.

"In the Middle Ages, we were often Beguines, lay women who lived in communities and did charitable work. After the Reformation, it was more complicated for women to live in communities in Protestant countries. Most members of Telea in those places worked as nurses in hospitals, ran small businesses and got married, lest them be accused of witchcraft. Many fled to Catholic countries and set themselves up as nuns in small, enclosed properties. If they didn't challenge church authorities, behaved modestly in public and wore the appropriate outfits, nobody doubted them."

"How extraordinary! I had no idea!" exclaimed the Mater.

"Of course, that slowly changed. In the nineteenth century, we set up women's schools all over Europe and North America. During the twentieth century, we established health centres and women's hospitals throughout the world.

"Those are also forms of living in a community. We were well spread out in the Soviet Union. Less so in developing countries. In faraway places, women scattered Telea in small groups. But I digress. You were asking about old age."

"I assume that traditionally old women were cared for by their families. However, if you don't have a family or a community, what happens to those women?"

"Sisters always took care of sisters. If a woman became ill or frail, she would send a letter or a messenger to her Telea contact and soon a 'niece' would show up. Eventually, we created nursing homes. No member of Telea dies alone unless there is an accident or a rupture in communication."

"Thank you! You have given me a lot to think about. I think I will rest now."

The motorhome stopped on the way for everyone to stretch their legs, have a quick meal and use the bathroom. Leonor and Justine checked in with the Mater to see how she was doing. The Mater was trembling visibly again. So, since she did her best thinking lying down and the bed at the rear looked appetising, the shaking woman lay down and let her mind wander. Soon she was asleep.

Chapter Eleven

They arrived at Maison de la Toile around midnight. Everyone was exhausted, especially the two women who drove in shifts. The Mater was awakened gently, adjusted her scarf around her head, put on her coat and, as she exited the motorhome, she was delighted at a fully lit magnificent mansion. Even though it was a dark and cold night, two rows of staff stood to receive her, all women who were dressed in very old-fashioned uniforms.

An older, thin woman all in black moved to welcome the Mater. Her hair was pulled back, and she had a large stone visible over her long dress. As the new owner of the mansion walked towards the entrance, they all bowed deeply and then stood. The Mater was too tired to change etiquette just now.

"Welcome to Maison de la Toile. My name is Fatemah, daughter of Nura. I'm the housekeeper."

The Mater followed Fatemah into a majestic, rocaille, hall where a grand staircase seemed to flow up. Everyone else knew where to go except for Leonor who followed behind. The housekeeper looked at Leonor with surprise and lifted an eyebrow.

"This is Leonor, my new advisor. Please show her to a guest room. We are tired, hungry and thirsty. Send a tray with food and tea to our rooms as soon as possible, as well as our bags."

"Of course, Madame. I will show you to your suite, and then I will lead Madame Leonor to her room."

Fatemah led the way up the staircase onto a landing that led to two diverging hallways. She asked Leonor to kindly wait and led the Mater to the right until they reached the end. Fatemah opened the double doors, painted with birds and flowers and showed the Mater her suite of rooms. She entered a large and airy room, all white, with contemporary furniture in dark wood. The floor was a multi-hued wood parquet.

On the left side was a big desk with an ergonomic seat and, behind it, stood a large and empty bookcase. A magnificent window, in front, should frame the landscape, but it was a dark night, and there was nothing to see. There was a table and four chairs. On top of the table, a beautiful crystal vase with freshly cut flowers added a note of colour to the room. On the right, there was a door to another room, but before it stood a sitting area with sofas covered in white satin, white pillows, a coffee table and a large TV screen.

The bedroom was also an impressive white room with an ornate baroque double bed in dark wood, all carved with spindles and thin columns. The linens were all white, with a cotton comforter cover embroidered with silk thread. They looked plush and inviting. To the right, there was another door. Presumably the bathroom.

The bedroom also featured a chest of drawers in the same style as the bed, with a vanity mirror above it. A bench in upholstered white satin was placed at the foot of the bed. Except for a tall window covered in lace, all the other walls had floor-to-ceiling white cabinets. The Mater opened one of the larger doors and noticed a full-length mirror with interior lighting. She was pleased with all the storage space.

Finally, she entered the bathroom and was delighted by the modern and sleek décor, again all in white, with a plush bathrobe and thick towels. One could almost swim in the marble tub, rectangular but with a curved back to rest the body. A walk-in shower, a sink, a toilet and a bidet completed the bathroom features. Above the sink was an illuminated mirror and soothing vanilla candles had been lit.

Fatemah had been silent up to now, but she explained that all bedrooms had undergone thorough renovations in the last two years. Also, there was new electricity and plumbing all over the house. The Mater appreciated that her suite was warm with central heating. Both returned to the living room where there was already a silver tray with steaming lemon tea and small sandwiches.

"Thank you for showing me to my quarters. I will retire now, and I believe that Madame Leonor is still waiting for you. How do I call staff?"

Fatemah showed her the intercom behind the door with codes for different rooms. "You can call any one of us any time, but no one can call you. We need to knock at your door and ask permission to enter. There is a maid that lives on the premises. She has lighter duties so that she can be called to serve you during the night. Until tomorrow, Madame!"

"Good night! Please make sure that no one wakes me up. I intend to sleep until very late."

The Mater was delighted with her quarters and grateful for the white walls and décor, so unlike the entrance and grand sitting room. She needed a restful space. Later, she would add artwork and personal touches. She used the bathroom, undressed and slid into the bed. Good mattress, but it needed an over-mattress of memory foam and orthopaedic pillows, as she was used to. Letting her mind wander, the Mater let the images and impressions of the day come together until sleep took her away.

Since she didn't have a cell phone, The Mater woke up slowly, without any idea of what time it was. She used the bathroom, put on the bathrobe, walked to the intercom and called the kitchen for coffee. Interesting that she had no desire to smoke. That was a very good thing. She looked out the window and saw a beautiful winter garden and rows upon rows of plants.

Nothing flowered yet, but it would be magnificent in the spring. Shortly after, a knock on the door announced breakfast. A maid in her silly traditional uniform carried a tray with a pot of hot coffee and pastries. She removed the previous day's tray and asked if that would be all. The Mater invited her to sit at the table with her. The maid was shocked and said that she couldn't possibly do that. Madame Fatemah would kill her.

"Okay, you may stand. I would like to get to know you, as I like to know everybody who works for me. Tell me a bit about yourself."

"I'm Emilie, and as you can see, I am a maid here. I also live in the house in case you need something during the night. I'm right from Arles. Been born here and lived here all my life. I'm twenty-five years old, and I have had my necklace for three years.

"On Sundays, I have the day off, and I like to visit my family. They don't know about Telea, and I won't tell anybody. I took a hairdresser course and, if you would like, I can be your personal maid. I know that you don't have hair, but I could fix your wigs, help you dress and take care of you."

"I'm sure that you would do fine, but I don't need a personal maid. I can take care of myself. However, if I need anything done in the room, I will call for you."

Emilie curtseyed, took the dinner tray and left. The Mater realised that proximity to her person was a mark of status, just as with other powerful individuals. Once more she reminded herself to be careful. She drank a couple of cups of coffee, nibbled on a pastry and called for the housekeeper using the intercom.

Fatemah knocked at the door shortly after, waited to be welcomed in and greeted the Mater with greater warmth than the night before, although still stiff. "Good afternoon, Madame! I trust you slept well. How can I be of service?"

"I slept well; thank you. Although I will talk to Madame Leonor about solving this problem, I don't have a way to tell time, so I want you to gather all the house personnel so that I may greet them and, during this week, I want to meet personally with everyone. Please set up a schedule for the afternoons. I normally sleep in the mornings, so you don't have to concern yourself about me until I wake up. Please tell me about your role and about the house staff."

"I have been with Telea for fifty-six years and have served as housekeeper of Maison de la Toile for thirty-two years. I'm originally from a minor tribe in Saudi Arabia. My father molested me as a child, and my mother helped me to escape. In one of his absences, she stole a camel for me and gave me provisions, and I made my way across the desert. I made it to Oman, half dead from thirst and hunger. The trip took longer than it should have because I was young and didn't know my way. But I survived.

"In Mirbat, I was very lucky because I took a job as a maid for a wealthy family. I didn't spend any of the money I received, so within two years I had enough money to take a boat to Mozambique. All I had was a new dress, and the leftover money in my purse. Although I was Muslim, I sought refuge in a nunnery.

"Again, I was lucky because it was run by Telea. They found me a job with a Portuguese household, but every free afternoon I had I went back to the nunnery. They taught me to read, write and do arithmetic. I had found kind women who accepted me, and they gave me my stone which I have never split into another. It just grew through the years.

"The Portuguese family returned to Portugal in 1975, and they took me with them because I was fair-skinned, and they liked me. By then, I had received a contact in Lisbon which I sought as soon as I was able. She gave me all the information I needed about how to get to Arles and some money. I took the first train to Paris and then came here. I was received by your predecessor, worked as a maid and then became the housekeeper. That's my story."

"Thank you for sharing," said the Mater, "but I would also like to know what your responsibilities are. Tell me also about the staff and the security personnel."

"We have a chef and a kitchen maid, three housemaids and your predecessor had a personal maid. After the Mater's passing, I transferred the lady's maid to work as a housekeeper for the director of Ireland. It seemed for the best because she was inconsolable. As you may understand, the staff often develop affection for their employers if they are well treated.

"The plantation sends us handymen when we need them, and a gardener is assigned to work in the house garden two days a week. I'm in charge of the smooth running of the house and of anticipating your wants and needs.

"Every day, after your breakfast, I will come to you to discuss any unusual tasks and to know what the menu will be for the day. I will bring the chef's recommendation but, of course, you may change it at any time. We will do our best to please you. If there are any repairs that need to be done or any larger purchases, I will bring them to your attention.

"I don't deal with the household accounts. They are managed by, and the bills are paid for by our accountants who have an office in Arles. We have three accountants who live together in town and work together. They take care of both the house and the plantations' accounts. They take care of everything. I just send them the bills to be paid, and they also deposit our salaries in our bank accounts.

"There are also a dozen security women who work in shifts, just for our peace of mind because we are very well disguised as a commercial enterprise, with the plantation and all. We are at low risk for assault. All the main points of access have surveillance devices, and both the house and the plantation have video alarms. I believe that we are safe."

The Mater nodded her head.

"Thank you for that. After I get dressed, I would like a full tour of the house from the bottom up. Don't forget the mid-afternoon assembly of the staff."

"Madame, if I may… I'm seventy, but I still have many good years ahead of me. I had great affection for the previous Mater, and I think that she liked me as well. When she became ill, we transferred two nurses from our nursing facilities to take care of her, but I helped as well. I grieved when she died, as did all in Telea. However, you are the new Mater and, if you permit me, I would like to continue in my role as housekeeper.

"This is my home as well. I have a nicely appointed room on the third floor, with all the memories that I collected through the years. I vow to you that you have my absolute loyalty, that the secrets of this house are safe and that I will do my best so that you are happy living here."

"I would like you to continue as well. I appreciate your dedication, and I hope that you may come to have affection for me as well."

Fatemah bowed deeply and departed.

The Mater took another cup of coffee, now lukewarm and was very glad of this conversation. If Fatemah were to ask for retirement, where would she find another housekeeper? Everything needed to stay the same until the Mater had enough experience and knowledge to change things.

After a hot shower, the Mater dressed in her second outfit of beige pants and matching sweater, this time with a lower neckline. She wanted the staff to see her stones, and she only had another set of clothes. She desperately wanted a wardrobe, shoes and house slippers. She needed underwear. Her body was still adjusting to changes, and it would take some time until she would be comfortable seeing herself naked, with all the sagging skin.

Chapter Twelve

The Mater called Leonor to her suite and waited for a little while with the main door open. Her advisor came in, bowed her head and asked, "How do you feel? Are you ready to face the challenges of the day?"

"For now, I feel energetic, but later I might need a nap. Fatemah is going to show me the house, and I thought you might like to come along."

"Wonderful. I have been in my room afraid of getting lost or going where I'm not supposed to be. They sent lunch up to my room and Emilie, a chatty maid, explained to me about the staff. They don't know what to make of me because they don't know if I'm a guest or a staff member."

"You are a permanent resident of Maison de la Toile. You are my subordinate, but you are not staff. You will be my companion, eat with me and drive me around. I also want you to become my private secretary, besides being an advisor. You need to be busy, and I need help. What do you say?"

"I'm so absolutely delighted. I will be a great secretary, you'll see, and I will never break your confidence or your trust."

"I expect nothing less than that. Let's go downstairs now."

Fatemah was waiting for them in the living room, standing by the door. Both the Mater and Leonor looked around, taking a panoramic view of the hall, the staircase and the living room. The room was pastel blue with marble and gold trimmings. Not to the Mater's taste, but she understood that her predecessor had been stuck aesthetically in the eighteenth century. From a conservation point of view, it would be a crime to paint over everything.

However, the living room, while well-lit with abundant sunshine, was not welcoming, and the hall was cold. She liked the staircase, though. From there, they visited the formal dining room, the library and the dance hall on the other side of the entrance. All the rooms followed the same colour pattern and aesthetic. The furnishings were luxurious, but the seats were stiff and uncomfortable, and the Mater really had never liked rocaille. It was just over the top.

The Mater turned to Fatemah, "Please show me the basement so that I may rest my eyes." The housekeeper was none too pleased but said nothing. Through a hidden door under the staircase, they descended wide and practical-looking stairs and found themselves in a small hall. One of the doors led to an industrial kitchen, capable of preparing dozens of meals at the same time. Fatemah explained that when they gave formal dinners, she hired extra kitchen staff and servers. The chef was one of the women who had travelled to the Azores, so the Mater smiled in recognition.

Besides the kitchen was the staff dining room with walls painted white and a long beautiful, thick wood table and sturdy chairs. An amazing oak armoire from the eighteenth century with a marble counter and shelves above held dishes and glassware. It was a traditional French country dining room in all its glory. The Mater was envious of the staff. They peeked into the large pantry and followed the housekeeper to a smaller room with cabinets on both sides.

"This is where we keep the formal dishes and silver." She opened the doors and the drawers to show the contents. Centuries of silver utensils, trays and receptacles shined, all perfectly polished. The drawers contained embroidered tablecloths that matched the dishes. Antique French Limoges porcelain. Wonderful. The Mater found it impressive.

They walked back to the basement hall and entered a laundry room with an industrial washer and drier, another room with a table and other paraphernalia with an opposite door.

"Would you like to see the wine cellar?" asked Fatemah.

"I don't know much about wine, so I will trust your judgement on the matter. Let's continue."

The Mater and Leonor found themselves in a full gym complete with neon lights and its peculiar smell.

"This is where staff can train, but it's mostly used by the security team," explained the housekeeper. "We clean it daily, but it still smells."

"Perhaps when I feel stronger, I will train here too. Emani or another woman could guide me."

The last room was the most surprising: A computer lab with its own servers. All brand new.

"Wow! This is unexpected. Why did you install them here?"

"The council decided that we need to improve our IT capabilities and our internet presence. We still need to hire professionals, but everything is ready for you to decide."

"Welcome to the twenty-first century. Awesome!"

Leonor had been silent during the tour, but she immediately recommended the creation of a secure website and the need for hackers to confirm internet security.

From the basement, there was another flight of stairs that led to the third floor where some of the staff lived. There were four rooms with three beds each for the security personnel, one small room for Emilie, the night maid, a small suite of rooms for the housekeeper and a seventh empty room. Each room was well-appointed and looked comfortable. By now, the Mater was hungry and tired. So she returned to her own suite and asked for sweetened yoghurt and muesli as a quick meal.

After eating, the Mater was reminded by Fatemah that the staff was waiting for her in the ballroom. Wearing all her nanobot jewellery, she confirmed her appearance in the mirror. She wanted to look regal but approachable. With her baldness, simple suit and the jewellery well visible, the Mater presented herself to the staff.

"I wanted to introduce myself to you, and during the next few days, I intend to get to know each of you in turn. I understand that a big house such as this one requires a lot of effort to keep up, but I want you to know that I'm a woman who requires little maintenance. I tend to sleep in the mornings, but I'm a hard worker for the rest of the time.

"Madame Fatemah will assign one of the maids to clean my suite every day and that person will also bring up my meals. Madame Leonor will eat with me. In addition, if the main doors to my suite are open that means that I'm open to business, of a sort. If the door is closed that means that I want privacy and don't want to be disturbed.

"I look at you, and I can't help but notice that the maids' uniforms are woefully outdated. That will be resolved soon. In the meantime, I won't make any staff changes, but if any of you wish to be transferred to another position, please let me know.

"In regard to formality and etiquette, I expect that a simple nod will suffice. I don't want to diminish the stature of my office, but we live in a very different era that requires an easing of formality. The type of deference that I will most appreciate is discretion, work well done and prompt responses to my orders. For now, please line up and extend your hands."

The Mater concentrated and proceeded to transfer energy to each staff member. Their reactions were of surprise and gratitude. She could read their feelings, which was of great benefit in dealing with people. The Mater decided that her household would benefit from regular infusions of energy. The last one to place her hands in the Mater's was Fatemah. The energy transfer confirmed the housekeeper's commitment to her.

After the staff departed, the Mater informed Fatemah of her meal schedules and of her requirements. Then, she asked Leonor to join her for a light working lunch in what she considered her living room. "Please bring paper and pen upstairs because you will need to take copious notes."

Between soup and sandwiches, the Mater made lists until she was exhausted. She needed everything. First, a smartphone with the council's information and the accountants in her contacts. She needed two computers fully loaded with the usual software, one for her work and a personal laptop, as well as a good printer. She wanted a tablet and an e-reader for her pleasure.

And she needed clothes. Since her body was still reshaping itself, they could order a limited variety of items online for quick delivery, or Leonor could check the local stores. They discussed what kind of clothes she would like. Comfortable indoor attire, outdoor clothes and a couple of more formal suits to deal with the council. She also needed moisturising cream and make-up.

They discussed preferences. The Mater reminded Leonor that she too needed everything; therefore, she should purchase what she needed and liked on Telea's credit card. Since the stores in Arles should be open for another couple of hours, the Mater asked Leonor to go and buy the phone and the tablet immediately.

Leonor went in search of Lila, who had been their driver and was a member of the security team, to accompany her. That settled, the Mater felt her body shivering again and went to her already cleaned room, undressed and lay down in bed for a nap. She thought about the house. Although she loved her suite, she really was not comfortable with the public rooms. But they would do for the foreseeable future.

The staff seemed nice enough. Tomorrow she would start to meet each one, one at a time. She also needed to contact the council. Should she send an email or a handwritten note? She needed stationery. She needed sealing wax and would use her signet ring to make it official. She must remember to make a note of it before dinner. So many things to remember.

Well, this was her new life, with a quivering body and everything new. Her belly and breasts had looked tighter when she got dressed. That was a sign that the muscular contractions were working. Soon she would train her body for speed, endurance and core strength. She slept a little but felt refreshed although she still had no idea of the time.

Leonor knocked at her bedroom door, waited to be called in and excitedly informed the Mater that she already had some of the items on the list. They sat in the living room amidst boxes and bags. Soon the Mater had her phone set up and connected to the wireless of Maison de la Toile. It was close to dinner time. They decided to unpack the rest after dinner.

The Mater told her secretary to note that she needed abundant sheets of stationery with Telea's logo, sealing wax and a credit card. She had no access to money and no way to make independent purchases. Tomorrow, she would need to contact the accountants and ask the senior one to visit her promptly.

Dinner was set up on the table, and it was an elegant affair with white wine of Provence in crystal glasses, cold sparkling water, a consommé and a sole almondine in brown butter with vegetables and very small potatoes, served on a Limoges plate. For dessert, they had a marvellous Tarte Tatin with whipped cream. Everything was delicious. The Mater assumed that the chef wanted to impress her with this first dinner. She had succeeded.

The Mater asked Leonor how she had purchased so much stuff and if she had rewarded herself as well. Her secretary explained that Fatemah had loaned her a corporate card and that her items were already in her room. She handed her superior a stack of receipts for review while she unpacked the tablet, a computer for personal use, a printer, reams of good quality paper and boxes of ink.

"Tomorrow, while you sleep in the morning, I'll connect and set up everything for you. I suggest you wait until we have an IT woman to set up accounts for you. We must be careful and attentive to cybersecurity. You are not a regular woman. You are the Mater and your very existence is a secret. Perhaps we will need to set you up with a couple of fake identities for your personal internet browsing."

"Good thinking. We need to hire IT people very quickly and I don't know how to do that."

"I recommend you wait until after your meeting with the council. They should have inside information and help with the search. How about we check your clothes and see if you like them? Whatever you don't like I will return tomorrow."

"Regrettably, I can't wait. I want information on the council members before we meet, and I want to be able to access the internet as soon as possible. Perhaps the solution will present itself. But right now, let's check what you got."

The Mater gave Leonor back the stack of receipts and asked her to hold on to them if returns were needed. After, they should be sent to the accountants. The bags held a variety of clothing items in her current size from soft and comfortable-looking long dresses for indoors, to a couple of elegant suits, blouses, socks, underwear and seamless bras. There were velvet house slippers, low-heeled shoes and a pair of boots. Everything was elegant and understated. There was also a wool, embroidered large scarf to offset the neutral colours of the clothing and a Hermes silk scarf.

The Mater tried the clothes, and everything fit. She was pleased that the dresses and blouses were low cut to allow her to show off her stones.

Chapter Thirteen

The next day was glorious, sunny and crisp. The Mater left the house, wandered around the winter garden, noticed that everything around was well kept and was happy to see a herb garden close to the kitchen in the back. There was also a large kitchen garden waiting for spring planting.

A stone path led to two low-rise apartment buildings destined for staff. She didn't go in, but she appreciated the care of the design architect so that the apartment buildings did not clash with the architecture of Maison de la Toile. Her silver puffer coat was warm enough, but she needed to work. So back to the house she went.

The Mater spent some time interviewing staff and left the rest for the following day. From her living room window, she could see the expanse of flower bushes extending up to the gate and to both sides of the property. As soon as she had a wig, she would make time to check out the business side of the plantation. The evening was spent making more lists with Leonor of questions to ask, people to see and tasks to accomplish.

The leading accountant arrived in the mid-afternoon of the following day, bringing with her a corporate credit card with no name. It simply stated, 'Senior Director'. Her name was Martine Devereaux, she was a Telea member and had been responsible for the accounting of Maison de la Toile and the flower business for two decades. She was an assertive woman and looked middle-aged and well-coiffed, with little make-up.

Martine wore a lovely scent. She disclosed that it was a House de la Toile product and explained that the accounting of the business was challenging due to the number of seasonal employees, full-time employees and diverse products. She explained that it was a solid business, two centuries old. They sold fresh flowers all over France, scents to perfume companies, had a perfume label and produced and sold scented soaps in shops all over Europe. Finally, they had a laboratory that explored the health applications of flowers and herbs; however, it was a recent enterprise without any new discoveries yet.

Martine clarified that the business supported the day-to-day expenses of the house, but that any great expenditures, like the recent renovations, had to be paid for by the Banque de la Toile. She recommended that the Mater should have an extended meeting with Monsieur Antoine as soon as possible to understand the global accounting of Telea.

The accountant detailed the various bank accounts held at Banque de la Toile for managing the house and the business. They did not deal with any other bank, nor did they have any debts with any banks. The size of the checking account for Maison de la Toile was the same as that of a municipality. It was large, but they were an important employer in the area and the business was doing well.

The Mater reminded Martine to establish a work contract for Leonor and to pay her the rate of a senior advisor and her personal secretary. She should also guide Leonor in establishing a personal bank account with Banque de la Toile.

"I have need of an excellent IT department, but I would start with only one person. Considering the confidentiality necessary, who do you use for your accounting firm?"

"Both the Banque de la Toile and my firm use the services of a small company located in Marseille. For everyday issues, they have one staff member in Paris and another in Arles. Both women are competent, but I suggest you contact the company directly to set up your own team. They are all members of Telea, so your request will be a priority. I have their contact information on my phone. Here you go."

Both women took out their phones and exchanged contacts. Finally, almost as if it were an afterthought, the Mater asked if she knew of any investigator close by who could help her gather information on certain people swiftly and discretely. "That's very wise Madame. One should always be prepared with knowledge. If you are available tomorrow, I will send Simone duBois. She is a member of Telea, and we have used her services occasionally."

"Most excellent! I look forward to meeting with her. Before you go, please give me your hands." As it would become routine for the rest of her life, the Mater concentrated, felt the now familiar warmth and offered a boost of power to Martine. The experience was totally new for the accountant. Her eyes widened; she smiled and curtseyed expressing her thanks.

The rest of the day was spent interviewing the remaining staff, continuing to make lists with Leonor and having dinner together. The Mater needed time alone, so she spent the evening browsing documents of Telea for various facts, watched some TV series and went to bed early. She realised that her body started quivering when she was tired. She hoped this was not to become a permanent issue. It would be embarrassing in public.

On the third day at Maison de la Toile, as soon as she woke up, the Mater called the IT company, asked to speak with the manager and could almost hear the receptionist bowing on the other side. It was mildly amusing. She explained her needs and was transferred to the manager. They arranged for a meeting to take place at four o'clock, the same afternoon.

While the Mater was still having breakfast, Leonor entered the suite with two boxes, one perched on top of the other. One box contained printed stationery and the other a simple wig of sable brown hair on a Styrofoam head. She was very happy with both. Of course, soon she would have to go personally to a wigmaker to have this wig adjusted to her head and to order a set of wigs. She could have asked a wigmaker to come to the house, but she wanted to pretend to be a cancer patient.

It would be less conspicuous. She would make herself seem older and nobody would be the wiser. Of course, everybody in the house knew that she was bald, but the Mater wanted to restrict her true appearance to a select few.

From Fatemah, she received the contact information for the council and decided to call a first meeting in two weeks. This should be enough time for the investigator to find extensive information about each council member. The stationery was A5 size, made of thick, smooth cream paper, with the sign of Telea embossed in gold on the top centre. The envelopes were of the same paper with the logo embossed on the flap, and the inside was gold. It was lovely.

The Mater called for Leonor and together they decided upon an appropriate text and font for a first-time summons of the council ministers and their senior staff. The secretary then had the task of typing, printing and bringing the invitations for the Mater to sign and seal. She still needed the wax seals which had been ordered online from a specialty business. They should arrive soon.

A little later, Fatemah came to the door.

"Madame, there is a lady that would like to speak with you. She says that she is expected. May I present Madame Simone duBois."

A petite, young blonde woman dressed in a pink pastel suit entered the room. She really didn't look like an investigator, which was a good thing. Like everybody else who had met the Mater up to now, Simone bowed and then addressed her superior. "I understand that you have need of my services."

"Yes, I do. Please sit down. Are you any good at investigating?"

"Madame, I'm excellent because no one suspects me of being anything more than a fluff-head. From public records to private recordings, I have done it all. I'm quite a bit older than I look, and I have never received any complaints. Of course, not every client is happy with what I find, but the information that I uncover is thorough. In addition, I'm the soul of discretion. All my records from a job are expunged and all the information is for the eyes of the client only."

"Very well, I need you to investigate six people very quickly, in under two weeks. Could you do that? I don't need to know anyone's love life, but I must have whatever is public about them, especially their finances and if there are any rumours of wrongdoing."

"If it's mostly public information about them I can do that quickly, the rumours take longer. Who are we talking about?"

"The council. I have a meeting with them in two weeks, and I want to be prepared. They have had power for a very long time. Power tends to distort people's sense of right and wrong in favour of expediency. I want to know if that's true of any of them, hence wanting to know the rumours. Moreover, people in power in a closed system also tend to take advantage of their position for personal gain. I especially want to know if that's the case."

"I need to have any information about the council members that you may think of."

"I have never met them, so all I have is their names, addresses and contact information."

"Madame, in one week I will have their public information and hopefully some gossip. The following week I will pursue as much private information as possible in the allotted time. Do you want me to come to the house, or would you prefer I meet with you elsewhere?"

"Please come to the house. The staff has sworn a vow of loyalty and discretion. If I can't trust them, I'm in trouble. Here is my phone number so that you may contact me personally, and this is all the information I have about the council. As soon as I have a private email, I will let you know, and you can send information that way."

The Mater gave Simone a piece of paper with all the data. They both stood up, the investigator received an input of energy and left. The Mater was impressed with her claims. She hoped they were true.

At five minutes before 4:00, the Mater heard a car in the driveway. At the appointed time, Fatemah brought her guest into the suite. This young woman was a contrast to the previous one. She was tall and skinny, had short dark hair and was dressed in black jeans and a black turtleneck with a padded bomber jacket. Her smile was genuine, and thankfully, she did not bow. The young woman had piercings in her nose, and as she stretched her arm for a handshake, one could see the end of a sleeve tattoo.

"Hello! We spoke this morning. I'm in awe. I never met a Mater. My name is Louise, but I like to be called Lou."

"Welcome to Maison de la Toile, Lou! Please sit down. To begin with, I have many IT needs, but today I want you to set me up with a personal and secure email address and a simple password. I don't know if a VPN is the way to go, you tell me.

"In the basement, we have a full computer lab with what I was told is the best technology available. You need to check it out and tell me if something is needed. Once that is done, I want you to think big. I need a team of experts to set up and monitor Telea online. I want it to be secure against intrusion.

"I want to bring Telea to the twenty-first century. I want women to be able to receive untraceable emails and for them to be able to contact me or any regional director at will. Hence the need to monitor activity. I imagine a sleek website with a secret door only accessible to registered Telea members where another website would be layered. That would be Telea's meeting place. What do you think?"

"It definitely sounds awesome and doable, but it will take time, and as you said, I'll need a team of dedicated IT experts and people to input data. It would be silly to waste talent on a menial task. I'm just the manager of my small company. You own us, so we can certainly set up here.

"Would you be comfortable if we did the bank and the accounting business here too? Those systems are already set up, and there is a technician on each site. We just need to merge the data once a month. Also, I need to be sure that the servers can handle the traffic of hundreds of thousands of users."

"Well, let's go to the basement and find out." The Mater called Leonor to go with them so that she could take notes.

By dinnertime, the Mater had an email account, was registered on several sites including an e-reading site, had her credit card number associated with her accounts and everything was secured. Lou also looked at her smartphone and tablet and added a layer of security to both. The bad news was that the servers were only sufficient for current and short-term needs. The gym was going to have to be split, with a wall, to add several more powerful servers.

The Mater exchanged contact information with Lou, gave her a powerful boost of energy and thanked her for her work.

Dinnertime was an exciting event full of conversation about the day. The Mater and Leonor ate a delicious meat stew with still-warm bread and had an orange Bavaroise for dessert. It was a very good thing that the nanobots would burn the extra calories, otherwise the Mater would be fat again.

Once more the Mater wanted a quiet evening by herself, so Leonor left to join the staff in the basement because she wanted company. In the meantime, the Mater purchased several books from the e-reading company and ordered an e-reader. Until the device arrived, she would read from her tablet. So she settled into one of Octavia Butler's novels. When the maid came to clear the table, the Mater asked for mint tea and dark chocolate, if there was any. What a perfect ending to her day!

Chapter Fourteen

As promised, a week later, the Mater received her first report from Simone duBois via email. The news was not good. As suspected, they all had fattened their purses at Telea's expense. The value of each woman's holdings was above that of the Maison de la Toile. They had huge mansions all over Europe, investment accounts and loads of expensive jewellery.

The problem was that they had an enormous amount of institutional knowledge. If the Mater fired them all the Telea would stumble. She needed to reign them in and have enough time to find new women.

She needed to speak with Antoine. So she called him and told him to come to Arles with all the data necessary to describe the banking practices of the women in the council. The Mater also wanted a full, but succinct explanation of Telea's global banking.

Considering that she had her wig, the Mater decided to check out the business side of Maison de la Toile. She called ahead to make sure that the managers would expect her. With Leonor by her side, they walked to the buildings on the other side of the property. The day was clear with a hint of spring in the air. Under her puffer coat, with the wig and the Hermes scarf covering her head, the Mater felt a bit too warm during the brisk walk. It was good for her.

While they walked, she asked about her children and about Carrie. Leonor informed her superior that both her son and her daughter had returned to their home countries. That they had hired a solicitor and a lawyer to take care of the inheritance bureaucracy and that it would take some time. As far as Leonor was aware, they were both dealing with their grief well. That would also take time, but life continued, and they were both wealthy beyond their expectations.

Her daughter, son and their spouses kept their jobs in the meantime. That was a good thing to give routine to their lives. Carrie was not doing so well because she was depressed, and her sight was deteriorating. However, she had many supportive friends in her village, and with time, her mood was expected to improve.

It must have been the nanobots doing it, but the Mater felt emotionally distanced from her family and best friend. In a way, that was not a bad thing since she had effectively died. She was not the person she used to be. On the other hand, it didn't seem motherly or friendly to not care more. But she was not a mother anymore, right? Or anybody's best friend. The Mater was pensive on the rest of the walk.

Several people were waiting outside the building for the two women. They were mostly men and a single woman who identified herself as the lab researcher. The buildings were close to the road, with an office, warehouse, three processing plants and a small laboratory. The Mater introduced herself as Maria, the new owner of Maison de la Toile, and introduced Leonor as her private secretary. She didn't elaborate but informed the people assembled that if there were any serious issues that she should be informed of, Leonor was the point person to contact.

The general manager was an overweight man who showed them around. The warehouses were a mixture of storage and assembly plants. The flower export business would only start in full spring. For now, the fields were fallow, awaiting compost and the initial weeding. The scents from last year were still being bottled, filling orders for various perfume companies.

The perfume section was in full swing producing delightful soaps with tasteful packaging. The small lab was the last place to visit. The Mater noticed that the researcher had a small stone hanging by her breasts. It was almost concealed, but the stone peeked out from under her blouse. Therefore the Mater decided to have a private conversation with the young woman. She dismissed the men, and both Leonor and her superior entered the small space, closing the door.

"You must know who I am."

"Yes, Mater. It's a great honour to meet you. I'm Aleksandra, but everybody calls me Alex. I have a double doctorate in botany and chemistry from the University of Kyiv. I'm Ukrainian."

"I'm pleased to meet you. Please explain to me what you are researching right now."

"I was hired by the general manager to develop new scents. I needed a job, and I took the opportunity. It's not really my area of expertise, I'm sorry to say. However, I have a good 'nose' and I can produce foundation scents. The problem is that up to now I haven't found any new scents, but I have only been working here for about a year."

"When did you get your stone and who gave it to you?"

"About five years ago, I met my best friend who ended up sharing her stone with me. She explained about the Telea and swore me to secrecy. She stayed in the Ukraine, so we keep in touch via video calls. I have never told anybody about the stone or about Telea. Please believe me. It was a huge coincidence that I ended up working at Maison de la Toile."

"I believe you. Now, tell me what your dissertation was about?"

"I studied poisonous domestic and wild plants. Several poisons have excellent pharmaceutical potential, others are simply lethal in large enough doses. Some are stable compounds, others are unstable and cannot, yet, have much use."

"What a fortuitous coincidence! I used to have a large garden with many poisonous flowers. They are so decorative, but the animals know they are not edible. My favourites were daffodils, belladonna and foxglove. They are beautiful but deadly. Not even insects go close to them, so the flower beds always look pristine.

"I had a couple of fully matured angel trumpets going over the gate to my garden. They were impressive but needed to be pruned every year otherwise they would take over. What would you say if I asked you to concentrate on producing stable toxic compounds for Telea's use? Would you, do it?"

Leonor looked alarmed but said nothing. Alex paused for a while and was thoughtful. "Am I correct in assuming that you are asking me to create bioweapons?"

"Yes, that is exactly what I'm asking. Not weapons of mass destruction, but compounds that can be used in assassinations. I can think of a few men that need killing. However, any targets are hypothetical right now. I would simply like to have options in the future."

"I can do that, but I would need a large enough lab with a negative pressure room, proper filtration and an exhaust system. I will need personal protection suits. Basically, I want you to build me a biosafety class II laboratory with a corresponding biosafety cabinet that unlocks using my biometrics. Can you do that? Also, for now, I would like to work alone, and I want you to double my salary."

"That's fine. You will oversee ordering all the equipment and dealing with supply companies. Please ask an expert to design a lab for the future with room for up to four women, including you. I will designate a space on the property for that effect. As of now, Alex, you are the director of La Toile laboratory. Start planning and hire someone else to develop scents."

The Mater took Aleksandra's hands, gave her a boost of power and left with Leonor.

On the way back to the house, the secretary asked, "Are you sure you want to pursue this poison business? It seems distasteful, pardon the pun. We could lose the ethical core of our beliefs."

"Dear Leonor, I welcome your advice, but I want all the weapons that I can use. The world is a dangerous place for women and girls. Otherwise, Telea would not exist. Up to now, secrecy and concealment have been our policy, and rightfully so because we didn't have the means to defend ourselves against violent men without suffering legal consequences. We can't just go around killing people because we don't like them.

"However, in many parts of the world, men in general are a threat to women. Even in the West, there are many violent men who destroy women through direct actions or through legislation. The future is unknown, and I would rather be prepared. I'm sure that I will make many decisions that you will disapprove of. That is one of the weights of my power, there will be many more. That's one of the reasons I need you. You will be my moral compass and will try to keep me human."

"You know that I will die in a few decades and that you will carry on for centuries. The longer you live, the less human you will become. Please remember the person that you are now and choose my successor carefully, with compassion in mind."

"Remind me of that when the time comes."

Chapter Fifteen

Antoine du Pressy arrived promptly at the appointed time. He came to Maison de la Toile in a chauffeured limousine, carrying a heavy leather travel bankers' case. The driver went to the kitchen for a cup of coffee. The banker was presented to the Mater by the housekeeper who closed the door behind her. He bowed deeply.

"Welcome Monsieur du Pressy! A nod will suffice as a token of my office. You must be exhausted from your trip. Please let's sit at the table, and you can show me your graphs and charts. I want to be fully informed."

"Thank you, Madame. Not at all. I took the train and was met by the limousine at the station. I believe I should start at the beginning."

"Since the first Mater, every woman who receives a necklace sends a tribute of about 10% of her income. It's the price for good health, longevity and often prosperity. I can't speak for how it worked millennia ago, but as long as I'm aware, and we have records, every Mater had a man of business. This happened because women were often property themselves, did not have a legal status to hold a business in their name or simply because they could not physically defend their holdings against men. So a line of men in my family committed themselves to guard the assets received and invest the money.

"If there were no direct descendant, a son-in-law or a grandchild would take the mantle. Of course, we became fabulously wealthy ourselves by receiving 10% of the tribute. Not every banker was competent. Some were corrupt or visible in their wealth, and the Mater had them executed as a punishment and warning to others. But, by and large, we did our best.

"We have not been in France long, only since 1816, after the Napoleonic Wars. Europe was just too uncertain and fraught with instability due to its constant wars. The central office of the bank, for many centuries, was in Byzantium or Constantinople. Before that in Egypt. We were always called House of Telea, or web, in different languages."

"How did you manage to thrive through the centuries?"

"By being inconspicuous and never displaying wealth. As I said before, the few bankers who did not follow these rules were executed on the Mater' orders. Also, we have always had security inside the walls of our compounds. Even nowadays, our bank is always discreetly guarded. We have the best physical and online security that money can buy. We don't fire people for being indiscreet; we kill them. That's always the best way to keep people quiet."

"I approve. I'm sure that throughout the many centuries of Telea's existence, we women have done exactly that to any who betrays our trust. Continue, please."

"So, by accumulating the wealth that constantly arrives, wise investments and simply the beauty of compound interest, Telea has more assets than the largest bank in the world. One-third of the assets are invested in sovereign bonds, another third is invested in companies owned by Telea, and the final third is invested in the prosperity of Telea members themselves. Let me explain in more detail."

"We only select stable countries to invest our money in sovereign bonds. Since World War II, we have kept a substantial amount in US treasury bonds, in Germany and in Scandinavian countries. The interest is low, but so are the risks. In addition, Telea owns successful businesses all over the world. We were pioneers in green energy, for example, and have always supported women's cooperatives in the developing world.

"Finally, we operate micro banks by which we make small loans to Telea members to start their own businesses or to overcome economic challenges. It is from this third that we help, without return, in times of catastrophes, such as earthquakes, tsunamis or even war. In the long run, we profit. Please let me show you."

Antoine proceeded to show graphs and charts which illustrated his explanation. He added that the final third was used by the bank to pay staff salaries. While each business paid its own workers from its profits, there were some full-time employees all over the world, such as coordinators, directors and security personnel.

"How is it possible that ministers have become obscenely rich on your watch?"

"I suspect that some of the tribute is diverted directly into their accounts and never reaches the bank. Telea's records are outdated and need to be brought up to date. The bank can only deal with records provided by the ministers."

"I see. That will be solved with updated computerised records. From now on, I want you to bring me quarterly reports on our assets and expenditures. I have some ideas in my head that will require large sums, but I want to think them over before I contact you. Ah, I almost forgot, we will build a small category II laboratory on our premises. Please don't be alarmed with the cost."

"Of course, Madame, and with your permission, I will leave now."

The Mater called for Fatemah who escorted Antoine to his car and then called for Leonor.

"It's time to send out the invitations to the ministers. Have you addressed them all properly and printed them? Did we already receive the sealing wax? I will sign and seal them now. I want the letters delivered by courier."

She didn't relish the upcoming confrontation, but the Mater had two weeks to prepare, and then she would shake the council of ministers.

Chapter Sixteen

During the following two weeks, the Mater started doing physical activity. She also started training with Lila because Emani was busy searching through her contact lists to recruit more security personnel. It was wonderful to have a younger and stronger body! The rest of the time she planned and read reports. The Mater wrote copious notes, thought about strategy and, after dinner relaxed with her newly arrived e-reader or watched her favourite movies and series. This was a time of preparation.

One evening, Leonor insisted that it was time to call in a wigmaker and a dressmaker. So, after an enjoyable time searching the internet, they settled on a couple of choices. Leonor made appointments for a month after the council meeting. The wigmaker was in Marseilles, which would make it a day of being tourists and enjoying themselves.

For outfits, they settled on a minor clothes designer whose dresses and pant suits were minimalist, flowing and flattering. The Mater wanted a full wardrobe of elegant but comfortable clothing. Leonor planned with the designer for her to come to Maison de la Toile to discuss the order and take measurements.

Two days before the meeting with the ministers, Simone duBois came to the house with another report. The Mater was expecting her, and they talked alone with the doors closed.

"I'm sorry to add to your troubles, but you need to be particularly careful with the minister of finance and her immediate staff. Besides appropriating for herself vast amounts of tribute, Madame Stephanie Tassel has ordered the assassination of several women who refused to pay her directly. Her personal secretary, Melanie Foucault, is involved in contacting private assassins through the dark web. It's my recommendation that you terminate both as soon as possible."

"Don't worry about that. Their days are numbered. Who else?"

"They are all guilty of crimes. The minister of infrastructure uses subpar materials that can't withstand catastrophic weather or natural disasters. The minister of economy skims from the top of every investment. The minister of social issues and the minister of international relations both receive bribes. The minister of interior also receives direct payment from tributes but hides those women from the records. She often blackmails women to pay her above the stipulated 10%. They're all rotten!"

The Mater agreed. "I need you to continue digging. This should become your full-time job in the foreseeable future. Follow the money and find all the corrupt women. I want Telea cleansed of their taint. They will all lose their stones."

Simone blanched. Having one's stones removed by force was the equivalent of a slow death sentence. All the previous benefits of the stones were quickly reversed. Women developed cancers that spread swiftly through their bodies, developed autoimmune diseases and had strokes or heart attacks. They all died within a year of losing their nanobots' protection. It was as if the body turned viciously upon itself.

"Of course, Madame. May I have your permission to hire more investigators? I can't possibly do a job of that size all by myself. If all we are doing is following the money for the last decade, let's say, the investigators don't need to be members of Telea. Our secret will remain."

"Won't they ask why so many women are prepared to just give their money? No. I want you to find women with nanobots to help you. Perhaps you can network with our newly formed IT department. They can help with that. If that's not enough, find more women and pay them well.

"In addition, I want you to develop, enlarge and maintain a network of informers throughout the world. I want them to be ordinary women who wear stones and go about their daily lives. That's the beauty of Telea, we conceal ourselves in plain sight. These women are to report to you any threats to our organisation, any corruption or anything unusual that we ought to know. These women should be paid a fee for each piece of information.

"You are a very good investigator, and you are loyal to me. It's a natural fit that you should also be my chief of spies. I bet that the ministers have their own information network. Ferret them out, if it's possible, and see if they are prepared to change allegiance.

"I suspect that those women believe that they are being faithful to Telea, so it might be easy. See what you can do. Also, I believe that this work will take decades to perfect. Be my spider in Telea."

"Madame, I only speak French and English. How am I going to deal with information and tips from all over the world?" Simone looked concerned.

"The tips should preferably come to you through the website that we are going to create. Use a translation app or, if needed, hire translators. Please coordinate with Louise Ferrer. She likes to be called Lou. She will need to know your requirements when she sets up our website."

The Mater dismissed Simone duBois and reformulated her plans for the confrontation with the council of ministers. To that effect, she called a meeting with Leonor, her personal secretary; Emani and Manuela, her heads of security; and Fatemah, her housekeeper. She waited until they were all together and explained her requirements. In two days, heads would roll.

Chapter Seventeen

It was a perfect spring afternoon, sunny with a light wind. The rows of bushes had started to flower. Small, delicate buds. She could see the seasonal workers hand-weeding the rows around the roots. Later they would use small electric rotor tillers between the rows. In her private garden, daffodils and tulips were in full bloom. Today, it was time for war. Jarring thought amidst the beauty.

By four o'clock in the afternoon, the driveway had several cars, but the Mater waited for Fatemah to come and inform her when they were all assembled in the ballroom. She could imagine their discomfort downstairs, waiting, without any chairs or refreshments.

Half an hour later, the housekeeper came to her suite to inform her superior that the minister of finance had just arrived with two staff members. The Mater understood the snub of lateness for what it was. Posturing. She checked herself in the bedroom mirrors and approved of her baldness, her black pantsuit with a matching low-cut blouse and her display of stones. Her only make-up was a carefully applied neutral lipstick. Taking a deep breath to calm herself and to concentrate, the Mater descended the stairs and made her way sedately to the ballroom.

She had instructed Fatemah to remove all furniture from the large space, leaving a throne-like chair by the wall opposite the door. As she walked in, she was pleased to see her whole contingent of security guards in attention by the walls. They were armed, as instructed. Groups of women milled around and hushed as the Mater made her way to her chair and sat down with a regal look. All eyes were on her. She noticed their elegance, their air of superiority and the challenge in their eyes. The housekeeper locked the door and stood in attention.

"I am the Mater! I am the Mother of Stones!" she declared in a clear voice. "Since I don't know you, please come forward, introduce yourselves and submit to me."

Instead of following instructions, six of the women separated themselves from the others and stood side by side.

"I am Stephanie Tassel, minister of finance, and I declare no allegiance to you."

With a voice dripping with disdain, Stephanie continued. "You are a nobody without any pedigree or relevance. Your bloodlines are suspect, and I refuse to bow to you. I have no idea how or why the search committee settled on you, considering the many daughters of the first one. However, I am a grand dame of France! I am a direct descendant of the previous Mater. I should be in your place, and you need to be crushed for your impudence, bitch!"

The six ministers held hands and as a line walked closer to the Mater. Everyone could see electrical blue sparks gathering in their hands. Immediately, the security personnel withdrew their handguns with laser sights and red dots appeared on the heads of the ministers and their staff. They were ready to shoot, but the Mater, with a hand sign, told them to hold.

The Mater focused on Stephanie, concentrated with all her might and forced those sparks to come to her. She simply absorbed their power, all of it. Her own jewels sparked blue light, the Mater felt engorged with so much power and developed a dull headache. Stephanie crashed to the ground while the others disentangled themselves and fell. Manuela, the warrior, checked on the fallen Stephanie.

"She is dead; all her jewels have burned out. Mater, please note that under her tunic, the finance minister had a belt made of stones. Against our rules, these women," and she pointed to the other ministers, "must have been stockpiling stones for years."

They all looked dazed and one of the defeated women started crying. The Mater looked at her own hands and noticed that they were shining with power. She must be glowing. While the warriors placed themselves behind each minister or remained with their guns drawn, Fatemah and Leonor continued to guard the door. Everybody else fell to their knees. They had never seen so much power and were terrified.

"Melanie Foucault, step forward and come close."

A woman lifted herself and ran to the door. A security guard held on to her and forced Melanie to approach the Mater.

"Please! I have nothing to do with the insurrection. I'm just her secretary." Melanie wailed pointing to the dead minister.

"Actually, you are much more than that. I have evidence that you were the one to commission the assassinations ordered by Madame Stephanie. You are not only part of the insurrection, but you were an active participant in over a dozen murders of Telea members, just in the last decade. Who knows what you did before! You are, therefore, sentenced to death."

Melanie screamed as the Mater absorbed all the power from her stone. Melanie crumbled to the floor, next to Stephanie. The room was in absolute silence, interrupted by one woman in the back of the room who vomited. Nobody moved to help her.

The Mater then ordered the remaining ministers to stand.

"As of right now, all your homes and places of business have been invaded by Telea's security personnel. All your electronic devices and those of your family members have been confiscated. All the contents of your desks have been boxed, and they are checking for any hidden compartments. Your bank accounts, that we know of, have been frozen. For the next while, my investigators will find all of your other bank accounts and passwords.

"All your assets will revert to Telea. Your mansions and your jewellery will be sold. You and your heirs are bankrupt. That is the price you pay for stealing from Telea, which each one of you has been doing with impunity for decades.

"Besides being guilty of rebellion against me, you are each guilty of various crimes. Step forward, minister of economy, Marie Lambert. For the last decades, you have been appropriating funds from every investment. You have defrauded Telea and our companies. Besides being bankrupt, now you will surrender any stones that you have in your person."

"You can't do that! Please don't do that," Marie wept. "I will die soon without my stone. I have a couple more with me. Have them but let me live."

"The problem is that you tried to kill me, along with these others. Who's to say you would not do the same in the future? At least you will have a year to live, however painful that may be."

"Guards, please remove any stones that Madame Marie may have on her person."

As one security person searched and patted her down, they found not three, but five stones. Marie was deflated, however she tried to grab the guard's weapon, but Emani was attentive and swiftly shot her in the chest.

The Mater stared at the remaining ministers and asked, "Is this the way you want to die? Without saying goodbye to your families and good friends?"

"Remove all the stones you have; otherwise, I will have you stripped naked and kicked out of the house in your birthday suits."

The remaining four ministers had nine stones among them. After witnessing the outcome of their peers, the women were resigned to their fate. All were in shock about the ruthlessness of the Mater. They had thought her unaccustomed to power and easily subdued. All those whom the council had been in contact with had reported upon her kindness and easy-going manner. The sentencing of the ministers was unexpected and swift and very, very bitter.

"Please leave my sight. I am done with you, but I want to leave you with a reminder that you will be watched, and your activities monitored. If you break your silence, I will go after anybody that listens to you. Don't try anything foolish against me or Telea."

Directing her attention to the members who were still kneeling, the Mater declared, "Stand up and listen closely. I assume that since you were the advisors to the ministers, you are all implicated in their crimes. However, I don't have any evidence against you. Hence, you will keep your stones, and you will live. If you fully cooperate with the investigators and help us understand the extent of corruption within Telea, you will regain some trust.

"However, those of you who do not cooperate may not like your new assignments. You will each be sent separately to work on our projects in the developing world. Your supervisors will be informed of your circumstances and my suspicions. If for three years I receive positive reports about you, each will be free to live and work where you want.

"On the other hand, if you try to run away from this exile you will be hunted and killed. Remember that each regional director has the power to monitor your stones, which will be a beacon in your pursuit. If you cause trouble where you are placed, you will lose your stones and suffer nanobots' withdrawal. It's up to you how you will face your exile.

"As you exit, show your identification to Manuela over there who will scan your cards. We will be in touch very soon."

The forlorn woman stood up and started to leave when a woman with curly hair and make-up running down her face called out, "Mater! Please hear me. I have important information. Please let me stay with my family, and I will tell you all that I know."

"What could you possibly tell me that would warrant a lenient sentence?"

"My name is Marguerite Coulier. I was the secretary to the minister of economy. I know that the ministers were and are still a threat to you, but you have an even greater danger that you know nothing about. Please let me explain and allow me to stay in France with my family."

"Very well," the Mater conceded. "Wait until we everybody else leaves and tell me what this danger is all about?"

Marguerite composed herself, looked around the room until she was certain all of her colleagues had left and explained. "It all started during the last decades of the previous Mater's reign. As you know, she was French and Roman Catholic and, although she lived beyond a human being's length of time, she never stopped having her faith, even though she practised quietly. I know these things that I'm about to tell you because I oversaw the distribution of all donations from Telea. The minister of economy would make her decisions with the Mater, and I would send the money to its destinations.

"During the twentieth century, the Mater started to unravel emotionally and became more and more concerned about her soul. That was the time that she started making donations to the Catholic church and seeking forgiveness for her sins. At the time, in 1932, she was living in Madrid and heard of a young priest who spoke of visions and of a new way lay people could reconnect with Jesus, through obedience to the church. That's exactly what she was looking for. We must remember that she believed in the divine right of rulers, therefore she felt that his sermons and practices were the answer to her spiritual angst.

"The problem is that she funded and promoted the growth of the Magisterium Ecclesiae, one of the most radically conservative movements of the Catholic church, beholden only to the Pope himself. They are the most authoritarian arm of the church and believe that the Pope is the only true interpreter of the truth and that his authority extends to civil matters. They are a powerful network that even today has brokered accords between the Vatican and sovereign states, called Concordats.

"Throughout the rest of her life, she betrayed Telea by aiding an organisation that seeks only power. They supported and had ministers in the worst of regimes, including Franco's in Spain and Pinochet's in Chile. Many thousands of people were killed, disappeared, or were tortured. The Magisterium Ecclesiae was founded during the last years of Emperor Constantine, during the Nicene Council, and it operates like a web such as ours. They place people in positions of power to control information, public policy and legislation. They are a menace to women's equality.

"The previous Mater didn't surrender her stones because she viewed it as a suicide, a capital sin in the eyes of the church. But it didn't end with her death. The minister of economy continued to fund the Magisterium Ecclesiae and had private meetings with at least one of its leaders. I don't know what they discussed, but I'm certain that many of our secrets have been shared with those men. They will come after you! They will come after all of us!"

The Mater was pensive, and finally, she replied. "I believe that you are right and the information you bring is very valuable. I grant you the right to live in France, but you will help us in confirming all your information. Also, I want the names of the people she met and the current leaders of the Magisterium Ecclesiae."

After all the visitors had left, the large room seemed even larger, and it stank of vomit. A large pool of blood stained the parquet and death added its own stench.

Three bodies were left on the floor. The Mater addressed the remaining women, her warriors, "What do we do with the bodies?"

"Well," said Emani, "the two without bullet wounds can be driven to separate hospitals. They died of massive strokes. Marie is another matter. With a fatal chest wound the police would be called, and we don't want that. I suggest we bury her right here on the property in a grave deep enough that it won't be disturbed.

"Tomorrow, I will go to a plant nursery and buy a tree to grow over the grave. With mulch around it, nobody will know or suspect anything. I believe the staff will continue to be silent regarding all Telea matters."

The Mater agreed with the plans and went to her suite, followed by Leonor. The security personnel carried the bodies to separate cars and drove off in search of remote hospitals. Emani stuffed Marie in a large plastic bag, used rope to secure the covering, carried the burden to another car and drove to the end of the property where there was a small grove. The maids cleaned the floor and aired the ballroom.

In her living room, the Mater sat on the sofa and started weeping silently.

In a worried tone of voice, Leonor asked, "Are you alright? What can I do for you?"

"I have never killed anyone, and now, I've killed three women. What kind of person have I become?"

"The one that still asks that question. Marie was a murderer, and you passed the sentence. The other two wanted to kill you, and so did the other ministers. And, in the process, you discover that you have another skill. You can absorb the power of the stones into yourself.

"I grieve for you because you lost another piece of yourself, but, during your very long life, you will be forced to do this again. Just do it for the right reasons. Please don't kill anyone just because you don't like them."

The Mater smiled and wiped her tears as Emilie entered, carrying a tray with a bottle of Oban, a crystal and silver ice bucket and two crystal glasses. The maid looked scared. Certainly, the recent events had reached the kitchen, or she had been one of the maids to clean the ballroom. The Mater was sorry about her reaction, but she dismissed Emilie and poured herself a whiskey neat.

"I hope that we are safe now from the ex-ministers," said Leonor. "However, I'm afraid that the remaining have months to stir up trouble and create mischief. You would do well to order some fatal accidents. I'm sorry, but there could be serious retaliation. They still may have bank accounts that we know nothing of."

"You are probably right, but I just can't picture myself right now ordering their deaths. However, we do have a very serious issue with the Magisterium Ecclesiae involvement. If the ministers were working together with the Catholic church and revealing our secrets, none of us would be safe. They can be ruthless and very dangerous. We need data. We need information, but we will deal with it tomorrow. Right now, I need a long bath, dinner and solitude in that order."

They shared a second drink and Leonor left to talk with Manuela. The protection officer agreed with the danger assessment. They needed to be vigilant.

Upstairs in her bathroom, the Mater poured bath gel, let the bubbles accumulate and reclined into the hot water with a loofah in her hand. She wanted to scrub the sorrow and guilt away. Her mind knew that there had been no other choice, but she kept seeing the blood on the floor and the crumbled bodies.

For the rest of the evening, both the Mater and Leonor were subdued. At dinner the conversation was brief, and the secretary left after dessert. The Mater could not focus on reading, so she watched a mindless TV program and let her mind wander to the afternoon's events. The killings, the news about the Magisterium Ecclesiae, but also her new ability. It had revealed itself because she had been angry.

She must not let her emotions get the better of her. The Mater suspected that with time, she would become progressively more emotionally detached. She would lose empathy, but she would be even more serene. On the other hand, perhaps the nanobots coursing through her body had reacted to the threat to her safety and that might be the trigger.

In a box, on top of the coffee table, there were the collected stones. Each was a large amalgam of nanobots that could easily be split in two, so she would have double the stones to give away. That was a good harvest and, if she were honest with herself, she had also increased her power. That was the good outcome of many days of planning.

The next day, after breakfast, the Mater called Manuela to discuss security. What were the most likely circumstances for an assault? Would they come to the house? Manuela thought it was unlikely because the house was too large and well-protected for a small group to act. If she were to plan an assassination, Manuela thought that the best conditions would be outside and soon, while her guard was down. Was the Mater planning any excursion? Perhaps a trip to town?

The Mater replied that indeed she planned to go to Marseille with Leonor in a month to have wigs made and to visit the tourist attractions. Also, she would like to go to Arles and explore.

Manuela was thoughtful for a bit and said, "Madame, you are inviting death. Until everything is sorted, you should not leave the property. When you leave the house to go to the garden, you need to tell us, so we can protect you. Leave the curtains drawn in your rooms and don't stand by the windows. An excellent shooter, with the right equipment, could kill you from the street. For now, it's my experienced assessment that the risk to your person is high."

The Mater agreed with her assessment and promised to follow Manuela's recommendations. She dismissed her bodyguard and called Leonor to cancel her appointment with the wigmaker in Marseille. Instead, she would order the wigs from the company's website, and they were expected to send someone to the house to do the fittings.

The Mater called Simone, the investigator, to find out if they had managed to figure out the passwords for the various computers that had been confiscated from the traitors and their families. The IT team had achieved success with most of the computers, simply because many of the desks had been searched. It is amazing how much we write down just in case. Most phones were not accessible, but the laptops were yielding substantial data that needed to be shifted through in detail. This could take a long time.

What about the ex-ministers themselves? Where were they? They had moved in with friends and family, and it was too soon to assess if they were a threat. Then, she told the investigator all that she had learned about the previous Mater's involvement with someone within the Magisterium Ecclesiae. Could they ascertain what was leaked about Telea? Doubtful. Could they defend themselves against such a powerful institution? Time would tell.

The Mater was uneasy after her conversations. She had always been a planner and a woman of action. Now she had to rely on others to keep her safe when she was convinced that her life was going to be in danger in the foreseeable future. Yesterday the Mater had been feeling guilty for the three deaths. Today she was sure that the guards should have killed them all and should start thinking about killing those in the Magisterium Ecclesiae who knew about Telea. They needed to identify the individual people in the Catholic organisation who were aware of Telea's secrets.

For the moment, the main preoccupations were solidifying her power, ensuring her safety and learning more about Telea. She needed the contact information for all the district directors. The Mater called Simone again to inquire if the rest of the staff of the ex-minister of interior was cooperating. Someone had the information she required. The investigator disclosed that the secretaries had been so terrified that they were blabbing all they knew. She should have that list by the end of the day.

The Mater was also worried about the power vacuum that the elimination of all her council of ministers entailed. She could not possibly assume all their responsibilities. Therefore, the Mater decided to appoint interim ministers until the confusion settled down. She would contact the regional directors and ask them to suggest names. Contrary to her predecessor who had surrounded herself with French women, the Mater wanted a diverse council of ministers, representative of all the women of Telea.

For the next weeks, with Leonor's help and with the list provided by the ex-ministers' secretaries, The Mater called over two hundred regional directors. The time difference was an issue because it was the middle of the night for many of her contacts. The other problem was a common language since many women spoke English with difficulty so, for these times they got a translator. In every case, the Mater introduced herself, inquired about the situation for women in their regions and asked for suggestions for the position of ministers. She wanted women with high education, experts in the fields for which they were applying, with administrative experience and able to work in a team. If she received hundreds of applications for only six jobs, the rest of the women would be invaluable in other positions.

The one thing that continued to worry the Mother of Stones was the identity of all who knew about Telea in the Magisterium Ecclesiae. Marguerite has given the names of the men with whom the ex-minister of economy had meetings with, but there could be others. Certainly, the leadership must know about a vast network of women who themselves yielded a lot of power.

Not everything was about work though. With spring in full bloom, the Mater made it a habit of visiting her personal garden regularly. It was a way to escape the confines of the house, putter around with plants and enjoy a bit of time in the sunlight. The staff had placed garden furniture in the front and back of the house, so she enjoyed sitting outside, reading her reports and making notes on the margins.

She wore a large hat to provide protection from the sun and was always accompanied by a couple of security guards who monitored the surrounding area. They kept looking at the trees in the back of the property and at the apartment buildings behind Maison the la Toile. Emani explained that if a sharpshooter got to the roof of the apartment buildings, they would be in trouble. Therefore, the back of the house was closely monitored.

On a lovely Sunday afternoon, when part of the staff was away for the weekend, the Mater decided to plant some annuals around the flower beds. The gardener could do the job, but it was such a pleasant activity with the warm soil. Leonor helped with the plants while Emani and Nikola, another security guard, kept watch.

"Emani, come and—" a sharp pain bit her arm. Stunned, the Mater saw the blood flowing from her bicep and threw herself on the ground. Emani jumped on top of her while Nikola withdrew her side weapon and looked for the source of the shot.

"She yelled: We're under attack!" Leonor started screaming.

"Be quiet! Help the Mater!" demanded Emani.

With Leonor helping the Mater, the four women crawled until they reached the screen provided by bushes. Another shot missed.

"Keep crawling! Follow the bushes!" Emani whispered urgently. And then, she too was shot in the shoulder. She fell backwards with the force of the impact. Emani and the Mater were bleeding profusely, and Nikola kept watch, silently now. They heard more gunshots from the grove of trees. Then silence.

With the Mater and Leonor between them, the two security guards held their guns steady, even though Emani was in great pain. The Mater just clenched her teeth. Her whole body trembled. Must be the nanobots trying to repair the damage to her body. Leonor held her hand over her mouth, with eyes wide open. They stayed that way until Manuela arrived up.

"The shooter is dead, and you need a doctor. Leonor and Nikola help me take both the Mater and Emani inside. After that, Leonor call Jeanne d'Arc Clinic and ask for Doctor Justine Clairvaux. Tell her it's an emergency and to bring surgical tools."

Inside the house, the Mater and Emani sat in the formal living room while Manuela gave first aid to both. Blood covered the floor, marking their way in. While they waited, the Mater asked what happened.

Manuela explained, "Since the events with the ex-ministers and the information we have gathered about the Magisterium Ecclesiae, we have been waiting for something like this to happen. So we set up shifts every day in the grove, across the road and on top of the apartment buildings. A shooter would have to use one of these spots, and it would have to happen during the day for visibility.

"I'm sorry we missed his presence, and you got hurt. It was a man, and he must have set up during the night with extraordinary patience because we never noticed any movement. He was perched on a makeshift platform above the ground in one of the trees. Again, there was no noise during the night to warn us of any construction. He must have brought the platform with him and installed it silently. He was a professional and your luck was that you were crouched on the ground behind plants moving unexpectedly."

"Did he have anything on his person that might indicate who hired him?" asked the Mater.

"No, nothing. He was clean. No identification, no papers, just a bottle of water beside him and a finished sandwich wrapper. However, we took a picture of his face, and we'll fingerprint him. We will check all the databases and come up with a name and history."

Her arm felt better, and the bleeding had stopped. As they left the room, the doctor rushed in. "Oh, my goodness, what happened?"

"We were shot, but it's going to be fine. Please take care of Emani first. My nanobots are starting to repair the wound."

"Let me check if there is an exit wound or if the bullet is still in your arm."

After observing her patient and cleaning the wound, the doctor declared herself satisfied that the bullet had gone through. The Mater would have a full recovery. However, Emani's wound was more serious.

"I must operate on this shoulder; however, this is not the place to do so. The first aid will hold until we get to the clinic. By now, there should be nobody there. Let's go!"

Justine called for help and Manuela and Nikola supported Emani to the waiting car. On the way, the doctor called Kyong, the nurse, to meet her at the clinic.

When the Mater walked out of the formal living room the staff was assembled in the grand hall waiting for instructions and worried.

"Thank you for your concern, but everything is under control. Madame Fatemah, please have someone clean the blood and bring me a mint tea and a scotch upstairs."

After cleaning herself of blood and soil, the Mater noticed that the wound was almost closed. She put on clean clothes and called Leonor.

"Please bring me the addresses where the ex-ministers are staying. By tomorrow evening, the four will be dead."

The Mater then called Aleksandra, the botanist researcher, and explained her requirements. An hour later, the researcher was shown to the Mater's suite and gave her a box with the items that had been requested.

"Four of these injection vials contain 100 mg. each of digoxin, a digitalis preparation. These are overkill, but I presume you want a fast effect. The other four vials contain Botulinum toxin, also known as Botox, in very high concentrations. They will kill very fast.

"I just heard downstairs about the attempt on your life. I presume that you want to even the score and eliminate further threats. You are right, of course. Please remind whoever is handling these to be very careful and to use latex gloves."

"Thank you, Alex, for your quick response. Please see yourself out."

Leonor entered the living room, nodded her head and asked, "Do you have everything you will need to rid us of those monsters?"

"Yes, I do. Now it will be up to Manuela and her team to see if they are up to the task. I can't order them to commit assassinations against their conscience. One thing is to kill in the heat of battle or to kill in my defence. Another thing altogether is to kill in cold blood after careful preparation. Let's see what they say. In the meantime, I worry about Emani. Wait with me."

By now, the tea was cold, so they sipped the whisky. They waited for hours, had a simple dinner and waited some more. None of the women could concentrate enough to read reports, so they decided to watch an old TV show, the mindless kind.

It was close to midnight when they saw a car come up the driveway. It was the team. The Mater, Leonor and Fatemah were waiting in the grand hall Doctor Justine Clairvaux entered first, followed by Manuela and Nikola supporting Emani.

"First, she needs to go to bed. She is semi-conscious, but the anaesthesia will wear off soon. I'm going to set up a drip with pain medication. Please carry Emani to her room, and I will be right behind you.

"Madame, there were no problems with the surgery, but Emani might lose some mobility in her arm. Thankfully, it was her left shoulder, and her right side is dominant. However, I don't know if she might see combat again. Nurse Kyong will be here shortly and will keep vigil. I will return in the morning. Now, I must see to my patient."

Fatemah and Emilie carried medical equipment upstairs, and the Mater waited for Manuela to report.

"Madam, I once more truly regret your injury and the fact that we were not thorough enough."

"No matter, I am almost healed. I'm only concerned with Emani. She should be fine, but we are her family, and I worry."

"Now tell me what you did with the shooter's body."

"By now, the other guards must have finished the job. My instructions were to dig a deep grave, bury the body and the weapon and remove all his traces. Tomorrow, we will buy a tree and plant it over the grave site. At this rate, we will have a forest soon," Manuela said chuckling.

The Mater smiled grimly and stated her desire to assassinate the remaining ex-ministers. Would Manuela and her team, do it?

"Madame, we are all devoted to you. We are twelve women united in keeping you safe, so if it takes killing those who threaten your life, we will do it. Just to be certain, I will ask each guard separately. How would you like us to do it?"

"Each ex-minister is staying in a different city therefore the police should not connect their deaths. l would like it to be done by tomorrow night. I received poison injections for you to use, but you must be careful not to spill the contents on yourselves, and you must wear gloves.

"You are the expert, but I suggest you separate into four teams of three women. One woman is the driver and lookout, and the other two subdue the targets and inject the poison. You will be one woman short, with Emani down. In this box, there are two types of poison; either one will do the job. Tomorrow is Monday, a workday; therefore, their family and friends should be out of the houses. Find them alone, be inconspicuous and be fast. What do you say?"

"I would prefer to have more time for surveillance, but we'll make do. However, the danger is that you will be unprotected."

"I doubt very much that anything will happen tomorrow. Whoever ordered the assassination will be waiting for news. That's why they won't be expecting such a swift reaction on our part.

"Talk with your team, rest and be ready to leave early. You will arrive back at different times. I will wait up until all four teams are in."

Chapter Eighteen

The Mater could not get to sleep that night. Ethical and moral issues kept swirling around in her mind. She simply could not allow herself or her personal guards to become routine killers. The current situation demanded ruthlessness, but in the future, she needed to be guided by compassion. Otherwise, what was the point of Telea, if not to protect women?

Women needed protection from men. Not all of them, of course. Her own son was a model human being. But enough men were brutalisers and killers that women throughout the planet needed Telea. However, she now realised the extent of corruption and evil that women were also capable of.

The first Mother of Stones knew of it personally because she had been raped and discarded by her small tribe. Men had raped her and used her, but the other women of the tribe had excluded her in her hour of need. That's why she kept the stones a secret from women at large, keeping their power contained within her own daughters. Women were as capable of cruelty as men, they just did it differently.

It occurred to the Mater that when this crisis was over, she should write a manifesto of ethical behaviour to be disseminated amongst women of Telea. Women needed to be held accountable for the quality of their interactions with their sisters, especially the district directors, who were major nodes in Telea. They were, or should be, the moral and ethical guides for all the women in their jurisdiction. Their power should be for protection and nourishment.

At a certain point, she got out of bed, dressed and went to check on Emani. Kyong, the nurse, said that the patient had no fever and was resting comfortably with some help from morphine. The night was calm and quiet, so the Mater went back to bed and slept until late.

The following day, with Leonor as a helper, the Mater started writing notes about the limits of power within Telea and in the world, the mechanisms of energy exchange and ethical behaviour within the sisterhood. She exhorted women to be careful of harming others but to be vigilant in the protection of themselves and their loved ones. Whenever possible, they should appeal to the civil arms of authority like the police and the judicial system. Women should be politically involved to enact legislation that promotes and protects their human rights.

Only the district directors had the power to punish Telea members who transgressed by withdrawing their stones. Accused women needed to be given the right to defend themselves and unequivocal evidence had to be presented. However, the Mater had to approve the punishment. All removed stones had to be sent to the Mater with an attached report.

Actions against men had to be approved by the district directors and carefully planned to avoid police scrutiny. Only rapists and murderers who had escaped justice should be killed. All other perpetrators, such as criminal harassers, should be dealt with, using the minimum force required.

The Mater realised that she would need to create the equivalent of a written criminal and ethical code. This was more complex than her initial nightly reverie. A team of Telea lawyers would need to work on this.

Tired of working for hours, the Mater and Leonor had a beautifully presented dinner; however, they were so anxious about the pending assassinations that the food seemed tasteless. They spent the evening quietly.

At a certain point, they visited Emani to see how she was recuperating. The patient was sitting up, chatting with Kyong. Her shoulder was bandaged, and her left arm was immobilised. She clearly looked haggard, but she was alive. The nurse informed the visitors that Emani's condition was improving, but that it would be painful for some time. After the wound was fully healed, she would need extensive physiotherapy to regain movement in her shoulder.

"Thank you for protecting me. I owe you, my life!" said the Mater. "Besides being my chief army recruiter, you will be a military adviser to the council of ministers that I will appoint. For now, follow the nurse's and the doctor's instructions and take your time getting well."

After they returned to the Mater's suite, she received a phone call from Manuela. The warrior reported that all the cleaning operations had been concluded; however, there were a couple of issues that had required quick thinking. She would explain the details upon arrival, which would be several hours later. Manuela suggested that the Mater should sleep in the meantime.

Leonor asked to be dismissed and went to bed. The Mater, who did her best thinking during the late hours, stayed awake much longer and continued to write notes about the criminal and ethical code of Telea. Exhausted, with her muscles quivering but without much discomfort in her arm, she went to bed

Early in the morning, Fatemah knocked at the Mater's door and announced the arrival of the first team waiting for her in the living room. The Mother of Stones wrapped herself in her bathrobe and joined the fatigued women. They had driven all night and were exhausted. However, the leader, a muscular woman called Frieda, reported that the team had surveyed their target for hours until they found her alone walking to her car.

They caught up with her, confirmed that she was Gisela Stein and quickly injected the poison in her neck. They left her on the ground and drove off. Frieda added that it had been dusk and that there had been nobody on the street. Nevertheless, they soon exchanged vehicles, left the car they used in an airport parking lot and drove home.

The Mater thanked the team and ordered them to bed. For herself, she decided to shower and get ready for the day. This was a highly unusual decision for the Mater who normally would have just returned to bed, but she was anxious to receive the teams' reports, and this was just the first one to arrive. She ordered coffee and orange juice to start her day and called her chief investigator, Simone duBois, and Lou, her senior IT person and hacker, to join her in a meeting as soon as possible. She wanted reports on their activities.

Within an hour, both Simone and Lou arrived. Their investigations showed that at least six regional directors had been accomplices of the disgraced ex-ministers. Up to now, the others looked clean, but there was still a lot of data to analyse. The Mater asked them to find the contact information of the security guards in those jurisdictions so that the collaborators could be arrested and questioned and have their stones removed. Their property should also be confiscated if there was evidence of illicit wealth at Telea's expense.

"Have you found the names and contact information of all members of the Telea yet?"

"Yes," Lou answered, "those were in the hard drive of the ex-minister of interior. What would you like us to do?"

"I want our website up as soon as possible in the way that I explained to you. A secret website with individual passwords within a visible, public website. Once this is uploaded, I want you to send a message to every woman in Telea informing them of the website and requiring them to register on the secret site, so that we can post information and any woman can report abuses, corruption or even their needs.

"Do you have a web designer available? Make the public site an innocent-looking business site, like a travel agency. Within a few weeks, I would like it to be ready to send and receive information from our women."

"What about those women who don't have a computer or a smartphone?" asked Simone.

"You should confirm with the district directors how many women need devices, and I shall set a budget aside to purchase smartphones in bulk and have them sent to the regional directors for distribution."

"However," pressed Simone, "there are many places in the developing world without electricity to charge those phones. What do we do in these cases?"

"Let me know about that too. I will have my personal secretary order and purchase solar phone chargers from manufacturers and have them shipped to the regional directors in those areas.

"In two weeks, I would like to have a progress report which you may send by email. If there are any problems, please let me know."

The Mater called Leonor to attend to her and instructed her personal secretary to contact phone manufacturers to purchase sturdy and reliable smartphones. The same for solar chargers. That done, they waited for the assassination teams to arrive.

The second team reached the house as they were having a late breakfast. They interrupted their meal, and the Mater was informed that the ex-minister of the Interior was dead. They had surprised her during an afternoon jog and left her where she fell. There had been no other runners on the path. The reason for their delay was that they had to drive from Metz, and it was a long way back. The Mater told them to go and rest.

The third team arrived shortly after. Their target, the ex-minister of infrastructure, had been killed in La Rochelle in the hotel room where she was staying. Her death would be attributed to a heart attack.

Finally, the last team arrived in the early afternoon. It was a two-person team comprised of Manuela and Nikola. They had surveyed the house on the outskirts of Lyon until they were sure the target was alone in the house. They had both entered the house from the back, surprising the ex-minister of social issues in the kitchen. She had cried out, attempted to flee and hit her head on the counter.

Manuela was about to inject the poison when a younger woman came running with a gun. Manuela plunged the syringe, Nikola grabbed the gun, and it went off, the bullet lodging itself in the ceiling. They subdued the woman who subsequently disclosed that she was the eldest daughter and that she had been the one who had ordered the Mater's assassination.

Her mother had confided in her, and she had decided to take revenge by contacting the Magisterium Ecclesiae and asking for help in eliminating the Mater. The daughter too was poisoned, and her stone removed. Manuela and Nikola grabbed garbage bags from the kitchen, ran to what looked like an office on the first floor and placed everything from the desk into the garbage bags. They opened all the drawers on the desk to check for any hidden notes.

The purpose was to find out who the daughter had been in communication with at the Magisterium Ecclesiae. That was the most important piece of information. However, they could not leave the space of an obvious crime scene, so they quickly went to the kitchen, grabbed notes and cookbooks and placed them in the drawers. When they did that Nikola noticed a sticky note on the fridge with a phone number and the name 'Cooperator Alain Gerard'. She placed it in her pocket.

However, now they had two corpses instead of one. No one would believe two strokes or heart attacks at the same time. Hence, they had a tricky situation. Audaciously, they decided to carry the body of the daughter between them through the front door. The body was placed in the backseat, and they drove off towards the mountains where they dumped the body.

They drove to Grenoble, where they left the car, and took the train to Arles with garbage bags and everything. A taxi had dropped them off at Maison de la Toile. They believed that they had covered their tracks, but it was a good idea to lay low for a while. Perhaps they could even visit their families for an indefinite period.

"Serbia and Brazil sound like excellent places to hide in plain sight. Leonor will make your travel arrangements while you pack. I will contact your respective regional directors for them to find you appropriate employment in your country. Thank you so much for all you have done for me!"

It was done. The Mater felt relief, but also a certain emptiness. A part of her soul had withered with the killings. She had ordered the deaths of her ex-ministers, had directly killed two women and Emani had been shot. This was not what she had expected when she decided to transform herself into this new person.

She did not grieve for the fatal victims. She grieved that her reign had started with so much conflict. She grieved for the woman that she had become. And she was extremely worried about the safety of Telea. The Mater closed the door of her room, undressed and went to bed. She lay in a foetal position for a long while, buried in the mound of comforter until she fell asleep.

When she woke up, it was late afternoon, and Manuela and Nikola had left. Nine active security guards should be enough since the danger had passed. The Mater dressed in a comfortable yet elegant pantsuit and called the housekeeper to inquire how the staff was doing.

"Everybody is relieved that you are safe. I'm certain that we can re-establish the house routines and Mademoiselle Emani is recovering nicely. I suggest, Madame, that you take some time for yourself to distract your mind from the past troubles."

"You are right, of course, Fatemah. Perhaps tomorrow I will visit Arles with Madame Leonor and a couple of security guards. We will make an outing of it, and I will play the tourist.

"Since I didn't have lunch, please ask the chef if it's possible for her to prepare an early dinner. In the meantime, have somebody bring me an aperitif and some ice water."

The Mater called for Leonor who joined her shortly after.

"How do you feel?" asked her secretary.

"I feel relieved, but also a bit hollow. One should not take killing lightly, I don't feel guilt or remorse, but I'm just not happy about any of it. However, it is done, and I would like to distract myself. How do you feel about going out tomorrow? We could visit Arles and pretend to be tourists.

"I would also like to buy a pair of jeans, a couple of T-shirts and sandals. The weather is becoming warm, and I don't have anything informal. I even had to borrow Emani's clothes when I decided to go out to the garden. They are now damaged, and I would also like to buy Emani a gift. What do you say?"

"What a great idea! However, in the next few days, with your permission, I would like to go to Portugal to get my things and to return my key to the landlord. I lived in a furnished one-bedroom apartment, so I don't have much.

"I know that we have a lot of work to do here, but I could also talk with some women to choose one to take over my previous role as provincial director. In addition, I have some women in mind who could apply for a ministerial role. I will sound them out. Would one week of my absence be too much?"

"Not at all. Just make sure that I have all the pending files on my desk and all the necessary contacts. If need be, I will call you." The Mater assured her secretary. It would be good for her to also have some distractions.

Their early dinner was tasty as usual. They had steak, fries, salad and a strawberry pie. After, they chose to watch a romantic comedy. Silly but good fun. The Mater ended her evening reading. She had started re-reading an Anne Bishop series, and it was just delicious. Leonor retired early since she had not slept during the afternoon like her superior.

Chapter Nineteen

The Mater had been confined for months, and it felt like forever. Therefore, leaving the house in the early afternoon was an exciting adventure. She was accompanied by Leonor, who sat in the front seat, and two guards, one driving and the other woman in the back seat, besides their superior.

The Mater wanted to go shopping first, so they went to the largest mall, walked around and bought what they wanted. Inexpensive clothing items, but much appreciated in the warmer weather. Considering that summer was coming up, the Mater even bought a black swimsuit and a couple of colourful sun dresses. Next, they looked for a jewellery store, and the Mater found the perfect gift for Emani, a gold, sapphire and diamond bracelet. It was a graceful piece that would contrast beautifully with her dark skin.

After shopping, they decided to have lunch on the outdoor patio of a restaurant in the old town area. The Mater decided they should all eat at the same table, so the four women sat down at a trendy restaurant, ate bouillabaisse and hot crusty bread and ordered a bottle of white wine. The security guards asked for sparkling water.

Although there was much to explore, especially the various museums and art galleries, the Mater decided that she would rather be driven around to see the sights. She wanted to have a general impression of Arles. Then, in the future, she would make multiple trips back to town. She was equally impressed with the Roman amphitheatre as with Frank Gehry's aluminium clad, Luma Arles tower. However, the flower plantations were breathtaking. She was fortunate to live in one.

Back at the Maison de la Toile, the Mater unpacked her shopping bags and retrieved Emani's bracelet perfectly gift-wrapped in a lovely jewellery box.

"Hello, Kyong! May I visit with Emani?"

"Of course, Madame. I will go to the kitchen to get a snack."

With the nurse's departure, the Mater felt somewhat awkward to be alone with Emani in such an intimate setting. She was just so beautiful that even looking at her hurt sometimes. The Mater placed the chair closer to the bed and offered Emani her gift.

The woman looked stunned, "Now, why would you do such a thing, Madame?"

"Because I'm grateful to you for my life, I'm grateful that you are my personal guard and just because you deserve it." And she added in her thoughts, *Because thinking of you makes me happy.* What a silly thing for a woman of her age to think! But wait! She was no longer a woman of a certain age. She was the Mater, she was rejuvenated and Emani, even wrapped up in bandages and looking tired, was a very attractive woman. Of course, she didn't voice any of her thoughts. She just smiled as serenely as she could.

After unwrapping her gift and seeing the contents of the box, Emani started to weep silently.

"Oh, please don't cry! If you don't like it, you can exchange it when you are feeling better."

"That's not it at all, Madame. It's just that nobody ever gave me jewellery. It's absolutely wonderful and beautiful, and it looks expensive! I'm crying with happiness and feeling ridiculous."

The Mater also felt ridiculous, so she held out her hand, and they touched for a moment. It was enough for now, so she stood up and said goodbye. Walking down to her suite, the Mater felt a shiver. These were not the nanobots working. This was the woman feeling happy.

The next day, Leonor left to spend a week in Portugal to get her things and talk face to face with several women. The Mater received new reports from her investigator, from the IT director and from her botanist. Therefore, she spent a large portion of the day reading and writing notes. She called the banker because she had not yet received the latest reports.

The Mater stretched and left her work at the end of the afternoon. She felt lonely and didn't want to dine by herself. She went upstairs and asked Kyong if she and her patient could have dinner tonight in the suite. The Mater explained her predicament. The nurse was flattered and added that Emani was perfectly able to walk down the stairs for dinner, that it would also cheer her up because the warrior looked melancholic today.

Emani raised the issue that she could only eat with her right hand. The Mater then called the housekeeper from her living room advising Fatemah to tell the staff that there would be three for dinner. And so, it was. At eight o'clock sharp, there was a knock on the open door, and the Mater waved them in. As usual, the table was set beautifully, and there were fresh flowers.

Both Kyong and Emani were casually dressed, as was the Mater. Emilie served them sushi followed by a variety of tempura vegetables and fish, Finally, for dessert, they had macarons. Emani appreciated that she only needed to use her right hand with chopsticks. They drank mineral water and white wine and talked freely about their experiences as members of Telea. A couple of hours later it was obvious that Emani was tired, so both nurse and patient left with their thanks.

During that week, Emani had meals with the Mater frequently and always for dinner. The nurse was no longer needed daily, so it was just the two of them.

It was great fun when the wigmaker arrived with four wigs that had been ordered online. One was blond, styled in a French twist for formal occasions. Another was a dark pixie cut. The third was dark, with straight long hair, and the last wig was grey with a short, elegant cut. The wigmaker made the appropriate fittings in all her wigs. They would be useful for changes in her appearance. The Mater wanted to blend in.

Another entertaining day was the one in which the clothes designer and her assistant came with sketches, fabric samples and measuring tape. The Mater liked the asymmetric, elegant flowing designs, especially the pants and tunic sets. She chose neutral tones and black in silks and cotton for the summer and wools for the winter. These would be the clothes she would wear when dealing with women from Telea.

The Mater also asked for indoor caftans in fabrics appropriate for the weather. These should be colourful and comfortable. In addition, she wanted shawls and cardigans which could be layered with the chosen designs. For the winter, she chose an oversized wool coat with a quilted inside layer. That should keep her warm. A scarf and a hat would finish the ensemble.

The designer asked about shoes and underwear. The Mater thought for a bit and decided that she would choose those herself in the shopping centres because she wanted a comfortable fit.

The Mater also requested a new uniform for the staff of pants, tunics and running shoes. Each maid was to receive six sets of work clothes, three for the summer and three for the winter. The housekeeper would choose her own uniform, so the designer needed to consult with Fatemah and provide as many sets as the housekeeper saw fit. The clothes designer spent a long time measuring all the women in the house. With the order completed, the designer promised to return as soon as possible for fittings but warned that an order of that size would take some time.

The Mater decided to try her pixie wig. She put on jeans and a T-shirt and called Emani on the intercom to ask if she needed anything from Arles. It was still too early for her personal guard and healing friend to exert herself. So with two bodyguards in tow, the Mater went to town. On the way, she changed her appearance to that of a younger self.

The bodyguards were startled but said nothing. The Mater's goal was to buy shoes and underwear. They went to the shopping centre where they had been before where she chose a general shoe store where she bought a pair of Doc Marten boots, a pair of low-heeled pumps and house slippers. Next was the underwear store.

This was more complicated because most stores only displayed silly and frilly things. The Mater wanted comfort above all, but she realised that with her new clothes order, she would need appropriate foundation garments. So, this time, she went to an upscale Italian store where she explained her needs, and the saleswoman was very helpful. She finally stopped at a chocolatier and bought a box of truffles for Emani. Time to go home for dinner. The day had been full of feminine endeavours, but it had been exhausting.

Chapter Twenty

Juan Carlos Cristóbal was not pleased. He sat at his desk at home, which he shared with his mother, and he wanted to throw something or break someone. However, his famed stoicism and personal discipline asserted itself, and he took deep breaths to calm his anger. His home office, like the rest of the house in Barcelona, was of a traditional style with floor-to-ceiling bookcases of literary tomes, legal reference books and a large collection of theological and political essays. He was an Associate of the Magisterium Ecclesiae and, as such, he was celibate and committed to a life of striving for holiness.

In addition, he was also the vice president of Vox, an extreme right-wing party in Spain. He had been groomed since his adolescence to become a voice of Christ in the world, and to that effect, he had become a constitutional lawyer and a rising political power in conservative Europe.

Juan Carlos had an ascetic look. He was tall, dark with an aquiline nose, but not a handsome man. His thin lips, large ears and penetrating gaze repelled women and men alike. There was something cruel about him. Nevertheless, on social occasions, he was a paragon of civility and charm. Right now, though, his cold fury, revealed his authentic self.

"We have spent a century trying to infiltrate and control the witches," he thought. "How could it have gone wrong?"

He had just received a phone call from Brother Alain Gerard, a cooperator from Marseille, and had just found out that the assassin he had procured was dead and that the new Mater had sent her own assassins to get rid of his tame witches. There was some danger that the Magisterium Ecclesiae would be discovered as their foe. Now, he had no other recourse than to come clean with the Prelate Manuel Echevarria, their earthly pastor. Of course, Prelate Echevarria knew nothing of the assassination attempt, but he was well-versed on the witches' web and their Mother of Stones.

In a twist of fate or the hand of the Almighty, the previous Mater had been a devout Catholic and had funded the Magisterium Ecclesiae. Every prelate since the saintly founder of their organisation during the Nicene Council knew of the existence of the women's Telea and had manipulated their leadership for the Works of God. They had been stupid and greedy, but it had all been to the benefit of the Holy Mother Church.

Since he could not delay the inevitable, Cristóbal dialled the personal number of the Prelate and, after inquiring about his health, explained the measures he had taken and the disastrous consequences. Javier Echevarria was appalled.

"How could you have ordered an assassination without my blessing? Now we have a mess on our hands."

"Prelate, please accept my submission and deepest apologies. I will endure whatever mortification you order in the name of Jesus Christ. However, I don't think they know of our connection. It's logical that they would blame their ministers and that's the reason why they were killed.

"We continue to operate in the shadows and perhaps, in the future, we will have the guiding hand of God in our endeavours to get rid of them. There are only four people alive who know of our involvement, Brother Alain Gerard, Bishop Joseph McKenzie who found the assassin, you and I. There is no way that the witches can find out details about us."

"You better pray that it is the case because the Holy Father does not need to find out about this. However, the witches will not want to reveal themselves, so a scandal is very unlikely. Okay, God bless you and ask your confessor for the appropriate mortification."

"Thank you, Prelate. I shall do as you command."

Juan Carlos Cristóbal was a genuinely devout man. He believed with all fervour in the tenets of his church and its teachings. He prayed several times a day at the altar in his bedroom; he went to daily mass and confessed weekly. He went to retreats at the Magisterium Ecclesiae facilities in various parts of the world, he endeavoured to follow in the footsteps of holiness, and he was a devoted son to his elderly mother.

However, at fifty-two years old he was also a skilled politician and an ardent public speaker. He could manipulate the masses as well as those in public office. He was intelligent, ambitious and ruthless with the enemies of the church. And he was a very busy man.

He called on his mother to tell her that he had a meeting, informed the maid that he wouldn't be home for dinner and drove his car to the outskirts of Barcelona where the Vox had headquarters. Municipal elections were on the horizon and Juan Carlos wanted to ensure a good result. He understood the importance of local power and of grass movements guided by the right person, himself, of course.

During times of economic austerity and declining quality of life, it was easy to manipulate functionally illiterate people who were resentful of their circumstances. Juan Carlos was very skilled at directing anger for his purpose and had amassed a significant following in the polls. He had also personally overseen the variety of election strategies and the hands-on approaches to dealing with deviants and godless communists.

After the meeting with his Vox companions, he attended a dinner party at the house of a magnate of industry where he mingled with other men of power. It was a pleasurable evening.

The next day, the newspapers had headlines about the dawn firebombing of a popular gay nightclub. Thankfully, there were no injuries as the place had been closed. No one had claimed responsibility, but there were insinuations that radicalised Muslims were possibly culpable. Before his breakfast, Juan Carlos Cristóbal went to mass, confessed to the local priest who was also his spiritual advisor in the Magisterium Ecclesiae and went home for his mortification. He closed the door to his bedroom, stripped his clothes to the waist and proceeded to whip himself. Afterwards, glad that there was minimal blood, he felt clean of his sins and with peace of mind.

***

In Arles, at the Maison de la Toile, life continued as planned. With Leonor's return from Portugal, the Mater engaged in the first phase of her plans to revitalise Telea. She needed to visit as much of the world as possible, and she would travel under the guise of being a tourist. Her French passport was a problem because she was not yet fluent in the language. So, with Simone's and Lou's help, her investigator and spy and her hacker, they contacted a master French forger and got the Mater a Canadian passport under the name of Claire Milligan.

To begin with, she wanted to know who Leonor suggested as the regional director for Portugal. Therefore, the woman was summoned for an interview.

She was called Teresa Ferreira, and she was a small woman with her hair tinted reddish, middle-aged and assertive. Thankfully, she did not bow when she was introduced by Leonor but nodded her head respectfully. The Mater invited her and Leonor to sit on the sofa and took for herself an upholstered chair. While Fatemah brought the tea and pastries herself, Teresa updated her superior on general issues of the economy and politics of Portugal, not knowing that the Mater had been Portuguese. Once the housekeeper left, the Mater asked her guest to speak about herself and asked Leonor to keep notes on the interview.

Teresa disclosed that she had been fortunate to be a child of a large middle-class family, from the mountainous region of Trás-os-Montes, near Galicia. She had gone to the University of Porto where she had received a doctorate in Social Work. At university, she became close friends with a professor of Portuguese literature who was quite elderly. This old lady, who loved medieval literature, one day explained the basis of her longevity and active life, demanded absolute secrecy and gave her a store.

Teresa was then introduced to other Telea members and made good friends with the women in the group. She had maintained those friendships and some of these women were powerful in their own right. They were politicians, judges, owners of their own businesses, financiers. Others had gone back to their places of origin and worked in non-profit organisations, or were teachers, nurses, artists and social workers. In sum, Teresa admitted to having a wide social network that would certainly help her work as a regional director if the Mater approved her candidacy.

"Use those contacts to recruit more women into Telea. Make sure that they will be discrete, though," reminded the Mater. "Here is our updated list of Portuguese women in Telea. We only have under five hundred women. However, your job will be full-time because you need to travel to meet those women regularly, you need to share your energy with them, and you will be my eyes and ears in Portugal. Also, we not only need to recruit more women to Telea, but we also need to recruit warriors, spies and social activists on women's issues.

"I understand that Portugal has a very advanced legal code protecting women and children, yet, on the ground, women still don't feel protected in a society that largely remains a patriarchy. Your job is also to rescue those women who fall through the cracks of legal protection.

"I want to build a women's hospital in the mainland and women's clinics in Madeira and Azores. These will be private health providers that will specialise in women's health issues. Consultations will be free, and all treatments will be based on a percentage of women's income. You will need to gather a team and start the process with the Portuguese Ministry of Health and all other pertinent authorities.

"Although you will choose your team, do you think that you can cope with this vast task?"

"Madam, I believe that I am capable, willing and energetic."

"I want to warn you that corruption will be swiftly dealt with and will involve removing the stones of any Telea members involved, you included. When stones are removed from a woman, all the benefits that the nanobots provide will be swiftly reversed and women usually die within a year. You will be dealing with vast amounts of money, and you will be well compensated. But you will be personally responsible for making sure that everything is legal and clean."

"Of course, Mater. I am a thoroughly honest woman. I will earn your trust. If you agree, I will quit my current job with the Portuguese Segurança Social and start immediately with the personal contacts."

"Consider yourself appointed the new regional director for Portugal. Leonor will give you the contact information for Ana, a very good lawyer who should be in your team. You will also need a secretary and a full-time accountant, especially as you embark on the plans to build the women's hospital and health centres. I want quarterly reports of your activities, of women's tribute to Telea and of all expenses."

As they stood to indicate the end of the interview, the Mater asked Teresa to place her hands on hers and transferred power to the new regional director. "This you must do with all the women as you visit them."

Leonor guided Teresa to the front door and rejoined the Mater.

"Leonor, I need the contact information for Ana. Just to be sure about Teresa, I want to call Ana and ask her to keep an eye on Teresa and send Simone regular reports. My chief spy will have her first contact in Portugal."

Thinking of Simone duBois led the Mater to call for her to come to the house with a report. That same day, the chief of spies and lead investigator came and brought some astonishing news.

"I'm so glad that you called for me because I have important information to share with you. Before she left, Nikola gave me a sticky note found in the kitchen with the name 'Cooperator Alain Gerard' and a phone number. I wrecked my brain trying to figure out what a 'cooperator' is until I remembered what you told me about the Magisterium Ecclesiae. So I found out that it means someone who is not a member of the organisation but collaborates with them in a variety of services.

"Then, the phone number indicated that it was someone from Marseilles. There are several people named 'Alain Gerard' living in Marseilles, but I phoned the number and pretended to be a lost soul in need of salvation wanting a contact person to be my spiritual advisor. I was invited to visit them, a couple with six children. Imagine! The house was modest and in need of renovation, with four bedrooms and a cluttered living room.

"They asked me why I didn't go to my parish. The couple were suspicious, so I gave them my timid smile and explained that I had just arrived in Marseille from Arles. I was dressed modestly without make-up. In a weepy tone of voice, I said that I needed spiritual help because I had just left the employ of a couple of witches, and I felt that my soul was in danger. They didn't find my description odd. They were not surprised.

"The woman comforted me in my distress and the man, Alain, asked if I had ever heard of the Magisterium Ecclesiae, a Catholic organisation for lost souls. I said that I didn't. He talked for quite some time about the path of holiness and that the church was aware of these witches that I spoke of. They gave me the address of a church in Marseille and the name of a priest that I should speak with. I left, after thanking them for their help.

"While I was there, I cloned his phone that was just next to me on a side table, so I had access to all his information. I went through his phone records, and I found a number for Barcelona. That's where I am. We are on the right path to discovering who ordered your assassination and who knows about us."

"That's wonderful work! Thank you! However, I fear you could have been in danger. I don't want you to take excessive risks. Find out who the phone number belongs to, and we will go from there."

Chapter Twenty-One

The next day, the Mater asked Leonor to contact the four regional directors from France, four from Germany, three from Spain, two from Italy and the remaining four from smaller countries in Western continental Europe. They were summoned to a meeting in Strasbourg within the month and should bring their personal secretaries. A formal letter would be sent shortly. Leonor was tasked to arrange a conference room in a hotel, book rooms and order a dinner for all regional directors and the Mater. She should also order dinner for the private secretaries in a nearby restaurant.

The Mater discussed with Leonor similar meetings with all the Nordic countries in the following month and Eastern European countries a month after that. She wanted to consolidate her power in Europe, before doing the same for the rest of the world. The Mater expected it would take her a decade to reach all the regional directors since other countries were larger, and it would take longer to visit them individually.

The fact was that the Mater did not relish the expectation of travelling. She had no wandering feet or desire to visit exotic destinations. She was quite content to stay at home. However, it was her duty to reach out to as many women as possible, regardless of discomfort. She would make sure they always travelled first-class, at least.

A month later, her first meeting with regional directors approached, and the Mater sent six of her personal guards to Strasbourg to confirm security arrangements. She went with Leonor, Emani who was sufficiently recuperated to accompany her and three personal guards. She left Maison de la Toile defenceless, but they would be fine. They left early, took the train to Marseille and boarded their private aeroplane.

Upon arrival and check-in, a pleasant hostess guided the Mater to her suite and informed her guest that all arrangements had been made in accordance with her wishes. The Mater asked for room service to bring her a bottle of cold sparkling water and checked the information booklet for attractions nearby. She then called Leonor and her personal guards to the suite and told them that she would like to go for a walk in the neighbourhood. Were they too tired? All the women agreed that it would be nice to stretch their legs, see the cathedral nearby and find a restaurant.

After dinner, Leonor and the Mater went through their notes. The meeting was due to start at two in the afternoon the following day, so they could choose to sleep in the morning or have an early breakfast. Leonor was to be available in the conference room an hour before the meeting to check if everything was as expected and to greet the guests. She should call the Mater when all women were assembled. She dismissed her secretary and decided to spend time reading the latest novel she had purchased.

After a solitary lunch, the Mater prepared herself for the meeting by dressing in a silk pantsuit with all her stones in evidence and carefully applied make-up. She put on her blond wig, confirming that the coiffure was immaculate. Without any notes, she waited for Leonor, grounding and centring herself for the upcoming challenge. This was the first time that she would engage with a larger assembly without being sure whether the women would be friendly or resentful.

When her private secretary came to indicate that all the regional directors were assembled, the Mater descended to the conference room. It was not a very large room, so the women gathered in small groups, without much space to wander around. The chairs and tables had been arranged in a semi-circle with an upholstered chair at centre stage. All seventeen women and their private secretaries stood waiting. They had all been briefed on the new protocols and etiquette, so when the Mater entered, they faced their superior and nodded, waiting for the Mater to take her place.

Leonor and Emani closed the door to the conference room and stood guarding it. The Mater walked to her seat and sat down majestically. Each of the security guards stood on the opposite side of the room. The room was silent.

"I am the Mater, the Mother of Stones, the centre and core of Telea. Please line up and come to me one at a time. Introduce yourselves and give me your hands as evidence of your submission to my authority," declared the Mater in a clear and authoritative voice.

It was the first time that any of them had done that. They had all come into their posts after the predecessors' inability to rule, so they were confused. These were proud women who had, up to now, governed their territories with little interference. After some hesitation, the women organised themselves into a queue. The first one was perhaps the oldest, with wrinkled features, bright eyes and thin white hair pulled back in a bun.

"I am Gina Lombardi; I'm the director of Sicily and Sardinia, and I submit to your authority."

She had to bow to place her hands in the Mater's hands. This was an old, feudal symbol in which the subordinate acknowledged the power of the suzerain. In exchange, the superior conferred authority over the territory and promised to protect the vassal. In the context of Telea, it was a most appropriate gesture. It also gave the Mater the power to briefly read her subjects. Gina felt like a sincere woman, devoted to the Telea and curious about her new superior.

"Dear Gina, thank you for making the effort to come to this assembly. I confirm you as director of Sicily and Sardinia. It's a pleasure to meet you. Please find a seat."

For the next half an hour, this scene was repeated thirty-three times, as all the remaining directors and their secretaries introduced themselves and took the oath. None of the women felt threatening and some even smiled at the Mater. This was a good beginning.

After the ceremony, the Mater explained very clearly her expectations and the consequences of corruption, neglect of Telea members and other major infractions. She also clarified the duties of regional directors. If there was any director who could not fulfil those duties, either for personal or health reasons, they could honourably retire and suggest the names of three women from which the Mater would select their replacement.

She informed the assembly that she was preparing a text on ethics and on expected sisterly behaviour from Telea members. Once the essay was complete, it should be distributed to all women in their jurisdiction. Later, after much thought and research, and after listening to women's input from all over the world, there would be a proper legal code. To that purpose, there was a break for half an hour, so the directors and their secretaries could refresh themselves and write down at least one suggestion for the legal code. Could they please give those notes to Leonor, her private secretary?

After the interval, the Mater indicated that because of recent events, she did not have a council of ministers, which was a very important node in Telea. Therefore, she wanted every regional director to consider names for those roles and to contact the women for them to apply directly to the Mater. Contrary to the past, she would select one woman from each corner of the world to be a minister. There would be six ministers.

One for each of the following responsibilities: Telea management, finance, social development, women's issues, defence and communications. Each candidate was required to have extensive education and experience in their area of interest, had to be able to work in a team and had to have an impeccable reputation. Besides that, they should be pleasant but assertive.

Finally, the Mater reminded her regional directors that there was a need to recruit more women to Telea and to expand the current number of warriors. Many women needed protectors, and there were simply not enough women in that role.

The rest of the meeting was devoted to what the regional directors considered problems that needed solutions. One, the director of Bavaria, already had a list prepared, which demonstrated excellent forethought. By the end of the meeting, the private secretaries of the remaining directors delivered their own lists to Leonor.

The Mater closed the meeting by reminding the regional directors that they were ultimately responsible for the well-being of Telea in their territories and that any serious issues needed to be brought to her immediate attention.

Once the conference ended, the women all returned to their rooms to rest for a bit and to change their clothes for dinner. The private secretaries and the warriors went for dinner at a restaurant close to the hotel, hosted by Leonor and Emani, while the directors would dine with the Mater.

At nine o'clock sharp, the Mater entered the dining room splendidly in a heavily embroidered, strapless golden gown. With her stones displayed, her perfect blond wig and expertly applied make-up, the Mater was magnificent. She looked like a woman in her mid-thirties, and all the seated women stood up out of respect. The room had been closed to other hotel guests, and the small tables had been set up as a long table with eighteen seats.

The Mater sat at the end of the table, and she scanned her guests. They were all dressed beautifully with their stone necklaces sparkling. The room looked marvellous with its cream walls, golden curtains and crystal chandelier, candles and flower arrangements.

The Mater felt relaxed and used the opportunity to listen to her guests speak about their regions, and the women they governed. Not all knew each other, so this was an occasion for them to get acquainted. Dinner was a tasting menu of delightful morsels of delightful food presented as works of art, all paired with the appropriate wines. As the evening progressed, the conversation became less formal, and the Mater made a point of talking with all the women. Finally, when she was ready to retire to her suite, the Mater invited her directors to arrange with her private secretary to come and visit her for a couple of days at Maison de la Toile, in Provence. She wanted a more intimate setting to get to know the women in front of her, away from formalities.

In her suite, after undressing, taking a shower and putting on silk pyjamas, the Mater sent a message to Leonor and Emani to visit her briefly before going to sleep. She didn't have to wait long. A knock on the door announced their arrival. The two women were a bit tipsy and very pleased with themselves. Rightfully so since they had organised everything to perfection. Both women looked gorgeous. Leonor wore a classic channel-style suit, just very short, while Emani wore a beautiful body-hugging white knit dress.

"I'm sorry to call you from what seems to be a fun dinner party. I won't keep you long in case you want to go to a nightclub or a bar to continue enjoying yourselves. I just want to thank you, especially you, Leonor, for the perfect job you have done and to get fresh impressions from you both about the private secretaries. Do they all seem okay to you, or is there anybody shifty? What do you think of the regional directors?"

They both said that they preferred to make it an early night because they had to be clear-headed for the next day. They chatted for a bit about their thoughts on the women they had met and how everyone seemed dedicated to Telea and that the Mater had made a splendid account of herself. With that report, Leonor and Emani left for their rooms, and the Mater decided to sleep since she was very tired.

Chapter Twenty-Two

On their trip back, most of the women were subdued since their previous day had been a long one. They chatted in low voices while the Mater read the lists of problems and possible solutions presented by her directors. They had been thorough, and the solutions seemed feasible. They needed to submit budgets, of course, but they would be content with her assent. In the end, the directors knew their territories well, so they were the best people to govern them.

A rented limousine, with a smartly dressed driver was waiting for the Mater at the airport in Marseille to drive her and her companions to Arles. There was another vehicle, a large van, for most of the guards. The Mater, Leonor and Emani sat in the back seat, while Laura, a personal guard, sat in the passenger seat in front. The limousine driver was quiet and took them swiftly towards the highway. However, before they merged into the faster traffic, the driver made a sudden stop, opened his door and ran away.

All the women were stunned for a second until Emani screamed, "Bomb! Get out!"

The four women tried to scramble out of the car. Emani, Leonor and the Mater were without safety belts on. They were able to run away quickly, but Laura was stuck in the front with her seatbelt on and struggling with her nervousness to open it. When the expected explosion took place seconds later, the impact and fire blaze killed the poor woman and threw the Mater and her companions to the rough ground. There was a car behind them that also caught fire, and the driver was killed with the impact of the debris and the blaze.

Besides scrapes and proximity burns, the three women were fine out stunned. Leonor started screaming until her throat was raw. Emani and the Mater hugged each other. The access to the highway was packed with stranded cars and drivers came to offer help. There was no sight of the driver. Soon they heard police, firefighters and ambulance sirens, and the guards who were in the other vehicle ran towards them, having abandoned their own van. They surrounded the Mater but did not remove their weapons because there was already quite a crowd, and it was best if they looked inconspicuous.

The Mater, Leonor and Emani spent about two hours with the police and refused to go to the hospital. The police officers wanted to know why they had been the target of an assassination attempt. Who were their enemies? Emani explained that they were a group of friends who had spent a weekend in Strasbourg and were on their way home to Arles. That whoever had planted a bomb must have made a mistake.

The Mater, with her new identity as a Canadian, introduced herself as Claire Milligan who was a supervisor at the Maison de la Toile. The ambulance removed the charred bodies of her guard and of the driver who had been in the car behind them. The police called for a taxi for the three women, and the ordeal was over for now.

After a sombre trip home, the Mater, Leonor and Emani sat in the upstairs living room in the Mater's suite drinking a scotch whiskey and reviewed the horrible events. The warriors had gone to the kitchen to do the same and to remember Laura, their friend, who had died. The Maison de la Toile felt the weight of their loss.

"How did anyone know that we would be returning from Strasbourg on this day?" questioned Emani. "I think that we have a mole in the house. That's the only explanation because the regional directors and their staff only knew that we had a meeting overnight with them. They couldn't be sure we would return straight home. And the culprits are no doubt someone in the Magisterium Ecclesiae, perhaps the person in Barcelona."

"You are right," said the Mater. "Therefore, we have two people to uncover. First, who in the house is telling tales to the Magisterium Ecclesiae and who is the person on the other side of that phone number in Barcelona."

Leonor added, "We also have to notify Laura's family and prepare for her funeral."

With Fatemah's help, they found the phone number for Laura's mother, and the Mater talked with her that same night. Laura was from Guatemala and her mother would be grateful if someone could send her body home, to which the Mater immediately agreed. The family would grieve Laura as it was appropriate, and the Mater could focus on finding and punishing anyone connected with her death.

The next day, the Mater woke up early, dressed and asked Fatemah to call all house employees to the ballroom. When everyone was assembled, she entered regally and sat on her throne-like upholstered chair. The Mater surveyed the room, observed that everyone, from maids and cooks to warriors, was all there, and then she announced, "There is a spy in our midst, and I am going to find out who it is right now."

"Someone has been telling house secrets to a man in Marseille. If you have done that, please come forward and explain your actions. If you do, I will let you live. Otherwise, I will read the mind of each and every one of you, and I will burn the stone of the guilty woman."

There was a thick silence that stretched to anxiety around the room. Nobody moved. Nobody spoke. Until there was the sound of a sniffle in the back.

"Come forward right now!" the Mater commanded and Emily, the housemaid, walked diffidently and crying to the middle of the room

"Talk or I will burn your stone!"

Emilie started wailing and sobbing. Everybody else stayed silent. The Mater waited for a few minutes and then lost patience. "Bring her here so that I can read her," she said to the guards.

"Oh, please no! I will tell you everything. Please don't kill me It was me, but I was just chatting with my uncle. I didn't mean any harm."

"Who is your uncle? And where does he live?"

"He is a good man, Madame. He didn't do anything wrong, I'm sure. He is Alain Gerard, and he lives in Marseille. We talk about once a week and with my aunt too. He asks about the house and about you, and I didn't see any harm in telling him things.

"Sometimes, he asks me about the things on your desk. I think that is weird, but it doesn't hurt to tell him what there are. I know that I'm supposed to keep secrets, but I didn't think right, and they're family. I'm so sorry! Please don't kill me!"

"Do you also talk to your family in Arles about me and about the house?"

"Oh no, Madame, because they don't ever ask questions. They are not interested and besides, they have more interesting jobs than mine."

"As it stands, you have done a great deal of harm in talking about me and my secrets with your uncle. So, to partly make up for that harm, you are now going to tell me everything there is to know about Alain. After that, I'm going to find you another job in a place more suitable for your skills, like a Buddhist nunnery in Asia.

"You will be closely supervised, you will know the meaning of silence and perhaps in the future, I will let you return to France. You are simply a very stupid girl, and I don't kill people for that. If you don't comply, I will simply have your stone removed. Do you understand?"

Emilie kept crying while the staff went back to their tasks. Two guards stood by Emilie as she went to get her personal belongings while the Mater called for Simone, the investigator and chief of spies, to attend to her immediately.

About an hour later, Simone appeared at Maison de la Toile and was made aware of all the new information. Fatemah brought Emilie to the Mater and Simone in the upstairs living room where she was interrogated about Alain Gerard. They learned that he was a devout Catholic, went to church regularly with his family and alone and was a good husband.

Emilie added that he had married Emilie's aunt and was a good provider, working two jobs to support his large family. He worked as a driver for a rental company in the evenings and was a plumber for a construction company during the day. He was a good man, Emilie was sure. In the meantime, someone from the closest nunnery was already downstairs waiting for her and would take her to Sri Lanka where she would stay for the foreseeable future in a Telea's Buddhist monastery.

Chapter Twenty-Three

Juan Carlos Cristóbal could not believe that the witches had escaped again. He had meticulously planned the intended assassination, had one of his Vox underlings fly to Marseilles to install the bomb and had even given Alain Gerard enough money to retire from his driving job. No one had expected the swift escape from the doomed car or that an innocent man would die as collateral damage. This gave him a feeling of guilt and sin.

The silly niece that worked at Maison de la Toile, that witches' den, was a God-given opportunity to figure out their plans. Of course, the girl was barely literate so searching the desk was hardly useful. On the other hand, she was excellent at gossip and had provided quite a lot of information in this regard.

One of his problems was that although Juan Carlos was familiar with the institutional structure of Telea, he had no idea if the powers he had heard about were real. The previous Mater was a very long-lived woman but didn't seem all that remarkable. Perhaps even her reported longevity was a tale to impress the gullible. He had met her in his youth, and she was an authoritarian older woman, quite full of herself. He didn't understand how a successor was chosen.

He didn't even understand the reason why so many women felt devotion to her. What he was sure of was that the Mater yielded enormous power and was the richest woman in the world. If only the work of God could get access to that money! If only he could incorporate those wayward souls into the loving hands of the church! He needed to cultivate more spies and more influence in the upper echelons of Telea. In the meantime, he had political work to do in Spain and in Europe.

***

The following week went by quickly as the Mater continued to read reports and made contacts with her core people. She asked Alex, the botanist and chemist, if there was any progress in the development of new plant-based poisons and what was the status of acquiring permits and engineering plans to build her new class II laboratory. Everything was going according to plan, but it would take a few months before construction.

On the poison side of things, Alex had started a visually stunning garden in the English cottage style close to the trees in the back of the property. There she had planted large amounts of foxglove for digitalis, deadly nightshade, poison hemlock and belladonna, among others. Those were easily accessible plants because of their beauty. She had simply ordered the bulbs and plants online. In addition, she had thrown to the ground a variety of wildflowers seeds.

In one year, the garden would be in full bloom, ready to enjoy the view and to harvest. Stone paths allowed for easy access and Alex had already ordered a trellis with an arch to sustain angels' trumpets. On the shady side of the garden, close to the trees, there was a bench that allowed for rest and fruition of the dangerous beauty. All these plants would be distilled, purified and concentrated. They could be ingested or applied through injection.

The Mater contacted Antoine, the banker, via video call, just to know if things were going well in the financial sector. He had no concerns and just hoped that the Mater would quickly appoint a minister of finance to ease his burden.

Next, she called both Lou, her IT person, and Simone, her investigator and chief of spies, to meet with her. Over a pot of tea, the three women analysed the data that had been found in the dead ministers' hard drives and the contents of their desks. Lou and Simone identified over a thousand women who, unwittingly, had bypassed the tribute flow to the Banque de la Toile by paying directly to the corrupt women. However, those women had been contacted, their names had been included in the regional directors' lists and had changed their payment procedures. These women were victims and had no idea of the fraudulent schemes. Both Lou and Simone considered the investigation closed.

Simone informed the Mater that her own web of spies was slowly increasing and that all European directors were under surveillance, just in case. Most spies did the job out of a commitment to the Telea and a monthly fee; however, Simone additionally maintained a few men and teenagers who were happy to receive extra cash. The spies also reported on threats to women's issues or to individual women. Just under two hundred women had been rescued in the past months and been relocated to schools, women's shelters, or nunneries. Most of these women would eventually become Telea members.

Lou was also pleased with the results of her team's work. They worked in the basement of Maison de la Toile, which was enough for their current needs. The Information Technology team would in the future require a larger space and an increase in staff, but the work was progressing well for now. They had completed the website design. At first glance, it looked like the website of a travel agency; however, there was a login for a different layer in which Telea's logo was displayed, and women needed to further confirm their identity.

Upon admittance, the site provided a variety of information including an email link for women to directly contact the Mater. These emails would be constantly monitored and submitted to their superior who could then answer them herself or delegate another woman to do so. There was one staff member assigned full-time to the website.

With respect to the information of Telea members, Lou had chosen a teenager who wore the stone, to input data, while another in Lou's team developed an organisational map that illustrated the connections between members and the nodes formed by regional directors. In large countries with great population dispersion, perhaps the Mater would consider having a number of sub-directors who could give more direct assistance to the women on the ground. The Mater thought that it was a great idea once the full mapping was completed.

"About the telephone number in Barcelona, I have an idea of who it is," offered Simone. "I believe he is called Juan Carlos Cristóbal, and he is a highly placed member of Vox, the Spanish extreme right-wing party. The problem is that in order to confirm the information, I would need to call the number directly with some sort of excuse. I'm afraid of alerting the man to our inquiries.

"What if the phone number is only used for specific purposes, and he has another cell phone for daily use? If he is the man who ordered your assassination, he is very well-known and killing him could raise more problems than solutions. How do you want to play this?"

"Perhaps it is best to simply monitor his activities and see where that leads us. Do you have someone available in Barcelona?" asked the Mater.

"Yes. He is a private investigator, and I can hire him to do long-term monitoring of Juan Carlos Cristóbal. With such a delicate matter, it's best to deal with professionals. He will assume that we are some left-wing organisation looking for dirt on a Vox leader."

With the meeting concluded, the Mater spent the rest of her workday reading the information that Simone and Lou had left for her analysis.

Soon, the Mater started to receive her first reports from the newly confirmed directors. As expected, Gina Lombardi was ready to retire, and she submitted three recommendations for a replacement. The Mater understood her position and, according to the recommendations, she selected one woman to be the regional director of Sicily and Sardinia, and the two other women were nominated as assistants with full-time responsibilities, one in Sardinia and the other in Sicily.

Leonor came to the Mater and asked for an assistant. She explained that the volume of work was such that she spent her days typing and simply needed help with the expanding labour. The Mater suggested that she use the website to advertise. This would be the first test of its reach. Leonor would choose her assistant, but the Mater wanted to be part of the interview process considering that she would be privy to Telea's secrets.

Since they had already had the experience of planning and implementing a conference with directors, the Mater decided to proceed in the same manner with the planned meetings in Scandinavia and Eastern Europe. Russia itself would be left for another year, since their relationship with the West was currently precarious, at best, and they would require extensive counterintelligence measures to evade Russian spying on most foreigners.

***

Before the Mater could embark on her travels, she wanted the problem of Alain Gerard, the driver in her assassination attempt and uncle of Emilie the spy, solved to her satisfaction. Their foe had lost a source of inside information, but the danger continued and needed to be addressed before she felt safe. Hence, the Mater asked Alex, her botanical chemist to supply another couple of doses of 100 mg of digoxin, a digitalis preparation that would induce heart attacks. She talked with Emani and asked her to choose two of her fellow warriors to re-enact the previous assassinations this time on one man, Alain Gerard of Marseille.

The next day, with two vials of poison in their hands, Emani, Lila and Rebekah left for Marseille. Rebeka was a very experienced operative since she had served four years in the Israeli army and could easily subdue Alain. Emani was going as the driver and lookout, while Lila would help with any unexpected events. They decided that the church where Alain went regularly to pray was the perfect setting. After checking the interior of the building, they were pleased that it had dark corners and was dimly lit. They positioned themselves standing before the last pew, a couple of metres apart from each other, and they waited, pretending to pray.

Alain Gerard had the habit of stopping daily at the church after his work as a plumber. So, when they noticed him enter, dip his fingers in the holy water and cross himself, they were ready. The church had one nun in the front pew and perhaps a priest in the confessionary. They needed to be quiet. Alain sat on one of the last benches and then knelt in prayer.

Rebekah and Lila swiftly flanked him. He looked up startled, but before he could make noise, Rebekah closed his mouth and nose with her right hand and plunged the syringe into his neck with her left hand. They left silently, but Emani stayed behind for a couple of minutes in the shadows to see if there was any commotion. Alain crumbled and knocked his head on the bench in front of him. The nun looked back to see what was amiss, but the body was hidden between the pews, so she returned to her devotions. Emani left the church quietly, and they made their way to Maison de la Toile.

***

The political strategy meeting was going well. The participants, who were Barcelona's Vox coordinating committee, had decided on the lists for a municipal election. Juan Carlos was pleased with the choices. As the vice president of the party, his was the first name on the list, and he was certain that there was a good probability that he would be elected to the city council. That would be an important victory because the party was increasing its popularity, and he could bring the right proposals to the city council.

These proposals could counteract the pressure from women's and LGBT+ groups. Spain was ready for a return to family values, and he would be the one to bring detailed proposals not only to the city council but to the national coordinating committee the next time they met in Madrid.

His phone vibrated, and he saw that he had a message from Marseille asking him to call immediately. Juan Carlos Cristóbal excused himself from the table, went to an adjacent room and dialled the number. It was answered by a weeping Martina Gerard saying that Alain had been found dead of a heart attack in church. She was desperate with grief and worry about what to do with her life and six small children. Juan Carlos was stunned and needed to regroup his thoughts quickly.

"What about your niece, Emilie? Can she help you?"

"What are you talking about? My husband is dead, and you are asking about a silly girl? I haven't heard from her in three weeks. I need help now, just like my husband helped you before."

Juan Carlos heard the implicit threat in her words. She knew too much, but he could not bring himself to silence her, not with six children needing their mother. Consequently he did the next best thing. He bribed her with a promise of a monthly deposit in her bank account.

"Don't worry that it will all be fine. God will provide, and I will personally help you financially. Have you spoken with the rest of your family in Arles?"

"Yes, I called them, and they are on their way to help me with the funeral. However, no one has heard from Emilie. My sister called the house, and they were told by the housekeeper that she was fired for violating house rules. But she didn't come home. My sister is frantic with worry."

"Perhaps they should call the police to investigate. Who knows what goes on in a house of witches?"

Juan Carlos terminated the call and told the meeting participants that he had an emergency. He didn't go home, but instead made his way to his parish church and to his spiritual advisor. He needed to unburden his worries and find peace in his soul. How did those blasted women kill Alain? He was certain that it was a homicide and not a heart attack. But how did they do it in a public space where people had just finished hearing mass? It was just like the assassinations of the ex-ministers weeks before. Heart attacks and strokes.

Could they have identified him? Was he next? Juan Carlos Cristóbal decided to plan ahead. No more assassination attempts for the foreseeable future and let the witches be until an opportunity presented itself. It was time for him to focus on his own political career. He had to win a seat in the European parliament and create strong ties with the conservative parties of the continent. He had a future, and the will of God would be manifested as he ascended the ladder of power.

In the meantime, the Mater was also playing a long game. With her face-shifting ability, she was very difficult to identify as the head of Telea, therefore as long as her household continued to be committed to her safety, there was no reason to worry about Juan Carlos Cristóbal who she was certain was at the centre of the power games of life, death and money in the last decades. She would keep him under vigilance indefinitely. And time would shape the form of his punishment.

***

For the next decade, the Mater, accompanied by Leonor and Emani and her ever-present security guards, visited every regional director in the world. Some visits were simple, such as going to Canada and staying a couple of days in each province. Others were exceedingly more complicated, as was the case of some countries in Africa, South America, or Southeast Asia, where roads were at times non-existent. That was once the case in the Brazilian Amazon where they visited villages by motorboats. Some trips were very dangerous, such as when the Mater travelled through Somalia.

In most countries of the developing world, their safe travels involved hiring local male mercenaries because the female warriors would not be accepted. So the Mater made herself look old and wore her grey wig under her head coverings, and all women, depending on local customs, wore abayas, hijabs, niqabs or burkas. In these cases, they always travelled on high alert with their weapons concealed under their voluminous clothing.

In most cases, she came home broken-hearted with the plight of women all over the world. While climate change brought unspeakable hardships, war, famine and brutality were common and gratuitous. They all ravaged the lives of people, but the worst victims were women and children. Men spread terror through the most misogynous acts of terrorism. Telea's schools and health centres were destroyed all over Africa by Da'esh and Al-Shabaab.

Children were kidnapped while teachers and health personnel were slaughtered. In the United States and in South America, gangs and drug lords destabilised whole communities and Telea's assets were the targets of violence. And as always, machismo kills, and patriarchy maintains its hegemony through rape and fists. Something had to be done to eradicate the source of war and terrorism, violent men. So the Mater started to have the most radical ideas.

In the comfort of Maison de la Toile, finally done with her travels for another decade, the Mater looked haggard from exhaustion. Even her nanobots could not fully mend her tiredness and broken heart. Therefore, she planned for the next decades. She had the financial resources, women with expertise and a fierce anger. Humanity would change, even if she had to kill a billion men to do so.

Part Three

There was a time of great persecution of the rights of women, social upheaval and wars. That is when the Mother of Stones shouldered a terrible decision that led to the death of millions, and she endured more sorrow than you can imagine. It was the equivalent of giving birth to a new world through blood and floodwater. Our Mater freed us, but if her actions were to be known in the twenty-first century she would have been vilified and destroyed and Telea would have fallen with her. Instead, she guided the world to a different paradigm of relations between the genders and brought forth the world we know today.

—Excerpt from a teaching manual, 2378

Chapter Twenty-Four

The tentacles of trauma are like barbed wire, knotted in the core of one's being, however, every person deals with it differently. Some curl upon themselves and let the barbed wire grow to the point of incapacitation. For some people, the trauma even changes their genetic make-up, while others unfurl the cutting edges of pain, and it becomes a weapon.

Lizzy Skybird lay in a hospital bed victim of her boyfriend's fists. She had never been particularly pretty, but her face was never going to be the same. Her recovery would take time for the bones to knit and the deep bruising to heal. She flinched at sudden noises and at healing hands approaching. They all felt like preludes to assault.

The police had found her half naked, covered in blood, wandering the freezing streets of Newmarket, Ontario, and brought her to Peel Memorial Hospital. Initially, Lizzy had screamed with fear and crouched away from the officers, however their gentle tone of voice and slow motions allowed the wounded woman to relax enough to be taken to the hospital in an ambulance.

Her jaw was broken, so she couldn't speak. With trembling hands, she answered the officers' questions with a written message: *Justin, my boyfriend. Justin Jackson. Jayjay.*

This wasn't the first time, of course. It started with denigrating comments that turned into fists pounding the walls. The apartment was full of holes in the drywall. Next came a single blow to the stomach. She called the police, and the court had placed a restraining order.

Justin apologised deeply each time. He loved her. She just made him crazy. Please give me another chance. Justin ignored the restraining order, and she forgave him. Until this evening, he clearly wanted to kill Lizzy because it was her day off and she had spent the afternoon with friends and didn't make dinner on time.

Justin worked in construction, and he was a big man. He also drank a lot after work and was a mean drunk. He thought that she was inferior to him because she came from the Anishinaabe reservation in Georgina. He thought that she was stupid because she hadn't finished high school. He wanted to control her absolutely and Lizzy didn't know what was going to happen to her life now that through the haze of painkillers, she thought of the future.

Lizzy was only nineteen years old and had left the reservation looking for a waitressing job. She found one in a sports bar that catered to hockey fans. Her shifts were different every day. Sometimes, she worked afternoons until evening, other times she started at eight until closing. Her income was not enough to afford an apartment, so as soon as Justin had started sniffing around and he had seemed an okay guy, she left the rooming house and moved in with him. Bad mistake.

Lizzy lifted her head and saw that she was in a room with two patient beds. Next to her was a figure all wrapped in bandages, with only holes for her mouth, nose and eyes. Her arms and a leg were held in casts held by pulleys. Lizzy heard moans of pain. This woman was in worse shape than her.

The next day, after extensive tests, an orthodontist and a plastic surgeon informed Lizzy that she needed extensive surgery on her face and that she would have to stay in the hospital for four weeks, but that full healing would take up to six months. The internist was pleased that no organs were damaged, but that she had extensive internal bruising. The following day, Lizzy was prepped for surgery and wheeled into an operating room, and after she woke up in excruciating pain. Her mouth was shut with metal wires, and she couldn't scream. Later, she woke up in less pain but very groggy. Days passed until a dull ache spread all over her body at the slightest movement and her face was no longer an enemy.

As Lizzy's slow recovery progressed, the patient in the next bed had her face bandages removed. She could speak, but her voice was hoarse. A couple of police officers came to get her statement. They asked for her name and the circumstances of her injuries.

"My name is Danielle Lavoie. Madame Jean Paul Lavoie, all I know is that I crossed a street in Aurora and was hit by a car. It was dark, but the car rolled over me, and I don't know any more."

"Madame Lavoie, you were a victim of a hit and run. Unfortunately, all we know is that it was a dark vehicle. No one remembers seeing a licence plate.

Either the witnesses froze, or the licence plates were covered somehow. Who would want to hurt you?"

She answered in a whisper, "I don't know." And closed her eyes while a tear fell down her mangled face.

"Where is your husband so that we can notify him? You had no identification in your person, so we were at a loss about your next of kin."

Danielle gave the officers her home address and her husband's phone number. She fell asleep while they were still in the room.

Lizzy heard the conversation and thought that it was odd that someone would cross the street without any identification. How peculiar. Soon after, a woman came to speak with her and said that she was a social worker and that her name was Laura.

Lizzy would be taken care of, but she suggested that she should leave Newmarket to be safe and perhaps move back in with her family. Her boyfriend had been arrested but was out on bail. Lizzy would need to give a complete statement in court. Would she be able to do it?

Using a notepad, Lizzy wrote that she didn't want to go back home, nor did she want to go to court. She just wanted peace and quiet. She was willing to leave town after the hospital. But where and how? Laura explained that the government would pay her a monthly income and that they could find her a small apartment in Barrie, a city far enough that she wouldn't run into Justin. Was that acceptable? The social worker said that she would return in a couple of weeks when Lizzy was feeling better.

The next day, a well-dressed and handsome man entered the room. He didn't hug Danielle but gave her a peck on her forehead. The woman closed her eyes and forced herself not to flinch. She must continue to show a serene demeanour because her life depended on it. Jean Paul spoke as if he were the most loving husband in the world. He asked what happened and Danielle responded that she really didn't know.

Why had she left her purse at home, he inquired in a mild manner? I must have been very distracted, his wife replied in an even tone. Well, he had to travel on business, but when she was released from hospital, she would have the best care. He intended to hire a nurse, and he would try to be home more often. Jean Paul left the room and his wife exhaled deeply and started to tremble. She felt like a deer caught in the headlights, unable to resist the danger.

Lizzy had been drinking her meals through a straw, but slowly the pain had diminished. She started to think clearly. She was emotionally fragile and knew that she needed help. It would take a long time for her to feel safe. Nevertheless, she also felt rage at the brute who had almost killed her.

It was a cold fury that had no outlet because she was powerless. But Lizzy also felt curious about her roommate. She got out of bed, sat close to Danielle and held her hand.

Danielle asked her name and Lizzy wrote it on a notepad that she carried. Danielle's voice continued to be weak, but the bruises on her face were less raw. Her arms and legs were still in traction, but she moaned less often. Yet, silent tears fell down her face time and again.

"What happened to you?" asked Danielle in a whisper.

"My boyfriend almost killed me," wrote Lizzy.

"My husband also almost killed me," replied Danielle.

"Why didn't you tell the police?"

"Because he didn't do it himself. He sent his minion, Frank, to do the job because, if I talk, he will just find another way to have me killed."

"I will have to run away. He will keep coming."

"I will have to go back and pretend that everything is fine."

"What if I kill your husband and you kill Justin?"

"What? What are you talking about and how could we do it? Of course, I want to be free of Jean Paul, but my husband is a rich and well-connected man. I can't do anything. I tried to run away. Left my purse at home and just fled. I want him dead, but I can't do it and end up in jail."

Lizzy was feeling frustrated by the slow writing of her thoughts. This was something that she was not used to, but she tried her best.

"Sorry that I can't talk. Have to write. Not good at writing." Another page, *"If I kill your man nobody will know. If you kill my boyfriend nobody will know. No jail. We be free."*

"You give me your info. I give you, my info. We each do it, no one will know. Need alibi."

"Let me think about it. I will let you know. Now I need to rest."

Lizzy tore the written sheets out of her notebook and ripped them into very small pieces. Having placed the loose bits in two garbage containers, she went to bed herself to think and to rest. She knew that she would leave the hospital in two weeks and that the social worker would arrange her transfer to Barrie. She would still not be able to talk for weeks yet, and she would remain sore until her body healed fully. But she could make plans for her freedom.

A week before her release date, Laura, the social worker, came by Lizzy's and Danielle's room. The young woman's face now was a medley of colours, from dark to yellow bruises and her nose was still held secure with tape. The ear lobe that had been torn and stitched back was itching. Her head and face hurt. However, Lizzy was sitting up on an upholstered chair browsing a magazine and her mind was clear.

The social worker cheerfully informed Lizzy that all documentation was in place and the requests for funding had been approved. She would be taken by ambulance to Barrie where another social worker would take over her case. She would have a fully furnished utility apartment, including a bed, bath and kitchen. She would also have specialists' appointments at Barrie's hospital, including a therapist for women victims of violence. Lizzy asked about money for groceries and Laura told her that her social worker at Barrie would take care of the monthly income. Since Lizzy had no questions, Laura left with good wishes for the future.

Danielle had been listening to the exchange and asked, "Do you think that you're going to be alright ?"

Lizzy wrote down a reply, *"I will do my best. Did you think about what I said before?"*

"Yes, I did. I don't know how to find Justin Jackson or how to kill him, but I will do my part. However, you need to take care of Jean Paul as soon as possible because I don't know how long I will last in his hands. He will kill me soon."

"I will take care of your husband. Tell me everything that you know. Details how to get to him."

And so, Danielle told Lizzy about her husband's mistress in downtown Toronto, about his pharmaceutical business in Québec, about his driver Frank and about his habits. She wrote down the addresses and her phone number.

"If you have expenses I will pay you, but I can only get money after Jean Paul is dead. He controls everything."

"Can you hold on for three months? Need time to get money."

"Please do it as fast as you can. I'm very afraid of him."

"Don't have a phone. Will get one. Will tell you the day. You get an alibi."

Next, Lizzy wrote down Justin's home and work addresses, plus his phone number, just in case it would be needed. She gave those to Danielle and destroyed the remaining notes.

For the rest of Lizzy's time at the hospital, both women rarely communicated. Lizzy had more tests and exams done and was told how lucky she was that her vision would not be impaired. However, she could expect continued pain for an indefinite period.

Chapter Twenty-Five

On the appointed day, wearing clothes from the lost and found, Lizzy was transported to Barrie and to her small apartment. As expected, her new social worker was there waiting for her and introduced herself as Nadia. She was a tall, Black woman from Kenya, with a no-nonsense attitude. But she was kind and patient with Lizzy. She immediately gave her several hundred dollars in cash and asked the young woman to sign a receipt.

There was food in the fridge, but Lizzy couldn't consume any of it because she couldn't open her mouth and chew. Therefore Nadia quickly drove Lizzy to the closest supermarket, and she chose appropriate nourishment for her condition, including many jars of baby food.

For the next couple of weeks, there was a flurry of activities, from opening a bank account to meeting her doctors and therapist. Lizzy also went to a Salvation Army second-hand store to buy some clothes and a warm coat and bought a cheap cell phone. If people were startled by her appearance, nobody made any comments. Everyone knew what a victim of battery looked like.

Once settled, Lizzy began to plan her next steps. There was a public library a few blocks away, so she walked there, used a computer and investigated all the internet could provide about Jean Paul Lavoie, entrepreneur, and husband of Danielle Lavoie. Next, she used an application to view the house and neighbourhood of his mistress. It was a good place to kill him, but she didn't have the strength for a physical confrontation. The best way would be to run him down several times with a car. That should do the trick. But where and with what car?

The vehicle should be no problem because, when she was younger, she had learned how to hotwire cars just for fun. All she needed to do was steal a car, kill the bastard and dump the car. Then she would take a bus home. Where?

Danielle had told her that to keep himself young for his floozy of a mistress, Jean Paul liked to run the trails around their residence in Aurora. However, in order to get to the trails, he needed to run on the road. So she just needed to catch him on the road in one of his daily runs.

Two weeks later, Lizzy felt strong enough for the endeavour. With latex gloves, she stole an older car from the parking lot of a large box store that was open twenty-four hours and drove south. Then, she sent a message to Danielle with the code words they had decided upon, *"A cold front is coming."* Nothing in the message could incriminate either of them, and Danielle was expected to delete all messages. Lizzy staked the property from dawn on.

It was a substantial house with a large lawn and garden in a secluded area. For sure, they needed a gardener for that. As expected, soon she saw a runner leave the front gate in the opposite direction of her stolen car. Lizzy steeled herself, started the car and simply drove over Jean Paul. She backed up and ran him over again and once more as she drove over the body as she continued on the road.

Next, she drove to the suburbs where she parked the car in another parking lot with the doors open and the keys in the ignition. The car wouldn't last much longer. She calmly walked to a garbage container, dumped the gloves and walked to the closest bus stop. She had to take two buses to get home, then a long walk to her apartment. Lizzy was exhausted, so she crawled to bed and slept all day.

In the meantime, Danielle was busy dealing with police officers and investigators regarding her husband's homicide. She had an ironclad alibi in her nurse who slept in an adjacent room and who, at the time of death, had been busy helping her disabled patient to the bathroom. The officers wondered why somebody would target both wife and husband. It was suspicious.

They found no evidence of a murder for hire. They investigated Frank, but he looked like a devoted employee, and there was nothing to indicate his involvement. Later, the police would widen the circle to question business associates, disgruntled employees and even neighbours. Nothing came up.

As soon as Danielle was able to stand and walk with the aid of a cane, she moved to Montreal to be close to the business and simply took over. As a widow, she received great sympathy, and the senior personnel were very helpful in guiding her through the management of a large pharmaceutical company. It helped that it was a private company with no board of directors. Jean Paul had inherited it from his father and had expanded the business. The company had debts but had also a very healthy income, and they had just placed on the market two new painkillers without the addictive properties of similar drugs.

Danielle was relieved but also traumatised by her ordeal of living with a monster. She vowed never to get involved with a man again. She simply did not trust her instincts in the romantic arena. She did think about Lizzy a lot and of her side of the bargain yet unfulfilled.

Eight months after leaving the hospital, Danielle had full use of her arms, but she walked with a limp. Her back hurt often, only alleviated with hot compresses and massage therapy. She was weary of using painkillers, which was interesting considering the vast income she was getting from its sales.

Danielle's debt to Lizzy became more pressing when she received a message asking, *"Is winter still coming?"* Therefore, Danielle decided to face her responsibility and called Frank to her office. He was still the driver and fixer, having switched his canine allegiance from Jean Paul to his new master. However, once he completed his assignment of killing Justin, he had to go. She informed Frank of his target; gave him all the information she had and gave him an envelope with a lot of money for his troubles. He promised the job would be done soon.

While Frank was on his way to Toronto, Danielle spoke with her chief of security and asked for a referral for a female driver and bodyguard. She said it would make her more comfortable. Then Danielle wondered how to get rid of Frank. She didn't need to worry because Frank never came back.

Apparently, he got into a fight using a baseball bat on a man called Justin Jackson outside a bar and Justin's friends, seeing their friend dead on the street, decided to retaliate. It didn't help that they were all loaded with alcohol. Frank died of a brain haemorrhage. He had no wallet, identification, or money.

Danielle sent a message to Lizzy, *Spring has arrived. Send banking information.*

The next day, Danielle transferred a substantial amount of money to Lizzy's account and called her.

"This is Danielle Lavoie speaking. Is this a convenient time to talk?"

"Hi, Danielle! My mouth is working again. I'm glad you called. I hope that everything is good with you. What's up?"

"Our arrangement is complete, and we are both free. However, I would like you to come to Montreal so that we can discuss the future. I would like you to work for me. I have an idea, and I think that you are the perfect person for the job. What do you say?"

"Oh, fuck! Yes! I'd love to work for you! Send me instructions and I'll be there."

Chapter Twenty-Six

Once Lizzy arrived in Montreal, there was a car waiting for her by the train terminal. She was driven to an imposing mansion on the outskirts of the city where Danielle waited for her. Lizzy's small, battered suitcase from the Salvation Army was taken to an upstairs guest room, and Danielle invited Lizzy to sit in a classy living room, several times bigger than her whole apartment in Barrie.

"I'm so very happy that you are here, and I see that you are much better," said Danielle to welcome her guest.

They spoke for a bit about their conditions and commiserated about their physical pain but did not disclose the emotional effects of their trauma. They weren't that kind of friends yet. Danielle seemed unsure about how to continue the conversation, so Lizzy prodded her.

"Well, I'm here and happy that you wanted me. But you spoke about plans for the future. What's on your mind?"

"I want you to work for me with helping other women like us. You and I had each other in the hospital, and I am wealthy. But most women are alone in their pain. I think that if I help them, I will feel better. I think that both of us will come to terms with what happened to us if we help other women escape, survive and thrive. What do you say?"

Lizzy thought for a bit and said in a dejected tone of voice, "I wouldn't even know how to start… I don't know anything about helping people get through the system. That's for social workers. I don't even have a high school degree."

"First, I want you to finish high school. I will hire a tutor, and you will quickly pass your exams. You will stay here until you are ready to go to university. I know that you are a very intelligent young woman, but you need help with schooling. While you are in university, I will pay for all your expenses, including room and board in the students' residence, and I will give you a monthly allowance.

"That should occupy you for the next four years. In the meantime, if you know of any woman who needs to escape her boyfriend, husband, brother, or father, you will offer them help and let me know. I will take care of them.

"While at university, I want you to study sociology, psychology, business administration and any other course that interests you. I want you to be involved in women's groups, in clubs, and I want you to become strong, so use the gym and take martial arts.

"When you finish your studies, I want you to be responsible for a network of women who will become assassins, just like you and me. We will help these women, and in exchange, they will help other women get rid of the monsters in their lives. You will have a high salary, and you don't have to kill anybody else, but you will manage the women, their training and their assignments. My part will be to finance the enterprise. What do you think?"

Lizzy was silent, digesting the information. The idea that she could restart her studies was appealing, knowing that she would have financial support was vital, but she was particularly drawn to a future in which she would make a career out of managing assassins. That was awesome! Like out of the movies. Above all, she would have skills and could reinvent herself.

"I want to be called Elizabeth. Lizzy is a kid's name. And, yes, I will do it, and I will not disappoint you. You are giving me hope and a future. Thank you!"

For the next five years, Elizabeth devoured every morsel of learning that was offered and gave Danielle the names and contact information of thirty-seven young women from McGill University alone. On the weekends, besides working on reading and writing papers, Elizabeth spent time placing posters all over town saying, *"If you are a woman who needs help escaping, call this number."* That's when Danielle needed to hire a woman to answer the phone because the calls came frequently and at odd hours. This new employee, Louise, kept meticulous records of every woman helped, and she was charged with picking up women at agreed-upon locations.

After that, another woman, Rebekah, would pick up the women in a different car and at a different location and drive the women either to the hospital, the police station or to a secluded place in the forest north of the city where there was a women's shelter. It depended on the woman's needs and wants.

Every woman helped had to promise to do a favour later, perhaps drive another woman to safety or give temporary shelter. Either way, a favour was owed. They all agreed. That's why the meticulous records were important because future help depended on these women who were now battered, terrified, or in shock. Most women simply wanted to be driven to friends or family away from their aggressors.

Other women clearly needed a hospital and were promised refuge, if needed, after being discharged. However, a small number of women were alone and wanted nothing to do with the criminal and judicial systems. They simply wanted to disappear. It was for these women that Sky Place was created.

Sky Place was designed to be as obscure as possible. Women were offered a simple set of elastic waist pants and tunic, soft shoes and a cardigan. It was a uniform so that no one could feel excluded. Everyone wore the same outfit, including staff whose only difference was a nametag. No jewellery was permitted and no make-up or perfume.

Throughout the very large building, there were blankets and soft pillows to provide comfort. Each woman shared a room with another, to promote friendship and emotional connection. Their meals and gatherings were in a large room which was set up as a cafeteria. The women received counselling, emotional healing and physical exercise. They helped run all the services, so each woman had chores to do, from laundry and cleaning to preparing and serving meals.

Some women left Sky Place after a couple of months; others had no place to go. Among these women, some chose to become the core of assassins while others would remain in supporting roles. They needed different skills, so Danielle hired women mercenaries to teach the assassins and retired spies to teach the others. When Elizabeth took over management of Sky Place, she added female martial arts experts.

However, she decided that they needed a home exclusively for the assassins because one never knew what tongues could be wagging. Up to now, the assassins had only been training. They had taken no assignments yet. From their new setting, they would let the women go loose into unsuspecting perpetrators of violence against women.

Danielle purchased an equally large place south of Timmins, Ontario. While the inhospitable weather was a challenge, the ease of road access and privacy supplanted the disadvantages. They took twenty-four women with them, half for support and the other half for killing assignments. Elizabeth decided to call the group 'The Cleaning Women' and their place 'The Cleaning House'. With time, their numbers would increase, and they would need other Cleaning Houses, but for now, they were set.

Twelve women were sent on their first job across Canada, with home support from their handlers who were glued to their computer screens. All the targets had killed women and were not in jail for a variety of reasons, most often awaiting trial on bail or on early release. Their names had been researched thoroughly and Elizabeth had decreed their deaths. All twelve Cleaning Women came home without leaving a trace. Some men had been shot, others had been poisoned, and two had been drowned while intoxicated.

Elizabeth continued to expand the network, and the Cleaning Women started to receive appeals from victims all over Canada. Therefore, they set up a Cleaning House in British Columbia. At this point, Elizabeth and Danielle decided that owing favours was not enough. Those women needed to start paying 10% of their life income to have a cleaning woman come and do her job. This offset costs but also bound the survivors to the organisation.

An accountant was hired who was herself a survivor of sexual assault and battery and she took care of the records and received the payments. While this was happening, Sky House continued to be busy accepting women victims of violence and most of those women continued with their lives knowing that they owed a favour.

One serious problem was the amount of money now received had to be laundered somehow. Their network was a criminal organisation in every sense of the word. Sooner or later the authorities would catch up with a cleaner or do a raid in one of the Houses. Something needed to be done.

Danielle one day received a written note from a woman who called herself the Mater asking for a meeting on a matter of mutual importance. However, the note had no return address. That was odd, but there was a contact number and an email address. It could be something related to her pharmaceutical business, so she sent a brief email asking for more information and sent her business phone number.

A couple of days later, Danielle's secretary said that there was a personal call for her and that the woman had said it was important. Danielle lifted the receiver and said, "Danielle Lavoie here. How can I help you?"

A voice on the other side of the line replied, "Please hold for the Mater."

"Hello! I'm called the Mater and I'm the head of an organisation that might interest you. I'm sorry, but I can't discuss anything with you on the phone, but I strongly entreat you to come to Paris, with your lovely protégé Elizabeth, to meet with me. If you agree and set the time, my personal secretary will send you details of a hotel that will suit us."

"Why would I go to Paris on your invitation? You know that I'm a busy woman and so is Elizabeth. And how do you know about her, anyway?"

"You will understand when we speak face to face, but the future of your organisation is at stake. So please meet me."

"In that case, would this coming weekend be agreeable?"

"Excellent! You will receive details today. It will be a pleasure to meet you."

Chapter Twenty-Seven

Danielle and Elizabeth were received at the airport Charles de Gaulle by a woman who introduced herself as the personal secretary of the Mater and later, at a marvellous boutique hotel, they were escorted to their rooms to freshen up. An hour later, they were led to the Mater's suite by obvious bodyguards, all four of them female. However, the Mater met them alone. She looked like a woman in her thirties, petite, but with an authoritative gaze.

All three women were dressed in pantsuits in sober colours The Canadians wore discrete jewellery while the Mater wore her torque and breastplate of nanobot amalgam and diamonds, plus a single nanobot stone hanging from a gold chain. The Mater knew it was excessive, but the nanobot stones were part of the story. She wore a blond, well-coiffed wig to mask her baldness, and she looked regal.

She welcomed Elizabeth and Danielle to France and made her guests feel at ease with refreshments. They spoke in English for everyone's convenience.

"It has come to my attention," said the Mater, "that you have a women's shelter called Sky Place and that you assist women fleeing violent men. That is a worthy cause. However, you use Sky Place as a source of women that you transfer to Cleaning Houses and train them to become assassins. That is a dangerous cause. Finally, you don't know what to do with the money left over after expenses. You need to launder that money, or it becomes a liability. Is all my information, correct?"

Danielle and Elizabeth were stunned. They thought they had been so secretive, yet this Mater knew all the crucial details that could get them locked up for life.

"How can you possibly know this information and what do you intend to do with it?" demanded Danielle, feeling a pit in her stomach called fear.

"Don't worry about my getting you in trouble with the Canadian authorities," reassured the Mater. "I found out about you two from my spies, of course. They exist all over the world to keep tabs on events that affect women. And both your women's shelter and your Cleaning Women affect women in a positive way. The problem is that you are overextended and don't have a global reach. I do.

"I would like your organisation to merge with mine. This is not a hostile takeover. This is an invitation to make a difference at a planetary level. You have resources that we don't have, specifically your pharmaceutical company and your Cleaning Women, and we have resources that you would literally kill to get."

"Who are you, and what is your organisation?" Elizabeth demanded to know.

"Before I go any further, I must have your word of honour that anything that I disclose will be kept secret and not shared with another human until or if I give you leave to do so. No one outside of our organisation knows about us because we have kept it secret. In the rare cases, where somebody didn't keep silent, that person was silenced forever. Do you understand?"

"Yes," said Danielle, "we understand, and I give my word of honour that your secret is safe with me."

"I also give you my word of honour that I shall keep quiet about this conversation," added Elizabeth.

The Mater explained that Telea was as ancient as agriculture and that the first Mater found a strange stone, that we today know to be an amalgam of nanobots. The Mater pointed to her metallic shining stones and declared that they were nanobots which gave the wearer an extended lifetime in good health. She added that if they joined Telea, both women would receive their own stones and reap the benefits personally.

Finally, she explained how Telea was organised and the goals of the organisation: to protect women everywhere and to promote women's rights. The Mater gave examples of the struggles that Telea projects were experiencing worldwide from misogynistic threats and how women's achievements were being undermined all over the world, including Canada. That's why she needed the Cleaning Women to train her own warriors and expand their reach globally. She needed Danielle's pharmaceutical company because she had in her employ experts in genetics, virology and the creation of vaccines.

"And what will you do with my experts? What would they achieve for you?"

"That I will only explain if you join me. I have been the Mater for over twenty years and, barring decapitation, I shall live four centuries. It is my duty to guide women worldwide into a better world. You could help the process without being in your precarious situation."

"We need to sleep on this. I don't know if I want to bow to you—"

"No bowing necessary. A simple nod will do," the Mater interrupted with a smile.

Danielle resumed, "As I was saying, I don't know if I want to submit to your will at the price of living longer. And I certainly am not giving you, my company."

"The company will continue to be your property. And your sales will expand in the developing world with my backing. However, like every other woman, you will have to pay 10% of your personal income as tribute. Not income from your company, but your personal salary and bonuses.

"Elizabeth will continue with her current responsibilities, just expanded. She will be a significant node in the Telea, and she too will pay tribute out of the substantial salary she will receive from me. I want your willing participation, not forced by threats, however, if you two refuse me, I may just absorb your Cleaning Women one at a time and set up my own laboratories all over the world. It's up to you. As you say, sleep on it and give me your answer before you depart for Canada."

Danielle and Elizabeth left feeling overwhelmed. Not only had the Mater known about details of the criminal side of their enterprise, but she was demanding submission to her will. It was unthinkable! On the other hand, if they were absorbed by Telea, they would increase their reach a hundred-fold, and they would have a community. Their lives had been lonely without peers to talk to.

In addition, they would have long and healthy lives. In Danielle's suite, both women rehashed the conversation and the astonishing information they received. The only thing holding them back was their pride.

The next day, Elizabeth and Danielle sent a message to the Mater saying that they were ready to accept. They were once more led into the same suite they were before, and the Mater received them with a smile. This time, she wore a flowing dress with an asymmetrical cut and low-heeled shoes. Her full set of jewellery was evident. The Mater sat down but didn't invite them to do the same.

In her hands, the Mater displayed two gold chains with small stones. She explained that the stones would grow and that in the future when the stones were big enough, they should share them with women they could completely trust.

She added that women adjusted better to smaller stones because their bodies would receive the nanobots more slowly.

One at a time, both women bowed their heads to receive the necklaces from the Mater, and she asked for their hands. She read their honesty and tentative commitment. That was enough. The Mater promised to protect them and asked for their submission to her authority. They both offered it freely. Finally, the Mater asked them to sit down and discuss details.

To begin with, the Cleaning Women needed to leave Canada and spread throughout Telea's communities of women. They would train other women and be dispatched on assignments as needed. Elizabeth would need to become a peripatetic supervisor. She would be subordinate to the minister of defence and to the Mater herself.

Next, a decade earlier, Telea had chosen bright young students and sent them to the best universities in the world to become scientists. They were now researchers or university teachers in the needed fields of bioengineering, genetics and virology. It was time to put them to work directly for Telea.

The Mater wanted several research teams to create a virus that only attached itself to the Y chromosome, perhaps mediated by neurotransmitters responsible for rage. Bottom line, the Mater wanted to target violent men on a large scale. Wars were escalating in many parts of the world, and she wanted to end all wars. Finally, given broad parameters, the researchers could produce their own lines of research, and the best results would be selected. The Mater wanted Danielle to manage the overall research effort.

"But that could kill millions of men!" Danielle exclaimed outraged.

"Yes, it could. Yet, if you think of it, how many women are today targets of men's violence? Every year, wars and misogyny are killing thousands of women all over the world. And if you think things are bad for middle-class white women, imagine how much worse it is if you are poor, Black, disabled, homosexual or queer. How many women are oppressed by patriarchy today?

"I want to break the back of patriarchy! I want to destroy the military industrial complex! I want to force the world, kicking and screaming, from the dark ages of oppression into a world fit for our daughters. That's my plan and, with your help and the help of hundreds of thousands of women, we can do it.

"I'm not comfortable with the idea of killing millions of unknown men just because some men are violent," Elizabeth added her reluctance to Danielle's.

"But you are perfectly happy killing specific men. I have dedicated the last twenty years to raising women's consciousness and empowering them. I have built schools, hospitals, health centres, sports clubs. I have provided money through micro-banking for women to become entrepreneurs. I have given support to women's organisations so that legislation can change to improve women's lives. What are the global results of these efforts?

"In North America, women's rights are being eroded, sometimes in draconian ways. In Europe, the same thing happens under the excuse of tight budgets and the decades-long war in Ukraine. In South America, women and children are dying in gang wars, and machismo has lifted its ugly head. In Africa, there are localised wars between nations too poor to afford food, but with enough money for weapons. There are gang wars in the cities and widespread terror from Islamic fundamentalists who destroy women's schools and health centres and kidnap young women and children.

"Not to speak of female circumcision and rape as a matter of course. Southeast Asia feels like a lost cause with the most stringent misogynistic practices. Just look at the situation of women in Afghanistan, Pakistan and Bangladesh. In India, the caste system has been reinstated, and the extreme totalitarian regime has crushed women's rights. In Central Europe, totalitarian regimes coexist within the European Union, which has become a joke with the devalued euro and people's daily struggles to put food on the table and simply survive.

"Those totalitarian regimes are the most conservative possible. In Russia, since Putin died, his successor has simply continued his policies and tightened the grip on women's lives and gay people. Interesting how women's issues are always correlated with queer issues. In Asia, things are not better. China has been forcibly inseminating women to combat low birth rates. The same with Korea and Japan.

"The only bright spot has been New Zealand where we have a strong and healthy presence. In all other places, our women live in constant danger of discovery and secrecy has been tightened. However, this means that we are not expanding as fast as I would like.

"That, in a nutshell, is our plight. Capitalism is in its death throes but, as any dying organism, it's at its most dangerous now. Economic and social asymmetries have never been so stark. Patriarchy and male domination are widespread and getting stronger. And then, we have the upheavals of climate change with millions of refugees on the move, leading to an increase in slavery, including sexual slavery. Many of our women have simply disappeared among the multitude of displaced people.

"And you are reluctant to do something about it? We have the means to create a better society, not just for women and children, but for the surviving men as well. It falls on our hands to do so. Of course, it may take decades before the research teams come up with a solution. Until then, we will continue to target individual rapists, murderers, slave owners and politicians whose laws oppress women, children and LGBT+ people."

Danielle and Elizabeth were silent, absorbing all this information. There was a sense of doom and helplessness. They had been so focused on their corners of the world in Canada, that they had missed the bigger picture. The two women were living a privileged lifestyle and had never been critical of capitalism.

As for climate change, it had never affected them personally, besides being happy that winters were shorter. In addition, their work with abused women had never, in their minds, been fully integrated into a critique of patriarchy. Therefore, the Mater's harsh views of the world challenged their liberal preconceptions.

"By the time we have an appropriate virus, decades may have passed," continued the Mater, "and by all indications, things will only get worse. We need to be prepared, and I need your willing cooperation in this endeavour."

Danielle responded, "We have just given you our oath of allegiance. We may be reluctant, but we will do our part. And, as you say, the fruits of research may take many years and a lot may change in the meantime. I will set up the teams and list all the necessary equipment they will need. You will pay for the expenses and will decide where it's safe for the women to do their research. They should be inconspicuous, and each laboratory should have category IV safety protocols. Send me the names and contact information of your researchers, and I will set up the teams."

Elizabeth also repeated her allegiance and asked for addresses of the women's communities, so she could send her Cleaning Women to safety. Next, she would coordinate their assignments. Finally, the two Canadians bid their farewells and departed.

The Mater was left thinking about her interactions with both women. She was pleased that they were on board and members of Telea. Time would tell if they were committed enough for what was coming. She also remembered her original thoughts on killing when, two decades earlier, she had faced injury and had retaliated against the ministers of her predecessor.

When had she decided to become a god and assumed the power to exterminate millions of people? Yes, she was in a way a resistor of patriarchy, but she was also power personified. She understood that resistance to oppression was a fundamental right because, as Karl Popper had said, you can't be tolerant of the intolerant. They will destroy democracy from the inside every time. On the other hand, Telea was not, at its structure, a democracy, but an autocracy and the Mater was at the pinnacle of that network. How to conciliate the internal contradictions of her position and maintain herself within the bounds of her ethical framework?

Killing is ethically wrong, except in self-defence. However, wars continue to be fought and killing is considered acceptable under these conditions. Resistance fighters had been killing for a long time, changed regimes and established new nations. These circumstances were also considered acceptable.

The work that the Cleaning Women did was, from her perspective, an acceptable way of dealing with the monsters of society. However, gendercide was a different order of magnitude. She was fighting a war against male violence and patriarchy, was that a justification for her actions, or was she simply a self-deluded monster herself?

The United States of America, Canada and Australia had killed millions of native peoples to occupy their lands. Stalin and Mao Tse Tung had killed millions in the pursuit of their vision of society. Throughout history, men had used death for their own purposes. Yes, they killed women, but their wars killed mostly other men who were young, poor and stupid. Only in World War II and only in the Soviet Union, twenty-seven million people had died. Not counting the over sixty million Jews, Roma, homosexuals and members of the resistance killed by the ultimate monster, Adolf Hitler, in concentration camps.

Was she going to be remembered as another Hitler? How would her own women react to the unleashing of a deadly virus that would target their own husbands and loved ones?

The Mater remembered her own beloved son who was a wonderful man. Would he be among the ones decimated by her unleashing death among men? What about her grandson? He had become, by all accounts, a good person with two sons of his own. Was she prepared to eradicate her own male descendants?

With the passing of time, the nanobots had petrified her emotions. She lacked emotional range and had no particular affection for people, except perhaps her personal secretary, Leonor, and her recruiter, Emani. These two women kept her grounded in humanity. For the rest, they were all tools of a vision she had of a transformed society. That's why it was fundamental that she grappled with ethical issues because she had no morals.

Chapter Twenty-Eight

Twenty-eight years after incorporating the Cleaning Women, Telea was expanding under dire circumstances. Europe was amid chaos following the detonation of a nuclear missile in the Ukraine. Russia was under threat from NATO, but the giant bear seemed defiant. Nuclear fallout had reached the South of France, Provence, where the Mater had lived for almost five decades. She decided that it was time to abandon the Maison de la Toile and look for another place to settle.

The regional directors of Eastern Europe and of Russia were in panic, afraid that the war would escalate. As a consequence, the Mater sent an email to all European members of the Telea that she was moving to Africa and that Telea would help anyone wearing a stone and their families to escape the European continent if they wished. To that effect, Telea rented an old cruise ship and started to move the war survivors to countries on the Atlantic coast of Africa. These refugees had lost everything in the ruins of their homes and many of them were suffering from radiation poisoning, so they wouldn't live long.

Most countries allowed those refugees entry and residency status. The ill ones were treated in or admitted to Telea-funded hospitals. Some women decided to live in Telea communities, while others with husbands and daughters rented homes and settled in.

After the initial voyage with war-torn refugees, the cruise ship made several more trips transporting those women and their families who were looking for a better and more secure life. In this case, they brought their belongings and much-needed cash and jewels. They too were accepted by most countries.

The regional African directors of Telea were very busy settling thousands of people in a variety of places, finding them work and providing support. Many Europeans decided that they would like a simple if hard life in agriculture. Others worked in fisheries. Many others with good education and training in a variety of professions had their credentials accepted and worked as lawyers, accountants, teachers, doctors and nurses. Their bank accounts were transferred to African banks.

Within a few months, Europe experienced a brain drain in favour of Africa and a haemorrhage of money. With the passing of time, seeing how successful those immigrants were in their new homes, other people, who were not of Telea, also made their way to various African countries.

In most cases, the arrival of immigrants was well accepted by the local population because their own standard of living improved with the infusion of cash. Businesses paid higher salaries, Telea in conjunction with local governments improved roads and various infrastructures, and many immigrants decided to live in the country, thereby improving the living conditions of their neighbours.

All Telea members were warned that they were not colonisers, but instead lived in those countries at the mercy of Africans. They were expected to adjust to local customs and be respectful and peaceful. On the other hand, Telea warriors and Cleaning Women provided protection when needed. There were a few cases in which gangs of men decided to attack groups of women just because they thought they could.

Those women with their bodyguards quickly and efficiently subdued them and left the warning that they were not to be messed with. Local women supported the newcomers' defence strategies and some even asked to learn. Soon, Telea expanded, and more women became warriors or support personnel.

For herself, the Mater chose Angola as her next place of residence, specifically the city of Huambo in the central plateau. It had the advantages of having an airport and having moderate weather due to the altitude. The country was a study of contrasts and social asymmetry. On the one hand, Angola had the richest mineral resources of all of Africa, where an elite lived like international jetsetters; on the other hand, it had the second highest infant mortality in the world.

It was a very rich country with very poor people. Luanda looked like any other capital of a developed country, while the interior was neglected. However, the Mater planned in terms of centuries, and she hoped to guide Angola into an international powerhouse.

This time, the Mater decided to present herself as a young woman to give herself time to age in one place. She brought with her Leonor who had become elderly and frail. She no longer worked as the Mater's private secretary, but she remained as a companion. One day, she would die, and the Mater would lose one important link to her humanity.

Emani still worked as a recruiter, but her days of being a bodyguard were over. She was close to eighty years old and no longer had the physical strength or the agility to move fast. She was still very good with weapons, though.

From reports that she read occasionally, her daughter was now a very sick old woman in a nursing home in the Netherlands, while her son had passed away peacefully in his home in Tønsberg, Norway. Of his two sons, one had died young of a drug overdose, and the other was a successful lawyer.

Her only granddaughter from her daughter was a university professor of sociology, lived in British Columbia, Canada and had three children: one girl, one boy and a gender-fluid child. They were all adults with varying degrees of success in life. Her great-granddaughter, Alyssa, was a teacher in an elementary school, seemed to like her job and was living with a tattoo artist. The Mater needed Alyssa to reproduce. Time would tell, but, for now, she wouldn't interfere.

Her occasional reports about her family were another thread that connected with her humanity. She intended to continue to be apprised of the lives of her great-grandchildren and their offspring. Nevertheless, she had other pressing matters to attend to, such as the transfer of her power structures to Angola.

The Mater purchased an old Portuguese colonial mansion in disrepair on the outskirts of Huambo. She then proceeded to have it renovated to its previous glory, but according to her taste. She designed gardens of native plants and had a swimming pool installed. This would contribute to her well-being. In the meantime, while renovations were underway, the Mater, Leonor, Emani and their bodyguards rented a house in a privileged area of the city.

Her old housekeeper Fatemah had died, and the Mater, in prescience, had years ago hired a new housekeeper from Angola. Her name was Glória Massano, and she had an impeccable resumé, having worked in private residences and international hotels. She had real experience in management. Glória was now in her seventies and was utterly devoted to the Mater. However, it was time for her to train a replacement, preferably a young woman.

The Mater placed an advertisement on Telea's website and soon they had several qualified candidates. Both Gloria and her superior chose a young woman of under thirty years old to become a housekeeper in training. She was from Matala, in the Angolan province of Huila and was called Marisa Mendes. She had received her necklace as a teenager in one of Telea's schools, was highly intelligent and articulate and had worked in several houses as a cleaner and as a housekeeper to the few rich and famous Angolans. Marisa was delighted to be hired and promised her commitment, her silence and her best work. After a few months, Glória declared to the Mater that she was satisfied with her apprentice.

The next order of business was to hire a new personal secretary. Again, the Mater wanted a young person so that she would not have to see new faces every couple of decades. This was an important choice because her private secretary would be privy to all her secrets and would also be a personal companion and advisor. She wanted someone highly educated and capable of understanding how Telea worked. She also needed to be efficient at secretarial duties and be a pleasant woman.

Once more she placed an advertisement on the website and once more received many applications. Leonor helped her select the applicants, and the Mater asked her friend and secretary to do preliminary video interviews. The Mater would accept the top three candidates for in-person interviews.

In the end, the Mater chose Maria Ramos, a young Filipino woman with a doctorate in business administration who was also highly recommended by her regional director. She struck the Mater with her sweet assertiveness, a combination of kindness and of a tough stand in terms of social issues. She also liked to read and watch films and series. Having common interests would be a source of conversation. Maria immediately began working by sorting documents and assorted items that were misfiled due to the move. She was attentive to Leonor and to Emani, and the four women frequently had dinner together.

The Mater then asked her current council ministers if they were willing to relocate to Angola. Her minister of defence was a young Zulu woman from South Africa, and she was happy to go home. With improvements in communication technology, she did not need to live in Angola and, if needed, Huambo was close by through air travel. Her other ministers preferred to go back to their continents and manage their responsibilities remotely, except her minister of Telea Affairs who was European and decided to join the Mater in Angola but settled in Luanda, the capital. Her responsibilities required frequent air travel, and she needed to be close to an international airport.

Next, the Mater turned her attention to financial matters. She contacted the Banque de la Toile in Paris and asked them to relocate to Luanda. The heir of the long-departed Antoine du Préssy, was now his grandson, a young man who had been tutored from birth to be the banker of Telea. His name was Édouard du Préssy, he was excellent at his job and less formal than his grandfather had been. His staff was also larger to deal with the increased demands of a chaotic European world. In contrast to his grandfather's time, Édouard's staff was mostly Telea members who had studied economics and finance at the best universities and then had been trained in the Banque de la Toile.

Édouard's commitment to Telea was absolute. All his ancestors had been bankers serving the Mater and his loyalty had been ingrained. He immediately agreed to open a new bank in Luanda, Banco Teia, and to close the Parisian Banque de la Toile. He would proceed immediately. Before terminating the video call, Édouard reassured the Mater that Telea's finances had never been better due to a substantial increase in interest rates and the fact that years ago, they had diversified their investments into more aggressive Asian markets. The future Banco Teia would be the most powerful bank in the world.

Once she was settled in her renovated residence, big enough to house her staff, the Mater renewed her interest in her long-term projects, the investigation and production of plant-based poisons and the research on a virus to reduce male violence. As recent events in Europe demonstrated, war was a monstrous hydra of death, destruction and suffering. And it affected not only mutual enemies but all their neighbours and beyond. Men made wars, but it was women, children, the elderly and the sick that suffered the most. Millions of people had died in the Ukraine, first with the decades-long war and now with the nuclear missile.

The Ukraine was no more, but the millions of sick, desperate refugees and the nuclear fallout would affect the region and Western Europe for generations to come. And it could escalate into a folly of mutual destruction. It was time to check in with her researchers. There were ten small teams of four specialities, each responsible for creating a virus and a vaccine. Her poison team in Arles, France, had decided to stay and continue their work.

First, she checked with the elderly Alex, her senior poison expert. She reported that the research concerning local plants was mostly completed. They were focused on further concentration and mixture of poisons, so they could be used dermally or aerosolised. A single spray would do the job of killing the target. She had already shipped experimental versions of those poisons to Cleaning Women all over the world.

Once she heard back on the effectiveness of their action, she would develop a final product. Alex also reported that she had selected a replacement from among her staff and needed the Mater's approval. Since she had confidence in Alex's judgment, her superior gave her assent.

After this conversation, the Mater called Danielle Lavoie, who was in her late eighties and certainly needed to select a successor. They talked about the issue, and since she had no children, Danielle had bequeathed in her will her entire pharmaceutical companies and her assets to Telea. She said that she was going to send the contact information of each team leader and that the Mater should speak directly with them. Danielle added that she wanted to retire as soon as possible because she was feeling the weight of her years. She suggested that Telea should hire her CEO, who also wore a necklace, as the head of the company.

She knew all about the business and was aware of the purpose of the research teams. She should take full control of the company. Her name was Lidia Mackenzie and Danielle thought that Lidia should renew her submission to the Mater before taking over the companies. Ever since her partner, Elizabeth, had died in a car accident two years earlier, Danielle had been struggling with the loss. She just didn't have the heart to continue living any longer and was planning on having medical assistance in dying, using the justification of her ongoing physical pain from her decades-long injuries sustained when her husband had ordered her death.

It was the end of an era for the Mater. All the women with whom she had connected decades before were dead or close to it. There were new faces surrounding her, new names to remember and her humanity was slipping away. The Mater wore her young face and a pixie wig in pink, the latest fashion. Her body was as strong as it had been half a century ago, but she still had the expectation of living at least another three centuries more. She wondered how many new faces and names she would have to endure.

Maria proved to be a delight. She was efficient as a personal secretary and an insightful advisor. Of course, she was aware of all activities of Telea, from the humanitarian to the lethal and all the shades of grey. But she was perceptive and understood what was at stake. She was also fun, diverting Leonor and Emani with jokes and running commentary on the ridiculousness of society.

Maria received from Danielle the contact information for all ten research team leaders and passed them on to the Mater who proceeded to call them, one by one. Six researchers said that they were sorry, but they couldn't design a lethal Y chromosome-specific virus. Some said that they understood much more about bioengineering and virology than before; however, their research did not have any practical applications yet. Two asked about being allowed to publish their work.

The Mater was furious and asked them what part of 'secret research' they did not understand. The Mater terminated their employment immediately and issued severe warnings about continued secrecy. The rest of the teams were allowed to continue their work. Perhaps they could study vaccines for diseases plaguing third-world countries.

One research team leader from Australia, Mei Yang, said they had not been able to design a virus that only attacked men, but that they had interesting results. One virus had different results in female and male mice. Once deployed in aerosol form, the males in separate cages died quickly of haemorrhagic fever. However, if the males were mixed with the female population, the most sociable mice were seen sniffing the ears of females.

The more aggressive mice died as if they were separate because the female mice would not accept their proximity. Upon multiple autopsies, they confirmed that the infected females developed swollen glands behind their ears and secreted a new kind of pheromones which seemed to provide immunity to the male sniffers.

"Would these results be of interest to you, Mater?"

"Interest? I am totally delighted. Please continue your research and see what happens to the offspring of infected mice. Do they carry the infection? Are the infected mice even able to reproduce? Are there unexpected and negative side effects in the offspring? Please discover everything there is to find about the effects of this virus. And congratulations on your work!"

The other three teams had developed different lines of research. The research team from India was pretty sure that they could reduce the viability of male live births. That was a potentially interesting venue. If you could reduce the male population through the reduction of male birth rates, you could possibly create a less violent society. However, what if the reduction was exponential and every generation had fewer males? That would be a disaster and men would end up being extinct.

Another research team thought that they could reduce testosterone in both males and females. The Mater was not sure that was a good idea for a variety of reasons, chief amongst all was the unknown consequences for the endocrine system. She told the researchers that it was an unacceptable path, but that it would be interesting if they continued to study hormones and gender differences.

The last group had developed a virus that attached itself to the Y chromosome, but it was too lethal, and they were having difficulties with creating a vaccine. The Mater told them to burn all the specimens and their notes and terminate their research. She would find them excellent jobs with all the backing of Telea, but she wanted the lab abandoned within a week, fully disinfected with level IV protocols.

So now the Mater had two venues that needed to be explored. Research would continue until one or the other virus was deemed safe enough for the continuation of humanity. The world needed males, they were important for heterosexual and bisexual women, and without males, humanity would disappear. The problem was not that there were men, but that there was uncontrolled male violence against each other and against women.

The Mater was not naïve to assume that women did not have the potential for violence. There were violent women, women who abused children and the elderly, young women who participated in all-female gangs and women who were simply evil psychopaths. However, in patriarchy, these women were infrequent and somewhat controlled by male power in society, expressed in male legal systems and male-created prisons. There had to be a better society, one in which female empowerment did not mean subjugation of males. A society that would protect its most vulnerable people equally and with mutual respect. She wanted a utopia and was certain that everything might go wrong. That was her deepest fear.

Chapter Twenty-Nine

Within three years, both research teams with promising results were ready for human trials. The team from Australia had conclusively proven that both females and males could be infected with the virus, that they could infect and transmit the illness in aerosolised particles and that females would become the vaccine by developing swollen glands behind their ears that produced powerful pheromones. The females rejected violent males and, if they tried to force themselves, adrenaline in females mediated a sour-smelling pheromone that was lethal to the attackers. The infection rate was 92% in mice. There were around 8% of mice who had natural immunity.

Finally, women with nanobot necklaces were as likely to be infected as the general population. They confirmed this by feeding mice with very small amounts of nanobot dust. They had lived longer and healthier lives than the control group. However, they were all infected by the virus that they simply called 'Y virus'. Although the birth rate remained stable, the offspring of the infected mice carried the same characteristics, with each generation having less aggressive males.

The research team from India was not as successful because each generation of mice decreased the proportion of males until they only had one male left to impregnate all the females. This proved that the virus would become endemic, and the consequences would be catastrophic for humanity. The Mater thanked the group for their efforts but asked them to terminate the experiments and to burn all their evidence and the building. Since it was an isolated building, it was feasible to do so without danger to neighbours. She asked them to move to Angola and work on the prevention and treatment of tropical diseases, including haemorrhagic fevers. They said that they were pleased to accept the challenge.

Now that the Mater had a solution for dealing with violent males, she needed to plan how to implement such a drastic measure. So she called a meeting of all her ministers and advisors, including Leonor, Emani and Maria. To minimise travel and because communication technology had vastly improved in the last decades, this was to be a video conference call.

"Sisters, I have a plan and the means to implement it, but I fear that some of you may baulk at it. I will understand your reluctance. Nevertheless, I will carry to term this plan that has consumed me for half a century. My goal is very simple. I want to eradicate male violence, and I want to stop all wars. To do this, a team of researchers has given me the means. This is what they created."

The Mater then proceeded to explain her efforts in the past decades and the details about the Y virus created by the Australian team.

"We are now ready to go into human trials, and I need your advice. How should we proceed?"

Except for Maria, Leonor and Emani, all the information was new and shocking to her ministers and other advisors. The minister of Telea Affairs could not contain herself.

"Mater, you surely know that we are all devoted to you and that we submit to your will. However, if you will permit my foul language, what the fuck? You know that I'm married to a man and that my two daughters live with men. Are you just expecting us to do nothing and see our beloved partners die?"

"I will explain it again as you obviously didn't grasp the details. If the men are not violent, and they hug you frequently so that they can smell your pheromones, they will be safe, healthy and even happier. We should perhaps set up hugging centres with women who wear the stones for those men who live alone."

One advisor from Asia asked a pertinent question, "What about the cultural norms that dictate that men should not touch women?"

"Well, most men in those countries have families with women who can hug them. The problem is that if the women in their hearts despise their men, their pheromones will sour, and the men will die quickly. That might solve the problem of forced marriages."

"I think that despite my commitment to you, you are heartless."

"I'm sorry that you feel that way. The fact is, that faced with a death sentence, most men will alter their expectations and behaviour. If they are good men, they can go to one of the hugging centres that we will set up throughout the world. Once it starts, we will need to make an appeal to generous women, whether they are members of Telea or not. However, if you think about it, there will not be any hugging centres in war zones.

"Either the men abandon their weapons and go home, or they will die. Once home, if they are violent, they will die. I expect that there will be millions of deaths in the first year. Then it will stabilise and become endemic. Societies will have to change. Women will literally become the source of life in all aspects, so I expect men to venerate women as life-givers.

"War industries will be disrupted, there will be economic uncertainty, and initially, there will be chaos. We, Telea, will need to position ourselves to take control and avoid unnecessary hardships and death."

"Our reputation will be destroyed once the world finds out that a secret society of women unleashed this plague. We will be vilified and hunted down," said the minister of communications. "We need to decide, I think, if we are going to assume public responsibility for the Y virus or if we let it spread initially, keeping silent and presenting the solutions as if they were new discoveries. Also, are we ready to go public with our existence?"

The women discussed and rehashed all points for a couple of hours. The Mater kept silent and only answered questions directed at her. After what seemed like a very long time, all women reached the consensus that it would be suicide to let the world know of Telea's existence and that they had been responsible for developing the Y virus. The only alternative was continued secrecy and continued involvement in the world under their philanthropic actions. Telea would continue to present a public facade of liberal humanitarianism while concealing its dark side.

Another point of contention was where to start human trials. Some women suggested that the creators of the virus should be the first infected. Others advocated that there were areas in the world where the virus should be released first. There was no consensus on the matter. So the Mater asked where in the world were women worse off? They all came up with Saudi Arabia and Afghanistan. Why not start there? There was a reluctant agreement. So that's where they would start.

After the meeting ended, all the women, including the Mater, were exhausted. She had a brief lie down, but her thoughts kept swirling in her brain. She couldn't sleep, so she decided to act. The Mater called Mei Yang, the lead researcher in Australia, and asked her to send two aerosol flasks to her residence in Huambo.

Mei reminded the Mater that each spray container would have many doses and that one spray would be enough to infect a person. Also, it would be best if each container was refrigerated separately. The Mater acknowledged the information and asked about how to monitor the spread. Mei replied that any epidemiologist could do that job.

She sent a message from Telea's website to a member in Saudi Arabia and asked if she knew of any epidemiologist from the area. As a matter of fact, there was a friend who worked in one of Riyadh's hospitals who had worked with MERS and was very experienced. She also happened to wear a stone. The Mater asked for her name and contact information. Then she called the current leader of the Cleaning Women and asked her to come to Huambo, Angola. She was currently on a job in Brazil but could leave it to one of her women to finish the assignment and would board a flight to Angola as soon as possible.

The next day, the Mater received a plain-faced woman, of indeterminable ethnicity and age who was called Clara Simmons and had been born in the United States. She looked tough and humourless but, after holding her hands, The Mater received images of brutal trauma in her life. She didn't inquire but gave her a strong boost of energy.

"I have an assignment that eventually will require all Cleaning Women to bring death to men. They will infect one man at a time with a new virus that will spread. Is that going to be a problem?"

"Every cleaning woman is a merciless killer. We don't do moral dilemmas. We follow instructions and complete assignments, that's all. Up to now, no one has been caught. Some of our older women are thinking of retirement, but they can do one more assignment before leaving. However, if they are going to spread a virus, what is the likelihood that the women will die?"

"No woman will die because this virus only kills violent men or those men without a woman in their lives. However, the women will also be infected, will have flu-like symptoms and will develop swollen glands behind their ears. If they are willing to hug men, those men they love will develop short-term immunity. Hugs will need to be frequent. I know! This is a strange virus, but it was created to give women control over their bodies and to destroy male violence."

Clara was thoughtful and said, "I think that I want to be one of the first to go on assignment. I have a teenage son who travels with me wherever I go. I sure want to protect him of any danger and of this virus in particular."

"Very well. You will go with another woman to Jeddah in Saudi Arabia. You will need to travel with a man, so your son might do, and you must wear an abaya and scarf. I suggest that you cover your face and wear black gloves as well.

"This will make you blend in with the population and keep your identity protected. Your son also needs to wear traditional male clothing. So you will give me the measurements of the three of you, and I will have someone mail your local outfits. Where is your home base?"

"Detroit. Interesting that it has a large Arab population. Receiving a package from Saudi Arabia would be inconspicuous, and we can all three leave from there."

"The virus should arrive today in a refrigerated container. You will need to keep it as cool as possible. The only serious problem is passing the containers through customs.

"There is another option. You gather here and go from Luanda to Riyadh, then to Jeddah. Once there you spread the virus as much as possible. Then you should get out of Saudi Arabia as soon as possible. That should be doable, though very tiring."

Clara agreed with the plan and a week later she departed to Jeddah with her son, Daniel and Aya, a Christian Arab also from Detroit. They travelled on Saudi Arabian passports and Saudi names. Four days later, the three had departed and were on their way to Angola where they made their reports and got back their own American passports. They explained that their strategy had been to release the aerosolised virus in crowded places, like inside packed buses. No one had noticed the sprays, and their job had been done without incident.

Of course, now they were having flu-like symptoms and were infected. In addition, they had probably infected the passengers on the planes and the taxi driver. Clara kept hugging her son, just in case, even though she did not have swollen glands yet. They rested in the Mater's residence for a week before going back to Detroit, where they would inevitably infect other people along their way and at their destination. Daniel was feeling well, so they knew the protection worked. Now they needed the assessment of an epidemiologist.

The Mater called the number for the Telea member who was also an epidemiologist and said that she had heard of a strange infection going on around Jeddah and that she should have a look at it. The Mater also asked for reports on the seriousness of the disease. Then, she asked Clara to anonymously contact the American Center for Disease Control and report a strange disease in Detroit. With this part done, now it was a matter of waiting for news.

It was not long before reports of haemorrhagic fever among men and transwomen started to appear in the headlines of newspapers and television broadcasts. It was not necessary to send more Cleaning Women since the virus had spread so efficiently. The Mater ordered Mei Yang, her lead researcher in Australia to send to Lavoie Pharmaceutical Industries a summary of her findings with the purpose of having Lavoie claim discovery that infected women's pheromones were the source of men's immunity to the newly discovered virus.

Most people did not believe that infected women had the power to save men simply by hugging them. Late-night talk shows had a field day riciculing such assertions. Experts demanded funding for appropriate research on a vaccine. Others wondered if MERS had mutated into a haemorrhagic fever. Others still defended the theory that it had to be one of Ebola or Marburg, Lassa fever, or yellow fever virus.

The Center for Disease Control in the United States and the World Health Organisation clearly explained that it was a new Middle Eastern virus and that its genetic composition was completely different from known haemorrhagic fever viruses. Still, weeks went by before someone decided to test the assertions of Lavoie Laboratories and found them true.

At this point, men started to take notice, especially when many specialists started to die. The hugging centres that had been set up by Telea and by many women's organisations started to receive lines of lonely and sick men. Mothers hugged their sons. Wives hugged their husbands.

Sisters hugged their brothers, and every kind-hearted woman gave hugs to complete strangers who, with downcast demeanours and pleading eyes, asked for a hug. Transwomen did better than men because many lived with other women or in queer communities where a lot of hugging went on A few transwomen died right at the beginning of the pandemic, but they were the first to heed the warnings and single transwomen asked for hugs from other women all the time.

What male researchers who survived could not understand was why some men who had wives and daughters still died. They also received abundant reports of men who attacked women for hugs and then dropped dead in front of them. And many thousands of men on the front lines of wars died hugging their weapons before military commanders decided to bring them home to their families. NATO quickly collapsed and Europe struggled to survive nuclear winters with its population vastly reduced.

Some male-only institutions were particularly devastated, like their old foe, the Magisterium Ecclesiae, with strict separation of the sexes in their establishments. Among the most affected were male prisons all over the world. It did not matter whether the men were in prison for theft, drug-related issues or homicide. They died at the rate of 20% per week until many prisons simply opened their doors to let the remaining prisoners die outside their walls. Obviously, the same did not happen in women's prisons, which constituted a dilemma of fairness.

Many women were violent offenders who continued their violence inside prison. However, most female prisoners were not violent. Many had drug charges, were arrested for killing violent partners or were thieves. Therefore most parole boards decided to free the non-violent prisoners and wait until they could decide what to do with violent women. In response to these decisions, Telea decided to set up halfway houses to prepare the ex-prisoners to live in a vastly changed world.

After months of intense group therapy and lessons in literacy and citizenship, most of these women ended up living a normal, non-criminal life. The exceptions were arrested again, but the prison system in North America had changed substantially following the Norwegian model of rehabilitation, with dignity, and personal empowerment to allow women to reset goals for their lives.

Cultures that did not value women were the most affected. Men were decimated before they asked for a hug or women gave hugs to men outside their immediate family.

Russia and its satellite states had exhausted much of their financial resources in the long war with Ukraine. They had become pariah states after unleashing a nuclear missile in Ukraine and had been expelled from the Security Council of the United Nations. Also, they were some of the most patriarchal countries in the Northern Hemisphere. So this idea that burly men should ask for hugs was preposterous.

They hugged their bottles of cheap vodka and died by the thousands every day until their mothers, wives and daughters joined voices in massive demonstrations through the streets of the main cities and took control of much of the local governments. With the help of Telea and of a few women's groups, Russian women set up their own hugging centres and forced their men to take loving hugs from them. It would take a long time for Eastern countries to recover financially and emotionally, but the death toll slowly abated.

In places such as Afghanistan or Saudi Arabia, corpses piled up with nobody to care for them. The leadership in these countries was also decimated and the men who had loving women at home simply could not overcome the cultural tabus. In places such as the United Arab Emirates and Qatar, with millions of male guest workers away from their families, the death rate was extremely high. Cemeteries needed to be expanded and men were buried in common graves.

Slowly, but surely, women in Middle East and Southeast Asian countries started to venture into the public arena and began to create some order out of the chaos. There were many highly educated women who were in hiding or had fled their countries who, although airflights were scarce, returned to help.

In China, hundreds of thousands of single men died because there was a severe gender imbalance in favour of males, and there were whole rural villages without a single woman. Many other hundreds of thousands of men died in the cities where for decades women had refused marriage to focus on their studies and professional life.

As soon as the first cases of infection appeared, regional and local Chinese governments instituted strict lockdown policies. That was the worst possible measure regarding combating the Y virus because it prevented single men from leaving their homes and seeking hugs. Millions more died until the Central Communist Committee decided to follow the WHO guidelines and instituted hugging policies. In this case, there were many failures because women did not volunteer to be huggers but were appointed to the task by local governments.

Men died suddenly in front of some women who hated being in this position. The local governments arrested these women and appointed others for the job, compounding the problem until they asked for volunteers. At this point, there was a serious gender imbalance in China, with women being the overwhelming majority.

In South America, gangs almost disappeared in a flood of death. The drug cartels collapsed because there were not enough men to produce and distribute drugs. None of those men were mourned. However, very few men in society died in comparison to other continents because, culturally, hugging and kissing was a common way of greeting. The same thing happened in Southern Europe.

Portugal and Spain were doing surprisingly well because, since they were not in the sphere of nuclear fallout, they received enough refugees to repopulate interior villages with very low populations. Therefore, these refugees revitalised the economy and diversified the genetic make-up of those countries.

In about a month, hospitals, which had been overrun at the beginning of the pandemic, saw a marked decrease in new cases. When patients showed up, nurses simply gave them hugs and cared for them for a couple of days before they were sent home. It began to be a habit for women to hug men even in professional settings. The offices which before were mostly cold, impersonal places, began to have colour and human warmth. Men began to hug each other as well.

In a few months, the relationship between the sexes changed profoundly in most of North America, except in a few pockets of isolated patriarchy. Women became appreciated as men's lives depended on regular loving hugs from women. They started to be listened to, and they spoke with newfound assertiveness. The old habits of men dominating conversation and of mansplaining practically disappeared. Divorce rates plummeted since men did not want to lose their wives and women understood that a separation could mean a life sentence.

Women finally broke the glass ceiling of institutional power considering that in male-dominated industries and services, many men had died. However, a deep financial recession hit the world since most companies were owned by men and most of them were dead. The market uncertainties were such that most stock exchanges simply shut down. Production and distribution were severely affected because many of those jobs no longer had enough workers either to produce goods and parts or to ship them worldwide. Women started taking those jobs, from industrial workers to garbage collectors, from fishers to farmers and every occupation previously male-dominated.

Job vacancies were abundant, and salaries rose substantially. Rents became affordable because so many housing units became available. However, people did not spend recklessly like before the Y virus appeared. They reused and recycled everything, setting up mini recycling units in neighbourhoods and across towns.

Within ten years, the socio-economic landscape of the capitalist world started to change with the economy becoming more circular, social asymmetries less pronounced and greater attention to environmental issues. Of course, it was decades too late, as the sea levels had risen substantially, and the waters swallowed small island nations and coastlines everywhere. The transformation of capitalism into a different system would take a long time and be uneven across the globe, with some regional economies in the Southern Hemisphere becoming eco-socialist, while in others, especially the previously called developed countries, capitalism lingered for longer. It was not surprising that it would be so since other economic systems in history also took centuries to spread across the world.

In Africa, the situation varied immensely depending on the area. Countries that already had received many refugees fared better than countries where Muslim extremists had ravaged the countryside with terror. Mali, Niger, Nigeria, Burkina Faso, Somalia and Mozambique saw a sudden decline in their total population as hundreds of thousands of men died in the jungles or in the deserts. Local wars ended for the same reasons.

Chad, Cameroon and the Democratic Republic of the Congo were the stage for much dying and killing, as large groups of women attacked their male oppressors and instituted women-led governments. That was unexpected. So, besides the Y virus deaths, in some areas of the continent, women actively killed any men suspected of being terrorists. Consequently, the gender ratio in many African countries was skewed in favour of women.

In Angola, like in all countries of the world, many men died, but the gender imbalance was not as significant because the strong Telea presence had prevented unnecessary deaths. During the first weeks of the pandemic, Telea widely publicised the need for women to give hugs and established hugging centres throughout the vast country. Local women joined the effort, and the dying was mostly limited to violent men or men who lived with women who secretly hated them.

As in many parts of the world, there was a sudden and substantial decrease in violent crime. However, some women did commit those crimes, so the Mater, in conjunction with a gender-balanced government, restructured the criminal code and the prison system. Angola was the first country in the world to define crimes against men as serious as crimes against women. This gave a strong message that both genders had equal standing in society.

In addition, the Mater decided that policing should be gender-balanced, therefore there was a wave of applications from women for police training. Police officers learned from Telea warriors about de-escalation of conflict, about conflict resolution that did not involve arrests and about the application of force when needed. There were no more weapons in the hands of police officers. Also, the standing army was dissolved as there were no wars and so many military personnel had died for lack of hugging.

Angola's penal system became a model for the world because it was designed in conjunction with local communities, according to traditional values of cooperation and integration in the community. The effect of hundreds of people checking out offenders' every move was a strong deterrent to criminal behaviour. There were no more traditional prisons. Instead, offenders were sent alone to small rural communities where they were given a job, lived with other people of the same gender, had some freedom of movement and a lot of neighbourhood surveillance. Soon South Africa followed Angola's lead and other African countries followed suit. The Mater was pleased.

Chapter Thirty

The Mater looked out of her bedroom veranda and was happy with the way her garden flourished. She would go for a swim later in the afternoon. She turned her attention to Maria and sat down in her private living room.

"I think that we should give a party and invite all regional directors of Angola to attend with their families," suggested Maria. "You would have some fun and relax, and I would take care of everything. What do you think?"

"I think that it is a great idea. Ever since we moved here fifteen years ago things have been difficult, but for the past couple of years most of Africa has been stable and Angola is becoming an economic powerhouse. There are things to celebrate."

"Yes, we have much to be happy about, especially about the reconstruction of the national health care here and the extraordinary drop in infant mortality. Also important is that it seems like every other woman wears a necklace. We have become ubiquitous. I'm only surprised that you have not yet been outed as the leader of Telea. You know that it could happen anytime."

"I fear it. I think that I want to delay being known for at least another century. Let's plan this party, and then, let's consider our exit from Angola. We are doing well, and the country and continent are doing well, so this is the time to think about moving elsewhere."

A month later, under a lovely blue sky with a gentle breeze, The Mater hosted a garden party for about forty people, with the regional directors and their families. The small, young-looking woman was wearing a simple flowing white linen dress with her seven stones, her torque and her ring. On her head, she wore a short and stylish wig and used no make-up, except for pink lipstick. The Mater wanted this party to be a relaxed reunion of friends.

There were children running around under the complacent looks of their mothers and grandmothers. The women looked stunning with their colourful dresses and elaborate head scarves, with their nanobot stones proudly displayed.

Three women brought their husbands, and one woman brought her wife and all were delighted to be presented to the Mater. Maria had outdone herself with preparations. The menu was delicious, the tables were beautifully set, and the children calmed down for the meal. The servers and the housekeeper also wore their stones proudly over their white outfits, and all seemed happy with how things were unfolding.

The Mater asked each regional director for news about their provinces. Of course, she was well-informed, but it gave the women a chance to talk and brag about their accomplishments. The conversation flowed easily and before long it was time for the Mater to say goodbye to her friends. As they left, she took their hands and each woman received a power boost. They were grateful.

After the guests had all left and the evening descended, the Mater sat with Maria outside. They were wearing added warmth in the form of thick shawls and sipping a lovely scotch whiskey.

"This day was perfect. Thank you, Maria, not only for today but for all that you do."

"You're very welcome. It's the greatest privilege of my life to be your assistant and friend."

"You know, I was born here so very long ago in a time of war. I'm quite pleased that we were able to bring peace to this amazing continent. The peoples of Africa will continue to evolve and one day, mark my words, Angola will be the centre of the world. Until then, where would you like to live, my friend?"

Part Four

As we conclude the history of Telea and the life of our Mother of Stones, the Mater, we need to understand our own society and your role in it. Although you are young, you have a voice in our communities and in our world. We all participate in the continuous creation of our common lives.

—Excerpt from a teaching manual, 2378

Chapter Thirty-One

Alexis jumped into the water and squealed with delight. The day was hot and muggy, so the water was delicious. Suddenly, all her friends jumped too, and the water was a turmoil of legs and arms and laughing children. After a while, naked boys and girls swam ashore to do their chores. After cleaning the sand from her body, the eight-year-old ran home with her feet slapping the boardwalk and used an outside hose to wash most of the salt and the rest of the sand from her body.

In the summer, it was fun to use the hose because the water started hot and then progressively became cold. Using a towel that she kept hanging for that purpose, Alexis dried herself and entered the three-bedroom house where she lived with her moms and her sister Oruba.

"Mama, I'm back. Can I have a snack before doing chores?"

"There is a sandwich in the fridge. Make sure you tell the fridge to resupply bread because we're short on it," said her housemother, Carla, from upstairs where the bedrooms were located.

Alexis ate her sandwich with a glass of fortified juice and told the fridge to get bread, multigrain. That same day a supply wagon would deliver the groceries ordered. Of course, they could have walked to the local grocery store, but it often didn't have the bread they liked, so there was an electric robotic wagon that made daily rounds in the village for extra products. Auntie Bekka, who owned the store, didn't mind because she didn't like having perishables because, well, they perished quickly. Alexis laughed out loud at the joke in her mind.

Her family, the Obango, was composed of five mothers and two fathers who lived close by to each other. The dads lived together, they were Nobuto and Drei. Her house-moms were Carla and Lovata. Her body-mom was Teresa who lived alone, and her two sister-mothers were Nadia and Lesoto. Alexis had other older sisters and brothers who lived in community housing and one young brother, Normo, who lived with her dads.

They all helped raise the children and together they owned a thriving fishery business with all adults working in it in various capacities. Their skin varied in tones of darkness, with Alexis's skin being chocolate brown. All had curly hair, but hers was difficult to manage because it matted easily, so she preferred to have her hair cut close to the skull so that she could jump into the sea anytime. Saltwater was not kind to curly hair. She envied her body mother's braids that glistened with sunlight.

Alexis' and her sister Oruba's chores in the afternoons included checking nets to see if they needed mending. If that was the case, they each had tools to do the mending. Their other chores were weeding a vegetable garden that consumed all their compost and was on the far side of their houses away from the ocean. Finally, they often had their own learning research projects. Mornings were spent with their holographic teacher, Susana, who guided their learning.

Alexis was very proud that she was a good reader, but not so proud about her math assignments. She felt that she was not very good at logical thinking, however, she was only eight years old, so she would improve. Her greatest pleasure, though, was drawing and her mothers and fathers spoiled her with gifts of art supplies that she kept well organised in her large room. Alexis was by nature a tidy child. She liked her things 'just so', while Oruba was the opposite, an exuberant child always singing, dancing and leaving her things all over the houses.

The children were frequently in and out of all four houses, either to hug their parents or to look for treats. Sometimes, they got extra chores, although play was an important part of the children's daily lives. When Alexis was small and her older sisters and brothers lived in the houses, they frequently ate outdoors to accommodate their numbers. Now they usually had dinner at the central closed pavilion which had a kitchen, a dining room and a bathroom so that the whole family could be together for a daily meal.

The Obango family lived in Angola in a village close to the town of Lobito and sent their fish daily to the city of Benguela, using a different version of an electric robotic wagon than the one used for groceries deliveries. All cargo vehicles looked the same except for size. They were all covered in small hexagonal solar panels that powered the wagons indefinitely, had space for the cargo and hovered above ground using antigravity technology. This way, the landscape was not scarred by roads, and there was no pollution. People moved around the village using boardwalks or small paths.

For those that needed to travel further away, the hovercrafts were sleek, also covered in solar panels, with comfortable seating inside and an area for luggage. The passenger hovercrafts were self-directed with the input of the destination set at departure. However, very few people owned a personal vehicle, except regional directors due to the peripatetic nature of their office and the Mater, for the same reason. Every village had at least two personal vehicles for use by their members who paid a nominal fee for the privilege.

In the last century, technology had been geared towards microprocessors, communication and energy. One of the best inventions was the hexagonal solar panel, no larger than the palm of a hand, but which, combined with hundreds or thousands of other hexagons, provided unlimited power for the units they were connected to. All vehicles had them, and the same for every rooftop, and even appliances such as lawnmowers. The family's two fishing vessels were totally powered by solar energy, as were their homes. House designs also used passive solar energy to heat inside and shade to cool them off, oscillating between seasons.

Having to deal with heat was a problem in Angola, except for those who lived in the mountains or central plateau. Her body-mom, Theresa, who was a regional director of Telea, and her teacher, Susana, both had explained that since the Mater took power, three hundred and fifty years earlier, the global temperature had risen three degrees Celsius. This had increased the dimension of deserts and had reduced the size of lakes and rivers, and the ocean had eaten away islands and coastlines. Freshwater was always a problem, that's why people who lived by the ocean were privileged because each house had its own desalination unit.

Every scientist's dream was to be able to decode the nanobots that composed the amalgamations called 'the stones'. They had not been able to do that, but in the process of trying, they concentrated on creating smaller and smaller machines with the appropriate software for their function. As a result of these efforts, a team of scientists in Korea invented transdermal implants that activated the cerebral cortex and allowed the user to visualise, hear and communicate information with their mind. These were never available to anyone under twenty-five years old because of concerns that this technology could interfere with normal brain development. However, simpler and less invasive devices were used in adolescents and young adults for learning purposes. An external visor that clicked and was secured to the head allowed students access to all the written information in archives and related videos.

Alexis knew the general history of the Mater's lifetime and of Telea because it was mandatory learning in her age group. As she grew, she would learn more details. It was mandatory learning for all children of the world, ever since the Mother of Stones, the Mater, had revealed herself to the world one hundred and fifty years ago. It had been a surprise for only a few people, as most women wore nanobot necklaces and were devoted to their leader.

The Mater's power was absolute, but she rarely exercised it, except to broker peace or to eliminate psychopaths. There was no cure for psychopathy, and they left a trail of emotional destruction wherever they went and were dangerous to the community. The Mater, as well as the regional directors, had the unfortunate duty of removing those women's stones and guarding them until their demise less than a year later.

In a society with fewer stressors than it had been in the past, mental health problems had diminished, but they still existed. There were cortical stimulators that helped with depression, but the best way to manage mental illness was the love and caring of family and community. For those unfortunates who had acute episodes of mental illness, such as schizophrenia, aerosolised medication was the best short-term intervention. For the rest, people learned to cope and to support each other.

In the year 2356, the Mater would celebrate her four hundredth birthday, and the society that in part, she helped create was vastly different from the one she was born to. To begin with, every woman after giving birth to two or three children received a nanobot stone. The delay was done to promote the birth of males in a society in which women outnumbered men. Some women chose not to reproduce, and some men could not see themselves having sex with a woman. In this case, men provided sperm for fertility clinics, and single women often found themselves as house mothers for their chosen families or living alone in the context of their extended family.

The family unit had changed significantly with several people sharing a common name and living close to each other. Polyamory was the norm, even though there were old-style families as well. Older women and men often decided to live in communities with their age peers, and that was also a kind of family. Men always lived close to women so that they could receive at least one hug a day with a good pheromone sniff. There were, nonetheless, people who were so passionate about their work, that they lived alone.

They simply had little energy left to devote affection to others, like Teresa, Alexis' body mother. That was fine too. There were no moral dictates about how people should live. The one imperative that everyone, including children over twelve years old, had to assume, though, was community participation, both through service to others and through community meetings and democratic decision-making.

Once the living Mother of Stones had a dream of participatory democracy, and it had come to fruition. Local power was the centre of community living, whether in villages or in cities, which were divided into large neighbourhoods. Frequently, there were people who grumbled about the quarterly meetings as boring and too long. However, they were all very glad that the garbage was collected, that pathways and gardens were maintained and that freshwater, though sometimes scarce, was accessible to all. Not everybody enjoyed local politics, but everyone had to participate in discussions and cast their vote.

Many resources of the community were commonly owned, so one could say that local power was largely based on cooperative living. The tribute that was owed to Telea, an income tax of 10%, stayed in the community for the most and covered common expenses. So, although there was personal property, there was very little of private property or of private ownership of resources.

Take the example of the Obango family, they owned their houses because they built them, or their ancestors did. They owned the business of fisheries and made a profit out of their work. However, their fishing vessels belonged to the fishers' cooperative to which the family paid 5% per year of their revenues. Since many people in Lobito were fishers, it was easier to streamline the ownership of resources, and the yearly maintenance of the boats was the responsibility of a family that serviced all fishing vessels. Cooperative living just made sense.

Religion had also changed substantially. With widespread literacy and with most people having post-secondary education, critical thinking had overcome faith. Some of the old beliefs still endured in small enclaves, but most people were atheists, revelling in the beauty of nature and of the universe. There was a fringe mystic adoration of the Mater, but that was a subdued faith.

Everyone knew the history of Telea and of the current Mater, most people understood that the nanobot amalgam that they wore was the same as the Mater, so it was clear in their minds that the Mater's longevity was a function of science, not mysticism. Still, people's devotion to the Mater was real, and there was surprisingly little rebellion to her rule. The Mater dealt with rebels by talking to them, finding out the reasons for their discontentment and addressing their issues.

Regional wars had simply disappeared, although there were still tribal tensions and occasional clashes. When these happened, either the Mater or her regional directors intervened as mediators. If the violence continued, the Mater ordered all women to leave the area. That was often enough of a threat to end hostilities. Women with children did not have any appetite for war, so those conflicts were often the result of domination attempts of one group of men against other men. If the behaviour was grievous, the Mater left them alone until they died of their wounds or of the Y virus, thus reducing the population of violent men.

The old superpowers had become irrelevant on the world stage and fragmented into smaller regions. The new superpower was Angola with its advances in technology, good population density and gender balance, high planes excellent for agriculture and rich of most mineral resources needed to supply its industry. Angolan ports were hubs of distribution not only of basic materials but of transformed products. High salaries, universal health and social care were common in Africa, but Angola's standard of living was the envy of the world and a model to be followed.

However, its superpower status was that of a benevolent nature. Long gone were the days of imperial expansion, whether through economic hegemony or military invasions. In the twenty-fourth century, regions looked first to improve the lives of their own populations and then helped their neighbours. That was Angola's role.

Europe had restructured its regional borders into more reasonable sizes. The atomic fallout of three hundred years earlier had disappeared and most of the land had healed. Nevertheless, what once had been Ukraine and Western Russia were now left to the wild. Through irrigation with desalinated water and using crops resistant to drought, Mediterranean countries were thriving, having adjusted their agriculture to climate change that had transformed some of their southern areas into deserts.

The old Maison de la Toile in Provence continued to produce flowers and scents, but those plants were adapted to arid conditions. Their old research on botanical poisons had been transformed into pharmaceutical products. It was a thriving business.

East Asia continued to have a serious gender imbalance in favour of women and family units had adjusted accordingly. Also, their demographics had improved with the influx of immigrants from more populous regions. The one zone of the world that worried regional directors was the Indian subcontinent which, regardless of their technological prowess, continued to have greater social asymmetries than the rest of the world.

In the Americas, there was a resurgence of native peoples whose fertility had increased with minimum gender imbalance. They kept a watch and protected the Great Lakes of the North and the rain forests, including the Amazon basin. Of course, local people enjoyed, and sometimes abused, local hallucinogenic drugs. However, the international traffic had been reduced to a trickle, and there were no drug wars.

Synthetic drugs were forbidden, and after the pandemic of the Y virus, women rampaged and destroyed every drug lab they could find. For a while, there were a lot of addicts in withdrawal. Then, women took control of the local cannabis and cocaine trade, plants that simply grew wild in their lands, and forbade the use of weapons.

The one thing that people sometimes regretted was the significant scarcity of air travel. Almost all travel was done by electric ships to reduce carbon emissions. Intercontinental vessels, just like the fishing vessels of Lobito, were all operated by many thousands of hexagonal solar panels with unlimited power, enough to transport cargo and passengers across the oceans of the world. Travel took time and was beyond the means of most people, so life was restricted to smaller landscapes. If there was a need, local councils would pay for international travel, but it was rare. In addition, all meetings, conferences and conventions were done online with very large communal screens providing context for the speakers' holograms.

Alexis' life was more restricted geographically than the lives of people in the twenty-first century who used to move around from place to place in search of adventure and new sights. On the other hand, she had access to entertainment and educational technology not even dreamed of in the past. When she looked at holograms of famous sites, she felt she was there, surrounded by the sounds and smells of the places she visited. When she chatted with her friends across the globe, she interacted with their holograms as if they were in front of her. Alexis was still a child, but she had a wider understanding of the world than many adults in the past.

With the passing of time, Alexis continued her studies in the community living campus in the city of Benguela and decided that she wanted to be a peacekeeper. To that effect, she moved to Luanda where the main peacekeeping university was located. Here, she studied how to de-escalate conflicts, how to honour traditions and keep the ancient stories alive. She studied how different communities organised themselves and the cultural differences between tribes and societies of the world. Alexis excelled in all aspects of her learning, including physical training, and learning how to subdue aggression. She wanted to work in Africa, which delighted her parents who liked to have her close by, as it were.

When Alexis was twenty-five, she fell in love and started her own family. Her male mate was Carlos Pereira, a descendant of European refugees. He was also a peacekeeper, and it was handy that they could go together on assignments. They were settled in Luena in the interior of Angola. Alexis missed the ocean, but she adored her husband, their two boys and one girl.

They decided, after nine years of marriage that they would like another partner, and they chose Carla, a teacher to join them. They selected the family name of Luena, since that was their home for the time, and Alexis went for a holiday with the children to visit her birth and caring parents in Lobito, leaving the new couple for an uninterrupted honeymoon.

Chapter Thirty-Two

It was during the visit to her original home that Alexis received a written letter from the Mater asking her to pay a visit to Casa da Teia, in Huambo, to discuss her future. The Mother of Stones had returned to her base in the central plateau. The house was not only her home but a historic building of great significance to Angolans.

Alexis was perplexed. How could the Mater even know of her? So she decided to have a long talk with her birth mother Teresa, who was a regional director of Telea.

"Mother, why do you think the Mater is interested in my future? I have a good life. I don't want it to change. Of course, I must go and visit. It would be very rude to ignore her, but I'm worried about what to expect. Do you know anything that might bring light to this?"

Teresa was thoughtful for a while, and then she responded as best as she could. "I'm not sure, beloved. We all know that the Mater is very old, and she has seemed tired at the last meetings I had with her. Perhaps she needs a new personal secretary."

"Mother, it can't possibly be that because I don't have the qualifications. Her last personal secretary trained all her life for that role. I'm just a peacekeeper, mother and lover. Could it be that she needs a personal guard?"

"I'm sorry daughter, but I can't seem to help you with this. You just leave the children with us and go to Huambo. Don't forget to pack a nice suit for the meeting."

The village sent her to the Mater's summons in a spacious hovercraft built for speed and comfort. However, it still took Alexis a whole day to get to Huambo. She stayed overnight in a community house and sent a message indicating that she was ready to present herself to the Mother of Stones. Shortly after, she received a notification to present herself to the Casa da Teia that afternoon.

The young woman carefully inspected her outfit of a sleeveless tunic over pants, made of synthetic silk brocade. Alexis thought that she looked elegant and capable with her suit and soft boots. Now that she rarely swam in saltwater, her hair had grown, and it was set in a mass of thin, long braids with gold beads at the end. Very elegant, indeed.

At the appointed time, Alexis knocked at the door of Casa da Teia, too nervous to admire the surrounding gardens that had been started by the Mater three hundred years ago. The housekeeper bade her welcome and guided Alexis to a beautifully appointed sunroom where she finally met the Mother of Stones in person. A very old, bald woman regarded her with clear brown eyes and a smile. The Mater was small and thin, dressed like Alexis in a suit of silk pants and tunic. However, what stood out were her seven stones interspersed with diamonds, proudly displayed on her chest, plus a torque, and a large signet ring on her left hand.

"Please be seated, my dear. I'm afraid that a summons from me might unnerve the best of women, but that was not my intention. And here you are."

Alexis nodded her head in respect and sat across from the Mater around a coffee table with lemonade and cookies. It was a warm day, after all.

"Mater, you called, and I came. I offer my submission and devotion to you."

"Dear Alexis, I'm glad of your courtesy, but the fact remains that you are not a member of Telea. You don't wear a stone. That needs to be addressed."

"Mater, you are right. Moreover, I already have three children, two of them boys, so I'm ready to receive my stone from one of my mothers, and I will gladly swear allegiance to Telea and to you."

"You are right, naturally, to be ready to receive your stone. Do you mind if I'm the one to offer it to you?"

"Oh my! What an honour! Of course, I would be humbled to receive my stone from your hands. But why me?"

The Mother of Stones surprised Alexis by laughing aloud. "Please don't be offended, my dear. When I received these stones, I asked the same thing. The only difference is that here before me stands a composed young woman and all I did was whine. That's why it's funny to me.

"As you can see, I'm a very old woman. However, I believe that I still have a few decades left to train my successor. Well, it happens that you are many times over the great-granddaughter of my body. I don't think that Teresa knows that. I have two other descendants who live in North America. But I would love it if the next Mother of Stones were African. That's why I invited you here. To offer to train you as the next Mater of Telea."

Alexis was stunned. All she could think of was that this had to be a mistake. She had two life partners and three children. She couldn't be the next Mater, even if it took decades to become one.

"Mater, respectfully, I don't want to leave my family. I just got a sister-wife that I want to live with. My children need me. Besides, I'm a peacekeeper. I don't have a clue about how to manage anything else besides my household."

"I understand your reluctance. However, let me assure you that your family will stay with you for decades to come. You will raise your children and be a partner to your wife and to your husband. The only difference in your life will be that the Luena family will live in Huambo, close to me, and I will be a grandmother to your children. You can visit your family of origin anytime you miss them. If you insist, you can even continue your chosen profession as one of my bodyguards.

"I have given great thought to this process. In the past, because Telea and the Mother of Stones lived in absolute secrecy, it was necessary to remove the new Mater from her family and surroundings. Telea faked my death, and I was reborn as a new person with a new identity, far away from anything and anyone I loved. Nowadays, that will not be necessary. Also, your transition can be gradual instead of being a life-threatening event. When your time comes to become the Mother of Stones, I will surrender my stones to you, and you will be able to take the mantle seamlessly.

"I have followed you all your life. I know that you excel at anything you put your mind to. I know that you are a composed and thoughtful woman. I am certain that in a couple of decades, you will learn everything there is to know about Telea. And you will be the first Mother of Stones to live among her people from the beginning. You will also be the most prepared to take the mantle.

"In addition, I want to appeal to your sense of duty. There is only one of you. There is no other descendant of mine who is African. All previous Mothers of Stones were European. It is high time for Africa to take centre stage in the world and proudly celebrate all that was achieved here in three hundred years. Be that woman! Prepare yourself to be the Mater of Telea, the Mother of Stones to the world."

"May I take a moment to think about it?"

"Why don't you enjoy the garden for a while? Walk around and breathe. Think about what your mothers would say. Then, when you are ready, come inside and give me your answer."

The garden was indeed beautiful and a solitary walk among the exuberant foliage and flower beds calmed Alexis' mind. She sat down on a bench and realised that everything the Mater had said was true. She didn't have the necessary training yet, but she understood Africa, its people, cultures and relationships with the land. She would be a good caretaker. However, the Mater was not solely talking about one continent, but the entire world.

That was an awesome responsibility. On the other hand, Telea was organised in tiers of management with extremely competent women responsible for each part of it. One day, what she really needed to become was the soul of the Telea, the Mater at its centre, the Mother of Stones.

When Alexis returned to the sunroom, the Mater stood up and serenely looked at her.

"Okay, I accept!" the young woman declared. "But you may come to regret the amount of work involved to make me worthy."

"You are already worthy, and I love a challenge. I may even live longer with my granddaughter at my side."

"Grandmother, may I have my stone now?"

"Of course!" And there were tears in the eyes of the woman who so long ago had been Sofia.

THE END